# CLAY ALLISON

❖

## LEGEND OF CIMARRON

## Also by
## John A. Truett

---

## MONUMENT IN THE STORM

---

## TO DIE IN DINETAH—
## The Dark Legacy of Kit Carson

---

# CLAY ALLISON
## LEGEND OF CIMARRON

———

*by*

# John A. Truett

*Illustrations by Stu Pritchard*

Printed and bound in the United States of America. No part of this book may be reproduced in any form or by any electronic or mechanical means including information storage and retrieval systems, without permission in writing from the publisher, except by a reviewer who may quote brief passages in a review.

Sunstone books may be purchased for educational, business, or sales promotional use. For information please write: Special Markets Department, Sunstone Press, P.O. Box 2321, Santa Fe, New Mexico 87504-2321.

FIRST EDITION

10 9 8 7 6 5 4 3 2 1

Library of Congress Cataloging in Publication Data:
Truett, John A., 1927–
    Clay Allison: legend of Cimarron/by John A. Truett. —1st ed.
        p. cm.
    ISBN: 0-86534-276-8 (hardcover)     —ISBN: 0-86534-308-X (paper)
    1. Allison, Clay, 1840 or 41–1887—Fiction.    I. Title.
PS3570. R813C53    1998
813' .54—dc21                                           98-17385
                                                        CIP

Published by       SUNSTONE PRESS
                   Post Office Box 2321
                   Santa Fe, NM 87504-2321 / USA
                   (505) 988-4418 / *orders only* (800) 243-5644
                   FAX (505) 988-1025

# From The Author

A writer doesn't create a book single-handedly. As the number of my books increases, I find myself becoming more and more indebted to the contributions of good friends, such as Roy L. Jones who evaluated my early manuscripts and accompanied me on the many research trips.

Much gratitude also goes to fellow writer and artist, Stu Pritchard, not only for his valuable suggestions, but also for his beautiful illustrations and jacket design, which enhance this book.

Barney Hubbs of Pecos, Texas, was a dedicated Clay Allison fan and over the years amassed an extensive collection of Clay Allison memorabilia. I can't personally thank Barney, since he's gone to that "big roundup in the sky" where he's no doubt whooping it up with his western idol, but I'm indebted to his son, Bill Hubbs, who inherited his father's priceless Clay Allison archives. Bill has graciously allowed me access to the rare photographs in his father's collection. The Museum of New Mexico at Santa Fe must also be included for making available vintage photos of Cimarron and Elizabethtown.

Another personal boost comes from Chuck Parsons, Magazine Editor of the National Association for Outlaw and Lawman History, Inc., and whose book, *"Clay Allison—Portrait of a Shootist,"* I used extensively in my research.

Then, there are my Western Writers of America pardners, Leon C. Metz, Elmer Kelton and John Duncklee, who have each extended a professional hand to assist this dedicated writer.

My deepest appreciation and thanks to all of you.

*John A. Truett*

# Forward

*I*n the year 1870, with northern New Mexico Territory under the control of iron-fisted Lucien Bonaparte Maxwell, another controversial figure arrived on the scene to leave an indelible mark on the town of Cimarron. That man was Robert Clay Allison, whose outlandish deeds quickly turned him into a legend.

Old timers never let truth stand in the way of a good story, and with more than a century of retelling, most accounts of Clay Allison's life have been twisted to such incredibility that many cannot be corroborated. There is no proof, for instance, that he dispensed with over twenty men; but when he did kill, it was only that he had to.

Even so, it is easy to see how a callow Tennessee farm boy was drawn into a life of violence, and why Clay Allison reluctantly took his place in history as one of the most colorful gunfighters in the old west.

# Chapter One

"*D*ang it, Clay, you all right?!"

Clay Allison winced from the stabbing pain in his forehead. "I don't know," he said to his brother, John, whose voice seemed to come from a deep well. Clay raised onto one elbow and opened his eyes a slit.

The cornfield was still there, peaceful under a humid morning sun. The Tennessee valley resembled a smudged painting from the blue smoke of crops being burned off nearby. An angry bee hummed away among the rustling leaves.

"Serves you right for playing jokes on me!" John said. He put an arm under Clay's shoulders and raised him to a sitting position.

"All I did was put a bee in your hat."

"And when I turned it loose, the durned thing was so mad he stung the first thing he came to—the mule. That's what kicked you in the head!"

Clay grumbled at his brother's chiding. Although two years younger, John was the serious one, but they both took after their father—eyes blue as the Appalachian sky and hair black as the crows that circled their fields. Clay tried to push up his six-foot-two frame, but slumped against the wagon wheel. "I can't stop the world from spinnin' around!"

John's irritation turned to worry. "Better get you back to the house and let Mama tend to that bump."

He pulled Clay to his feet and pushed him over the sideboard, then climbed into the wagon and propped his brother's head up against a pile of corn.

Clay put hands to his temples. "My head feels like a loaded cannon—it could go off any minute!"

John got into the seat and flicked the mule's reins. "Mama's gonna raise Cain when she know's you've been funnin' around again."

Clay didn't relish the thought of having to explain to his mother. Nancy Allison had raised her three children with a firm hand since her husband's death sixteen years earlier. She was strong of mind and body and made certain of two things—her children had a proper education and the farm produced enough corn and beans to give her family the kind of life God intended for hard-working people.

John pulled the wagon to a halt at their big log house just as the oldest son, Monroe, came in for the noon meal.

"Monroe," John called. "Help me with Clay!"

The somber heavy-set Monroe rushed over. "What's the matter, an accident?"

John climbed into the back of the wagon and took Clay's arm. "Mule kicked him in the head. He's still dizzy."

Monroe helped slide Clay down to his feet and John got out. Clay put an arm around each brother's neck.

"Still can't walk?" John asked.

Clay started to shake his head, but knew if he did the cannon would likely go off. "No . . . if you could maybe just lay me down somewhere."

Nancy Allison saw them through the doorway and came out to stand on the porch, both hands on her aproned waist. "Robert Clay

Allison! Have you been sneaking whiskey in the cornfield again?!"

The boys' older sister Mary came out with her husband Lewis.

"Mama," Mary said, "can't you see he's hurt?" She ran down from the porch. "Clay, that's an awful bump on your head—what on earth happened?"

John gave a quick explanation. "A bee stung the mule's rump and it kicked Clay in the head."

They helped Clay up the steps and into the house while their mother, with a suspicious eye, trailed them to the bedroom.

After Clay had been eased down onto his bed, Nancy Allison knelt to study her injured son. Scorn turned to pity at the sight of his ugly bruise. "Mary," she ordered, "get a towel and some cold water . . . and you boys, go eat your dinner. It's on the stove. Clay needs some quiet."

The three men left obediently and Mary brought in a towel and pan of water. Her mother placed the moistened cloth gingerly on Clay's forehead.

Clay winced in pain, then relaxed. "I'm sorry, Mama, but it wasn't my fault, honest!"

She took his hand. "I know, son, it never is. But you just hush up, now. The thing is for you to get better—I'm here to see to that."

In moments of trouble, his mother always took charge and things turned out all right. The sound of her comforting voice eased Clay into a restful sleep.

Two quarrelling blue jays outside the window roused Clay back to reality and he blinked, waiting for the explosion in his head. He had no pain, but his stomach growled from the tempting smell of fresh coffee and fried bacon. He must have slept the rest of the day and all night.

He got off the bed and onto his feet. Finding the world no longer spinning, he made his way out the back door and over to the large pump where he splashed cold water over his head.

As usual, the men had eaten early and gone to their chores before

Clay's mother and Mary had their breakfast. They were just finishing as Clay walked into the kitchen.

"Mama," he said, "you let me sleep the whole day and night!" He bent to kiss her cheek. Making her feel guilty might soften the harsh words she was probably saving for him.

"You needed that rest," she told him instead. "How do you feel, son?"

"Hungry as a bear right out of hibernation!"

"Sit down, Clay," Mary told him and got up from the table. "I'll fix you some breakfast." She cleared the table of dirty dishes and poured Clay a cup of coffee before working at the stove.

Clay took her chair and sipped at the coffee.

His mother's worried eyes had never left him. "I'm sorry I accused you of sneaking whiskey," she told him, "but you know how your father always preached against the Devil's drink."

"Mama, I was only five when Papa died. I don't remember everything he said."

Mary set a plate of eggs and bacon in front of him and he quickly began filling his empty stomach.

"I'm just worried about you leaving to join the Confederacy next week," his mother said, "and what will happen to you."

The country was being torn apart and surely Armageddon had begun, just as her husband, a Presbyterian preacher, had warned in his sermons. All the young men were going to war, many of them never to come home again. Luckily, her son Monroe and Mary's husband Lewis were too old to go. But Clay was leaving and she'd be losing John soon, as well.

Clay patted her hand. "Don't you fret none, Mama. I can take care of myself."

She heaved a tired sigh. "Well, if you feel like it, John and Monroe could use some help in the field. We've got to get that corn to market before you leave on Monday."

Clay finished eating and walked down the worn front porch steps to see Mary's husband Lewis give him a wave from the barn. Lewis, the oldest of them all, was better schooled. Every night after supper, he'd have his nose stuck in a book or newspaper. Lewis and Mary hoped to have a place of their own some day, but now they lived in a little cottage behind the main house. Clay waved back and made his way to the cornfield.

The sun's warmth silhouetted their big house and barn, standing in sharp relief to the distant blue-green mountainside with corn and bean crops glistening nearby. It would be hard on his mother and sister, Clay thought, with only Lewis and Monroe to do the work after Clay and John went to war. But he couldn't do anything about that. If the government up north would just leave them alone, things would be all right. The thought of it brought a dull pain back to his head.

Clay arrived at the cornfield to see the wagon partially filled with a mass of silky gold tassels and bright green husks. John's shirt, sweat-stained to a dark blue, clung to his back as he worked among the tall rows, cutting ears from the stalks.

"Mighty nice of you, little brother," Clay shouted, "to do half my work for me already!"

"Just gettin' in practice," John yelled back. "I'll be doin' *all* your work after you leave next week!"

Clay reached down and gathered the cut ears into a burlap bag, which he swung over his shoulder and carried to the wagon. The noonday sun beat down with unusual brilliance as he climbed up onto a wagon wheel and emptied the bag. Bright green husks tumbled out, glinting in warm sunlight like a mound of shimmering emeralds. The sight mesmerized him and he couldn't take his eyes away. The back of his neck tingled and a black cloud swooped down out of nowhere. He felt himself falling, then heard his brother's urgent voice.

"Clay, what's the matter? Wake up!"

Clay put a hand to his forehead. "I'm all right . . . just fell down, is all."

John had been on one knee beside him and now stood up with

relief. "How come you fell off the wagon?"

Clay rubbed the back of his neck. "Don't tell me I fainted—that's for women!"

"When a man does it, they call it blacking out. Maybe you shouldn't have gone back to work so soon—that mule gave you a really good kick!"

Clay got up and brushed off his pants. "It doesn't hurt any more. Now, don't you go tellin' Mama about this. I don't want her makin' a fuss!"

On Sunday, Mary helped her mother prepare a farewell supper in honor of Clay's departure. Nancy Allison even took her prized glass pitcher from its hallowed position on the dining room shelf and filled it with cool spiced apple juice. The cut-glass decanter had been passed down through the generations of Allisons and no one knew exactly where it had originated. Somewhere in the old country, Clay guessed. With his mother's passing, it would go to her daughter Mary. The pitcher was used only on special occasions and now its finely etched designs reflected beautiful red, green and yellow glints of light as Nancy Allison carefully poured juice into their glasses.

After breakfast the next morning, Monroe and Lewis said their goodbyes to Clay before going to their chores. John stayed at the house, since he was taking Clay into town.

Their mother watched with sad eyes as her son rolled his few belongings into a bundle. "My word, Clay" she said, "you'll certainly need more than that."

He laughed. "Just need enough to get me to Knoxville. I'll be wearing Army clothes after that." He gave her a hug and kiss.

"Now, get on with you, son. I'm not going to let you see me with tears on my face!"

Clay next gave his sister Mary a loving embrace.

"You take care of yourself," she said and dabbed at her eyes.

He climbed up behind John on their dull-brown horse and they started off to town where Clay would catch a ride to Knoxville. A heavy fog had settled around the Appalachians to the east, only their peaks showing like conical blue-green islands in a sea of whipped cream.

The two brothers rode in silence through a ghostly mist clinging to the mountainside and Clay looked around for the last time. "You never know how pretty this country is till you have to leave it," he thought aloud.

John dropped his brother off in town and they grasped hands in farewell. Each had a lump in his throat.

"You take care, now," John said and patted Clay on the shoulder. "Reckon it won't be long before we'll both be fightin' those Yankees!"

John got back into the saddle and turned the horse around. He didn't want to look back. After a few deep breaths of cold morning air he let the horse take him through the misty valley back home.

Army life proved to be a rude awakening for Clay. Instead of rushing into battle as expected, he joined the other recruits at Knoxville in a cursory physical inspection of their eyes, ears and open mouths, then donned an itchy uniform and suffered the rigors of drills and exercises. He worked hard at controlling his newly-honed temperament until one day at noon rations, it exploded.

The food slopped onto his tin plate was certainly not what Clay was used to back home and he began to eat with slow deliberation.

Seated next to him, a burly recruit cleaned his plate without hesitation, then watched Clay picking at his food. "If you don't like your dinner," the man said, "I'll eat it for you." He snatched a piece of the stale bread from Clay's plate.

Clay took a deep breath to hold his anger. "And you sure as the devil don't need it, so put it back!"

The man sneered and poked the crust into his mouth.

Clay jumped up, throwing a quick fist to the soldier's jaw, which sent him sprawling.

With fire in his eyes, the bully got to his feet and came at Clay, swinging both fists. Clay caught a blow to his left eye, then blocked a roundhouse to his jaw and landed a hard right to the man's face. The other soldiers gathered around, cheering on the combatants.

Their sergeant appeared, pushing his way through the group. He grabbed each fighter by his collar, holding them apart. "Which one of you started this?" he growled.

The burly recruit wiped blood from his lip. "That one tried to steal food from me," he said. "He's nothin' but trouble!"

"He's lyin', Sergeant," Clay said. "I didn't do anything!!"

"Well, you both'll have to explain it to the commander," the sergeant said.

The bully's lies got him excused, but Clay wasn't so lucky. First, his bruised eye was treated by the Army doctor, then Clay reported to the company commander. He stood at attention while the officer read the report.

Finally the commander looked up to study Clay's swollen eye and said, "Fighting isn't tolerated in this regiment. What's your excuse, Private?"

"It's the conditions, sir," Clay replied.

"How do you mean?"

"The men are edgy, wanting to get at the Yankees. But all we've done is drill, dig ditches and watch other units march off to battle. All this waiting just makes it worse."

The officer leaned back with hard but understanding eyes. "The men will get their chance when they're properly trained and we can put them into the field with hopes they'll survive. Until that time, you and the others will act like soldiers—and save your fighting for the battlefield. Any more infractions, Private Allison, and you'll be given duties less enjoyable than drilling and digging ditches!"

Clay returned to his tent and sat with dejection on a rickety cot. Nothing had gone right since he'd left the farm. The strange feeling kept running up his neck occasionally and he had to struggle to keep from blacking out. He found it harder to control his temper. Maybe if he could just get into the battlefield, face-to-face with the enemy, he could purge himself of the thing clawing inside his head.

Two cots away, a thin little man in horn-rimmed glasses sat cleaning his gun. Clay knew him as a quiet but dedicated soldier and remembered that inspection would be held that afternoon. He picked up his own weapon and began polishing the barrel. Soon the ruffian he'd fought earlier in the day entered the tent.

"Here, Private," the man said in a gruff voice to the smaller recruit. "You can clean my rifle. I'll take yours!"

Clay turned to see the ugly man yank away the small soldier's clean gun and throw a dirty rifle down onto the cot.

Clay's neck tingled and he rose in anger. "Give him back his weapon and clean your own damned gun!" he ordered.

The burly man sneered. "Mind your own business or I'll black that other eye for you!"

Clay doubled his fists. "I don't want to fight you again, so just give that gun back!"

"Looks like you didn't learn your lesson the first time," the man snorted. "Maybe this'll teach you." He threw a punch, but Clay grabbed his arm.

The other recruit jumped up in alarm. "Stop it, you two, or the sergeant will see you!"

Clay still held the man's arm as they glared at each other.

"Why don't you stop pushing everybody around?" Clay said through his teeth.

The big one gave a hard shove, sending Clay sprawling backwards over a foot locker. His arm struck a bayonet, which gave him a nice cut, and he grabbed at the bloody shirt sleeve.

"What the hell's goin' on here?" their sergeant yelped from the tent's entrance.

The bully pointed at Clay. "This soldier was makin' trouble. again. Only thing I could do was defend myself!"

Clay got to his feet as the sergeant walked over to look at the bloody shirt sleeve. "Come on, soldier," he said. "We better get you to the doc."

The company surgeon shook his head at the sight of Clay entering his tent. "I just got through tending to your black eye and here you come again!" He noted the injury and took out a bandage. "This is your second visit," he said while wrapping the wound. "What is it that makes you keep fighting?"

"I don't know, Doctor. Maybe it's because of a head injury I got some time back."

The surgeon looked up with curiosity. "A head injury? Do you have seizures?"

"What's that?"

"You feel dizzy, maybe black out."

"Something like that. It's just that I get mad a lot easier, now."

"Then I'll have to put in the report that you can't control your outbursts."

Clay groaned. "Doctor, if you do that, I'll get a discharge for sure!"

"That's exactly what I'm going to recommend. My guess is you have epilepsy and you'll continue to make trouble, whether you want to or not."

"But, Doctor . . . "

"I'm sorry, Private—it's for your own good, as well as the Army's."

With his arm healing and all the necessary papers signed, Clay rolled his few belongings into a pack and started back to the little Tennessee valley. After catching wagon rides and a lot of walking, he showed up at the house just as the morning sun peeked over the eastern mountains. Glad to be home, but worried about explaining the discharge, he decided to just tell it like it was. His mother always expected the truth and that's what he'd give them.

Nancy Allison saw him walking up the path and she ran to grab him in a tight hug. "Clay, you didn't write about coming home on leave!" she cried.

18

The others had come out, also, and grabbed his hand in welcome.

"Come inside," his mother told him, "you're just in time for breakfast."

They took their places at the kitchen table and Mary began putting on the food.

"Now, if only John were here," their mother said, "we'd all be a family again."

"John's been in the Army almost as long as you," Mary said, "but they haven't given him a leave yet. How did you manage it?"

Clay took a deep breath. "I'm not on leave. I was discharged."

They all stared in surprise.

Finally, Mary spoke. "What on earth for, Clay?"

"When that mule kicked me in the head, I guess it made me high strung. They said I was causing too much trouble."

"Well," his mother said, "those people don't know anything. Your place isn't in the Army, anyway, you belong here doing what you've been doing all your life!" She waved the subject aside. "Now, let's say Grace and get on with our breakfast."

She bowed her head and the others lowered their eyes as Nancy Allison gave the short blessing. After the Amen, they all began passing the plates of food.

"Clay," his mother said, "if you and Monroe have time tomorrow, maybe you could dig up a spot of ground next to the house. I'd like to get some vegetables started out there."

Clay and Monroe worked up a sweat the next day, hoeing their mother's vegetable plot under the hot afternoon sun. Monroe wiped a kerchief across his eyes and saw a line of Union soldiers riding past on their way south.

Clay watched them, too. He felt guilty being back home again while John was out fighting for the south.

"We had a bunch of those Yankees come through the valley while you were gone," Monroe said. "Whenever they make camp, they send out foragers to get food for their troops."

The thought of giving the Yankees anything rankled Clay. "Did you have to give those scoundrels something?" he asked.

"Didn't get to our place, but they nearly emptied the cellar from people down the road."

Clay and Monroe returned to the house for their noon meal and Clay brought out a shotgun. "It's not safe for you and Mary to be alone at the house," he told his mother and leaned the gun against the inside front door. "While the rest of us are working the fields, I want you to use this if any Yankees come around."

"My goodness," his mother replied with a shudder. "I hope I never have to fire that thing!"

The next afternoon, while pitching hay at the barn, Clay and Lewis saw a stranger ride up to the house.

"Danged if it don't look like one of those Yankees," Lewis said.

The man, in a dark-blue uniform and forage cap, got down from his horse and walked up the porch steps.

Clay put down the pitchfork. "You stay here," he told Lewis. "I'll go see that Mama and Mary are all right."

He walked to the house, quietly opened the front door and stepped inside. From the sound of their voices, Clay knew that Mary and his mother were in the kitchen.

Just ahead, in the dining room, the Yankee soldier stood appraising the house. His eyes fell on the cut-glass pitcher and he picked it up, admiring the flashes of color dancing from its faceted surface.

Clay's anger stirred. "I'll ask you to kindly put that back on the shelf," he said evenly. "Real careful-like."

The startled Yankee looked up with contempt. "The Union Army takes anything it wants!" he replied.

"I'm asking you just once more to put that pitcher down."

The man held the decanter out in front of him. "And the Union Army doesn't take orders from a Rebel!" He opened his hands, letting the beautiful pitcher drop to the floor with a crash.

Clay's mother heard the noise and came to the doorway. She uttered a cry of agony on seeing her heirloom reduced to shards of glass.

In a rage, Clay grabbed the shotgun leaning beside the front door. The soldier's hand went quickly to the gun at his hip, but he was too late. Clay fired and the blast threw the Yankee backward, spattering blood over Nancy Allison's freshly-scrubbed floor.

Mary appeared immediately at her mother's side. They both put hands to their faces and stared in horror.

"Clay, you've killed him!" his mother breathed in shock.

"He broke your pitcher, Mama," Clay said and leaned the gun back in its place.

Monroe and Lewis rushed up the porch steps.

"We heard a shot!" Monroe said. "Everybody all right?"

"Everybody but that no-account Yankee!" Clay told him.

Nancy Allison regained her composure and took charge. "Somebody will come looking for him," she said. "We've got to hide the body right away!"

Monroe and Lewis walked over to examine the dead soldier. "In the barn," Monroe said. "We'll bury him there. I'll take his shoulders—Lewis, you take his feet." They hefted the body past Clay and out the front door.

"Mary, get a pan of water and some towels," her mother ordered. "We've got to clean up all this blood." She snatched a broom and began sweeping up the broken glass.

Clay strode out to the barn and helped the others dig a grave in one of the horse stalls. After they had neatly buried the soldier and covered the ground with straw, a horse was brought in.

"If another Yankee comes looking," Clay said, "it won't look right if we're not doing our chores."

"Somebody ought to stay with Mama and Mary," Monroe decided. "Clay, you go to the house while Lewis and I work around the barn here."

Mary had just rinsed blood out of the towels and was helping her

21

mother pin them to the clothesline when two more Union soldiers arrived on horseback. Clay, busy chopping wood, paused as the Union captain dismounted and walked over the them.

"We're looking for one of our men," the officer said. "Have you seen any soldiers pass through here?"

"Nobody's been around here for days," Clay told him.

Unsatisfied, the men went inside to look through the house, then rode around the farm and gave the barn a thorough search. After agonizing minutes, the soldiers galloped off and Nancy Allison collapsed on the porch steps with a sigh of relief.

Clay put a hand on her shoulder. "Are you all right, Mama?"

Her tired eyes gazed into space. "Time was when a stranger came to your door, he was greeted warmly and you gave him something to eat," she said quietly. "Now, a body fears for his life when somebody stops by!"

Clay still burned with anger. "I'm tired of staying here and not doing anything about it! I'm gonna re-enlist with another regiment—one that'll take anybody, as long as he's willin' to fight!"

His mother took his hand. "I'm too old and tired to stop you," she told him. "I can only pray that some day I'll have my family back together again."

Clay found his second hitch in the Army better than the last, especially since he attained the rank of sergeant. But he'd earned it by practicing self-control and not mentioning his previous discharge. The Army seemed so desperate for men that no questions were asked.

The only thing worse than the last time was being assigned to a hastily-organized ragtag regiment of new recruits, pushing their way deep into the south as cleanup soldiers in the wake of fighting.

They had marched for days, stopping only to repair a bridge torn down by the Yankees or to clear a road blocked with boulders and felled trees. Then, there was the rain. Cold and driving, it turned them into miserable creatures slogging through freezing knee-deep mud until their toes had no feeling.

At last the rain stopped, but scouts reported enemy presence a few miles away. If the Yankees planned to sieze the nearby town, they'd have to cross a bridge—and Clay's outfit was the only group to stop them. Uncertain of the outcome, he and the others pitched their dog tents on the muddy ground and waited for orders.

Small fires were somehow coaxed to life and Clay, with his buddy Will Sykes, sat on their heels waiting for the coffee to warm.

"Better not take off your shoes," Will advised. "When they dry out, they'll be so shrunk you won't get 'em back on again."

Will Sykes, a lanky farm boy from Kentucky, furnished the only bright spot in the dreary war. With his blond hair and constant smile, he seemed to defy the hardships of Army life. It was his good humor that kept the others going.

A murmur of excitement down the line caught their attention and Will looked up with a new grin. "It's the mail rider! He must've been following us. Let's go see if we got anything, Clay."

"You go ahead," Clay told him. "I'm not expecting to hear from anybody."

Will rushed down the row of tents to a gathering crowd of eager soldiers and soon returned with two envelopes. "Hate to disappoint you, Mr. Sourpuss," he gloated, "but there's one for each of us!" He handed Clay a mud-speckled envelope.

Clay could tell it was from his sister Mary. Her handwriting was small with little girlish curlicues on the capital letters, something she'd learned at school. With a fresh warm feeling, he ripped open the envelope. But, as he began to read, his spirits wilted.

*Dearest Brother Clay. It is with my deepest sorrow I must inform you that our beloved mother was yesterday laid to rest next to father on the hill. She had not been ill, nor was there an accident. She was only in her sixty-sixth year, however I believe the terrible events of the last few months were too much for her tender soul to endure.*

Clay felt a stab in his heart and could barely continue to read through tear-filled eyes.

*Two weeks ago, a regiment of Union soldiers swept through the valley, destroying everything in their path. They took our horses and one of the mules, then burned the barn and cornfield before moving on. We are lucky to still have the house, although many things were taken by looters.*

*We know you have troubles of your own in your fight against the enemy, so please do not worry about us, for Monroe, Lewis and I are in good health and we pray that God will bring you safely back to us soon.*

Clay put his head on his knees, clutching the letter with a mixture of grief and anger. Because of the damned Yankees, his mother was dead. Now, he couldn't wait to face them so he could take out his revenge.

After a sleepless night, Clay dragged his stiff body out of the tent and began chipping dried mud off his shoes. The early morning air echoed with muffled sounds of men preparing or eating their meager breakfast while Clay and Will Sykes sat on a dry spot of ground beside their little fire. Will poured coffee into their tin cups and they put dried biscuits into their unwilling mouths. Suddenly distant gunfire cut the air, bringing every man to his feet. Just as quickly, an order came down the line: "Hold the bridge!"

Their captain shouted the command, "Fall in!" and the men rushed to take their muskets from the stacks that also held cartridge belts. Clay and the others each grabbed a gun, threw the belt over his shoulder and strapped it into place.

As the men raced toward the sound of action, they passed Doctor Benson Colbert and his stretcher bearers establishing a hospital tent to do their bloody work. The surgeon's grim face only added to the anxiety of young men going into battle for the first time.

The soldiers moved out into a line behind a low dirt barricade that faced the area of battle. All guns had been loaded the night before and were now at half cock, ready for action to begin. Each man's heart beat hard and fast.

There had been a lull after the first shot, but now came another, followed in quick succession by more. It was the enemy's skirmishers clearing the way for an assault. The captain in Clay's regiment ordered a group of men forward to counterattack. Will was one of them while Clay had to wait with the others for the onslaught.

In a moment, bullets zinged and whistled overhead, then the Confederates returned. Clay scanned each face but couldn't spot his friend Will Sykes.

"They're comin'!" was the report. "And they're comin' strong!"

Clay turned his eyes back to the area where some of his men had fallen. All seem to have been killed—except for one who struggled to get up. Somehow, Clay knew it had to be his buddy Will. He jumped over the dirt barrier and ran out into the hail of bullets.

"Come back here, you fool!" the captain yelled.

Clay ignored him. His only thought was to get Will back to safety. He stumbled over clods of dirt until he reached his friend and knelt down. "How bad you hurt?"

Will breathed heavily and smiled up through his pain. "Can't get up—it's my leg!"

The men in Clay's unit had been warned not to fire until ordered and Clay's neck bristled at the sight of a line of Union soldiers flowing over the ridge. Only two hundred yards away, they resembled giant blue beetles, not waving antennae but guns. He heard his own men give the Rebel Yell—shrill, long, high-pitched—as gunfire broke out from both sides. It was load and fire, as fast as possible. Nervous fear was now replaced by daring rage while shells exploded and howled overhead in a deafening roar.

With Clay's help, Will got to his feet and put an arm around Clay's shoulder.

"Come on," Clay said, "I'll get you to the hospital tent."

Each held his breath as Clay dragged Will through the hellish din of flying bullets, mixed with the screams of those being cut down, many never to rise again.

# Chapter Two

*W*ith only a few strokes of his saw, Army surgeon Benson Colbert cut off the man's right arm. The doctor gritted his teeth and threw the severed limb onto a bloody pile of other arms and legs that swarmed with determined green flies in the warm hospital tent.

Thunderous booms from a nearby cannon shook the portable operating table, but Ben ignored the din of battle and ran a sleeve across his damp mustache. He pushed up a pair of wire-framed spectacles and leaned down once more to sew loose folds of skin over the glistening white bone.

The young Confederate soldier, although half-conscious, watched with dazed horror as the bandage was applied to his arm stump.

After the final knot, Ben helped his patient off the table and gently eased the boy down to lie among other wounded, spread around like a slaughterhouse of neatly-butchered cattle.

Ben paused to wipe bloodied hands on the long bib apron tied about his slight, over-forty paunch. He had difficulty breathing the suffocating air with its stench of blood and excrement. Already, his

26

young medical assistant had staggered out in a trail of vomit, leaving Ben to work alone. Now, he moved from one patient to another, shooing away the endless flies as he checked for signs of reopened wounds.

The large tent shuddered from another roar of cannon fire as stretcher bearers came in again. Ben uttered a quiet oath. Supplies were running out fast, but he had no time to think about that. He gave the suffering man a quick examination and saw a gaping chest wound.

"Put this man outside!" he barked. "I've told you—arm, leg or head injuries only!"

Little could be done with chest and abdominal cases; most would die, anyway.

If he were easily moved to tears, Ben Colbert could have filled buckets. With each new mutilated body, he cursed the stupid war for ruining the lives of these men, some only young boys. Most of them would never walk again or have an arm to put around a wife or sweetheart.

The nerve-wracking sound of warfare continued and two more soldiers entered the hospital tent. One, teeth clenched in pain, dragged a bloody leg. He supported himself with an arm around the other's neck.

The able one worked his dry throat to speak. "My friend here got it in the leg—he's hurt bad!"

"Yes, yes," Ben muttered, "they're all bad. Let's have a look."

Ben could guess the extent of injury, but knelt down anyway and pulled away the torn trouser leg. The bone was shattered and he swore again. Earlier in the war, the old round ball of low velocity made clean injuries, easier to repair. But now they were using the conical *minie* ball that destroyed a bone when hit. So much for progress.

He stood up with a grave look. "What's your name, soldier?"

The wounded man couldn't answer and the tall one spoke for him. "He's Private Will Sykes . . . I'm Sergeant Clay Allison."

Through his foggy glasses, Ben sized up the young man. Clay Allison towered a little over six feet. Without his cap, a mop of unruly jet-black hair set off his angular face and small chin. Although self-determination shone from his hard-set blue eyes, it couldn't mask a glow of deep empathy.

"Well, your friend will die if I don't take off that leg," Ben said. "But regulations say I must have his permission to amputate."

Will Sykes, face white with pain, could only nod.

"You'll have to help," Ben said to Clay. "Take that pail and wash off the table while I tear off this pant leg."

Clay dipped murky water from a large barrel and sloshed it across the bloody operating table, turning the ground below into a quagmire of crimson mud.

"Now, let's stretch him out," Ben said.

The two muscled Will up onto the table and Ben took a wicked-looking knife from his surgical box.

With a frown, Clay started to back away.

"Don't leave!" Ben ordered. "I need you to hold him down!"

Clay hesitated. "Don't you have something to put him out?"

"Used up my chloroform on the last one." Ben rummaged through his field kit. "Have your friend wash down these opium balls with enough whiskey to make him drowsy." He handed Clay the medicine and a bottle of liquor.

Clay held Will's head up and he swallowed the opium balls with two large gulps of whiskey.

"He's going to fight it," Ben said. "You'll have to keep him from jerking around."

Clay took a deep breath and pushed down on Will's shoulders.

Ben wiped the blood-smeared knife on his apron and made a fast cut around Will's leg, just above the wound. With practiced skill, he scraped away bleeding flesh and peeled it up to expose the bone.

Will squirmed with a dull moan.

"Throw some water over it!" Ben ordered and picked up the handsaw.

Clay washed away oozing blood as the doctor moved his saw back and forth in a crunching sound through the bone. Despite the opium, Will screamed in agony and Clay grabbed his free leg to keep it from thrashing.

With the limb quickly severed, Ben added it to his gruesome stack of body parts, then tied a few arteries and folded loose skin flaps down over the bone stump. He used silk thread to sew everything closed. "More water!" he said.

Clay threw on some water, washing the blood from Will's amputation.

Ben patted the wound dry and looked over the glasses that had slipped down his sweaty nose. "You make a good assistant—my other ones either vomit or pass out!"

They placed the delirious Will Sykes, now half-sedated and half-drunk, onto a blanket where he lay rolling his head in agony.

The roar of battle at last faded to a merciful quiet, leaving the hospital tent filled with only moans of the wounded. Soon, the commanding officer entered to check on his men.

The tall middle-aged colonel resembled a scarecrow in a disheveled uniform with lifeless eyes that begged for sleep. Tired and beaten, he surveyed the misery spread about him. "What's your report here, Doctor?"

Ben sighed and wiped his hands again on the slippery-red apron. "Ten outside with chest and abdominal wounds who won't live." He looked around. "In here, six head wounds, six amputations and one with an eye shot out—all with hopes of recovery."

The colonel shrugged. "There'll be a few more, I hate to say. We've been outnumbered and the Yankees have taken the town across the river. We've lost a majority of our men. I have a burial detail working, now."

Ben had prayed he'd seen the last. "Where are the pack mules with medicine, Colonel? My supplies are almost gone. Any more surgery will have to be done without sedation and I'm down to my last bandage!"

The colonel shook his head. "The mules were either stuck in the infernal mud or captured by the Yankees . . . I'm sorry, Doctor."

Ben swallowed a growing lump of despair. He was lucky to have his own set of surgeon's knives and pistol-grip saw, along with his field case—but the little box was now almost empty.

The officer rubbed his chin. "The Yankees had a lot of wagons when they crossed the bridge, no doubt with a good supply of medicine. Maybe I could have two men sneak across the river into town and confiscate something for you."

Ben's spirits rose a notch. "I'd have to go with them—they wouldn't know which items to take."

The commanding officer shook his head. "Sorry, Doctor. I can't risk losing my only surgeon. It wasn't a good idea, let's forget about it. After we retreat you'll have all the supplies you need." He turned to leave and stopped at the tent door. "I'll see that warm food and coffee are brought in."

Clay wanted to get out of the stinking place, too, but glanced at the exhausted doctor. "Looks like you need help, Doc—you want me to stay?"

Ben relaxed for the first time since the start of battle. "You say your name is Allison?"

"It's Robert Clay Allison, but I'm 'Clay' to everybody."

Ben stuck out a blood-stained hand. "I'm Doctor Benson Colbert . . . and I appreciate your offer, Clay. I'll show you what to do!"

The sun began to fade as stretcher bearers carried in the last man. Ben and Clay could only wash the wounds and dry them with pieces of already soiled cloth.

After everything possible had been done, Ben removed the wretched apron and found a dry spot of ground where he sat down and leaned against a tent post. His eyelids closed like drawn window shades, shutting out the horrors of reality.

Not knowing if the doctor was praying or asleep, Clay looked down with respect and admiration. "You said 'hopes of recovery,' Doc. Does that mean some will die?"

Ben's eyes remained shut. "Most of the amputations will fester. Pus will have to be drained off, but that's to be expected. If there's bleeding, the wound will have to be opened and sewed back up. Without bandages and opiates, it won't be pleasant for the patient."

Clay glanced around the fetid tent with its mass of writhing agony and the pain-wracked face of his friend Will Sykes. "Doc, you've got to go across the river . . . I'll go along, too, and make sure nothing happens to you!"

Ben opened his eyes a crack. "The colonel won't allow it."

"After supper, when it's dark, we can sneak away and wade across the river at a shallow part. It shouldn't take more'n a couple of hours—they won't miss us."

Ben considered the possibility, then asked, "You have a family waiting for you back home, Clay?"

Clay realized how tired he was and sat down next to the doctor. "An older brother and sister and her husband, still on our farm in Tennessee. I have a younger brother, John. He's closer to my age. We always worked and played together. He went to war after I did." His eyes clouded in worry. "There was only one letter from John, so I don't know if he's dead or alive."

"What about your parents?"

"Pa died when I was five, my Ma, just a month ago." Clay gritted his teeth in anger. "My sister wrote me that Mama died after some damned Yankees ransacked our farm. The farm was her whole life . . . I guess what they did must've tore her apart!"

Ben caught the acid hate in Clay's voice and changed the subject. "Then my home's not too far from yours—Kentucky. When the war broke out it meant only one thing, killing and wounding of innocent young men. I just tossed a coin to see which side I'd help."

Clay turned to study the doctor's stern but kindly face. "I reckon you have a family?"

Ben frowned. "My wife died a year ago."

"Any children?"

"A boy, Steve. He's almost fifteen, now."

"With your wife gone, where is he now?"

"When I joined the Army, I left him in the care of my wife's sister Hannah."

The memory of gentle Hannah brought a glow to Ben's face. Torn with two emotions, he mourned the loss of his wife Nora, while at the same time felt guilty that her sister Hannah had filled the dark void in his heart.

"Dear Hannah," he said. "She'll have a rough time of it—Steve has a mean streak. At his age, he's ripe to take the wrong path." He shrugged. "It's my fault, really. I've been too strict with the boy. Never gave him the love a father should. But when this damnable war is over, I'm determined to go back and do the right thing!" He removed his glasses and looked for a clean spot, finally wiping the lenses on a shirt sleeve. "Enough about me. How long have you been in the Army, Clay?"

"This is my second go-around. It was easy to join up again since they didn't check my records."

"Sounds like you had trouble the first time."

"The discharge said something about 'epileptic behavior.' I was always gettin' into a fight with somebody."

Ben raised an eyebrow. "Then you have epilepsy?"

"They said it's because I got kicked on the forehead by a mule before I enlisted."

Ben nodded. "The frontal and temporal lobes of the brain are especially vulnerable when the front of the head is struck by a hard object."

"What does all that mean?"

"That a blow to the forehead can manifest epilepsy. Do you have seizures?"

Clay shrugged. "Guess you'd call it that. At first, I'd get this strange tingle in the back of my neck . . . a couple of times I blacked out. I don't do that any more, but I still get that feeling once in a while if my temper gets the best of me—or if I have a few drinks. Then I just explode!" He blew out a helpless sigh. "Reckon it's something I'll have to deal with the rest of my life!"

"You have partial seizures. But you must've learned to control it—you've made it to sergeant this second time."

Clay's face lit up. "Doc, you're the first one who understands me!"

Ben chuckled. "Well, I was schooled in surgery, not disorders of the brain. But the devil with it! You're as good as the next man. Just watch that temper and stay away from liquor—you should be all right."

Two enlisted men came in with containers of warm food and coffee. Clay helped Ben, going from soldier to soldier and lifting each one's head to put food into his mouth. After all had been taken care of, Ben and Clay sat on the ground to eat their own supper of greasy pork and rock-hard biscuits.

"You really want to go across that river?" Ben finally said.

Clay's blue eyes came alive. "Why not?!"

Ben glanced through the tent opening. "Well, looks like it'll be dark enough in another half hour."

While Ben Colbert ate the tasteless meal, he realized the only good thing about war was that it helped him forget his troubles back home. However, the conversation about young Steve had brought it all tumbling back.

But he hadn't mentioned the real problem—his younger brother Chunk. Chunk Colbert had gambled away his share of their father's estate and become a wastrel. As long as Chunk stayed out of Ben's life, he couldn't care less. The trouble was that his boy Steve admired Chunk's easy life.

Ben thought of the difference between young Steve and the sergeant eating beside him, now, in the hospital tent. He wondered if the selfish Steve Colbert would ever risk his hide for someone else, like Clay Allison was about to do.

# Chapter Three

*S*teve Colbert leaned idly beside the tavern door while his Uncle Chunk gambled inside. Steve wanted to go in, too, but Chunk would be playing high-stakes poker and didn't want a curious fifteen-year-old at his side.

Steve blew a strand of red hair from his face, impatient green eyes surveying the almost empty street. This small Kentucky town appeared much like his own, just a short ride over the mountain, where Chunk had picked him up on his way to school that morning.

At last, Chunk Colbert came out, looking suave in his dressy dark suit and red vest with a jaunty black hat atop rust-colored hair.

Steve thought it strange how his father and Uncle Chunk Colbert could be so far apart. Like comparing molasses to salt water. His father Ben Colbert, quiet and tight with his money, gave Steve only what was necessary. But to Uncle Chunk, tall, reedy and carefree, life was just one long poker game. Money passed through his fingers like running water. That's how Steve wanted to live. Someday he'd make money the way Chunk did. His uncle had already shown him how to use a fingernail to secretly mark a deck of cards before it was dealt.

Now, Chunk Colbert's steely eyes had turned grim, the left one twitching with irritation.

"How much did you make this time, Uncle Chunk?" Steve asked.

"That man cheats better than I do!" Chunk sounded calculating. "But just you wait—I'll get my losses back!"

An older man came out of the tavern, putting a number of bills into his coat pocket.

Chunk whispered to Steve, "You stay here and watch out for me." He pulled a slender knife from his inside coat pocket and followed the man around the corner.

Steve's freckles reddened with excitement and he looked again at the empty street. His breathing quickened as a woman appeared from one of the stores and started up the board walk. He scooted around the corner to warn his uncle, but stopped with a gasp.

The unlucky man lay on the ground with a crimson pool of blood forming around his neck while Chunk, on one knee beside him, wiped his knife blade on the man's coat. He stood up and ran fingers through some bills.

"What happened, Uncle Chunk?" Steve asked, gaping at the lifeless figure. "Did you kill 'im?"

"Only thing to do. Otherwise, he'd give a description and we'd both end up in jail."

Steve's forehead wrinkled. "It don't seem rightly fair to kill a man for just a few dollars!"

"Fair?! You'd better get that word out of your head right now, boy. Nothing in life is fair. Nobody's going to give you anything in this world. You have to take what you get, no matter how you do it! Now, come on. I'd better get you back home so your Aunt Hannah won't think you've been playing hooky all day."

"School's for little kids," Steve grumbled. "Can't I just stay with you, Uncle Chunk?"

"Not till you learn to take care of yourself." Chunk started for his horse, waiting in the street.

Steve kept arguing as he followed. "But I'm learnin' from you!"

"You'd have to know a lot more where I'm going."

Steve caught his breath. "What do you mean . . . goin' where?!"

"The war's turning this land into one big poor house. Those who have money are taking it west, to buy a new life. That's where I ought to be!" He put a foot in the stirrup and threw himself into the saddle.

Steve's eyes widened. "Let me go west with you, Uncle Chunk, I hate it here!"

They cut their talk as the woman Steve had seen earlier now walked up and gave them a hard look.

Chunk uttered a low curse. "Come on," he muttered to his nephew, "let's get out of here!"

He grabbed Steve's hand and pulled the boy up behind him, then dug a sharp heel into the horse's flank. It squealed in pain, kicking a cloud of dust over the boardwalk before galloping off.

With a frown, the woman brushed the dust from her clothes and walked away. On reaching the corner, she looked down at the grisly scene and uttered a scream of horror. Two men came running from the tavern to see what had broken the peaceful quiet of their law-abiding town.

Chunk Colbert worried about being recognized, since he'd been in the town before and was known by a few of the citizens. Now, with Steve hanging on for dear life, he raced his horse over the mountain trail, hoping no one was following. Arriving back in their own town, Chunk stopped at the schoolhouse and let Steve slide to the ground. The boy watched his uncle take a small container from a coat pocket and tip it to his mouth.

"I still don't know why I can't have a drink outta that bottle you carry, Uncle Chunk!"

Chunk laughed. "Now, just what would your Aunt Hannah say if you came home smelling of whiskey!"

"I don't care what she'd say—she ain't my ma!"

"Same thing. She's been taking care of you since your mother died and your father joined the Army. What would you do if she kicked you out?"

"I'd go west with you! We could work together, gamblin' and stickin' old men for their money!"

Chunk gave him a sharp look. "You can't go with me—and don't go telling Hannah or anybody else what we did! You just go on home and say you've been in school all day." He softened at Steve's dour face. "Don't look so sad, kid. Maybe I'll see you tomorrow." He punched a spur and the horse carried him away.

Steve kicked at a stone, thinking how funny it would be if he told his Aunt Hannah the truth—that he'd helped his uncle kill a man today.

Hannah James took another sheet from the clothesline and blew a wisp of fine brown hair from her hazel eyes; they sparkled in the afternoon sun, adding to the inner beauty of a plain face, still satin-smooth at the age of forty-one.

With just her and the boy Steve, she really didn't have an awful lot to do, but keeping house and cooking meals did take most of the day. The monthly stipend his father Benson Colbert sent from the Army paid the expenses; what was left over, she kept for herself in a sugar bowl on an upper kitchen shelf.

She picked up the basket of dried clothes and saw Steve walking up the path. He didn't deserve it, but she greeted him amiably. "What did you learn in school today, Steve?"

He eyed her slyly. "The value of money!"

"Where are your books?"

"Left 'em at school."

Hannah James had learned to be suspicious. "Have you been playing hooky again?"

He sneered in defiance. "What difference does it make? I know enough already!"

Hannah's patience crumbled. "If your ma were alive, she'd take a switch to you! Where've you been all day?"

His silence gave the answer.

"You've been with your Uncle Chunk, haven't you? Before your father left, he gave strict orders for me to keep you away from that brother of his!"

For months, Hannah knew the boy had been taking her money from the sugar bowl, little at a time. She didn't let on, thinking he was probably spending it on candy. Now, she realized he was giving it to his uncle to gamble with.

"There's nothin' wrong with Uncle Chunk!" Steve argued. "When he goes west, I'm goin' with him—he's gonna teach me things I don't learn at that durned school!"

"I know the kind of things he'd teach you! Now, I promised your father I'd keep you away from his brother and I'll do it, even if I have to hog-tie you!"

"So hog-tie me!"

Hannah spewed with frustration. "Now go wash your hands —supper's about ready!"

While they finished their meal in the darkness of early evening, Hannah tried to reason with the exasperating boy.

"Steve, I want you to understand that I'm doing the best I can for you, just like your father asked me to. The only reason I took on this duty is because your mother was my sister."

"And because you're sweet on my Pa!"

Hannah slammed down her soup spoon. "How dare you say such a thing! I admire your father. Benson Colbert is a fine doctor and everybody looks up to him. The Confederate Army was very lucky to have him enlist as one of their surgeons, and you ought to show him some respect!"

She got up to take away the dirty dishes, but in her heart knew what the boy said was true. Her devotion to Ben Colbert must have been obvious during all that time she kept Ben's house while her sister was ill. She wondered if Ben might have had some special feeling for her, too; she'd noted a soft look in his eyes when they said goodbye the day he left to join the Army.

"I don't have enough wood for the morning's breakfast," Hannah told Steve as she cleaned the big iron stove. "Would you please bring some in for me?"

Surprisingly, without an argument, Steve went outside to the wood pile and began rummaging through the pieces, selecting only what was necessary for next morning. With an armful he turned to leave, but froze on seeing a figure move in the nearby shadows. A familiar voice made him relax.

"Steve, boy, you've got to help me!"

"Uncle Chunk! If Aunt Hannah knows you're here, she'll take a broom to you!"

"I need you to do something for me."

"Sure, anything."

"That woman in the town today who saw us ride away—she told the law and now they're looking for me. I've got to get out of town, fast!"

Steve's heart skipped. "You goin' west, now, like you said?!"

"Yes, but you've got to help me."

"What you want me to do?"

"That money your Aunt Hannah gets from Ben, you know where she keeps it. I need you to get it for me—all of it—so I can get away!"

"What about the money you took from that man you killed today?"

Chunk growled in the darkness. "Had some bad luck in a game this afternoon."

Steve found his chance. "That woman saw both of us. That means they'll be lookin' for me, too—I gotta go with you, Uncle Chunk!"

"That's crazy, I can't have a boy trailing along!"

Steve held his anger. He wasn't just a boy any more, but he didn't want to argue and spoil this opportunity. "I'll get the money, but only if you take me with you!"

Chunk considered the situation. "Your father thinks a lot of you. I bet he'd really be hurt to know you ran away with me!"

"He'd be madder than a wet rooster!"

Chunk laughed. "I can just see him now!"

"Besides," Steve pouted, "he always made me go to school and do my chores before he'd give me any spendin' money!"

Chunk's voice turned conniving. "I could show you how to get all the money you want, and never work a minute for it!"

Steve gasped. "You mean you'll take me with you?!"

"All right, but I'll have to steal you a horse. Wait till Hannah goes to bed, then get that money and sneak out. I'll be waiting!"

Another dark chill of morning greeted Hannah James as she got out of bed and went to the kitchen. After starting a fire in the stove and setting the coffeepot to brew, she went to her nephew's room to wake him. But the room was empty and the bed not slept in.

*He's made good his threat*, she thought, *and run away with that Uncle Chunk.* She sighed with relief, glad to be free of the nasty boy. But she also felt heartsick for Ben—he would be devastated.

A loud knock took her to the front door and she opened it to see the town lawman.

"Hate to bother you this early in the mornin', Miz James," he said, tipping his hat. "We're lookin' for your sister's brother-in-law Chunk Colbert. He's wanted for killin' a man in Clarksville yesterday and stealin' a horse."

"I haven't seen Chunk Colbert since his brother Ben went to war," she told him.

"A witness saw him ride away from the murder scene yesterday. He had a young boy with him. You know who that'd be?"

"That must have been Chunk's nephew Steve. I've been taking care of him while his father's away. I was just going to report that Steve's run off during the night."

"With his uncle?"

40

She sighed in resignation. "I think so. Steve told me yesterday he was going to do it, but I didn't believe him."

"Do you know where they might've gone?"

"Only that Steve said his uncle was going west." Her eyes turned anxious. "If they're found, what will happen to them?"

"Go to jail and wait for trial."

After the man left, Hannah poured a cup of coffee and took stock of the situation. With young Steve Colbert gone, now, there was no need for his father to keep sending money and she would be out in the streets.

She went to the cupboard to check on what was left in the sugar bowl and smiled ironically to find it empty. The hardest thing, now, was to let Ben know what had happened.

Hannah sat at the little table and began writing a letter. As her pen scratched across the smooth lined paper, she prayed they would never find the two renegades. If his son were thrown into jail, it would surely kill Ben Colbert.

# Chapter Four

*T*he half light of a silver-arc moon cast eerie shadows on Clay Allison and Ben Colbert as the two moved through a stand of high swaying trees.

They quickly found the river bank and Ben looked with doubt at the intimidating purple stream. "We can't wade across here, it's too deep."

"If we go to a shallow place downstream," Clay said, "it'd be too far from town." He spied an object bobbing among the reeds. "We're in luck. There's a boat!"

They walked over and Clay pulled a small, rotting wooden hull up onto the bank.

"It's not big enough for the two of us," Ben said with disappointment. "And the front end is broken out."

Clay noted the doctor's heavier frame. "If you sit in the back, it'll raise the front end out of the water."

"What about you?"

"I'll swim alongside and make sure it stays up."

Ben got carefully into the rickety boat, then Clay took off his clothes, handed them to Ben and slipped naked into the frigid water, sucking his breath against the shock. He guided the craft slowly out into the dark moving stream, glad to see that Ben's weight kept the boat's nose high above the surface. It didn't take long to arrive on the other side and they silently moored the boat among some bushes.

Clay shivered, putting on his clothes while surveying the quiet street. Only a few Union soldiers guarded the supply wagons parked in front of some large buildings, evidently being used as headquarters.

Ben squinted through his glasses. "That wagon on the end is an ambulance," he whispered. "They must be using the building next to it as a hospital."

"Should be easy to sneak over there and raid the ambulance," Clay answered. "Nobody's down that way."

Ben shook his head. "It's probably empty. The wounded will be inside, and I'm sure that's where their doctor has taken his supplies."

"Then let's see if we can get in through the back."

The two moved quickly in a wide path so as not to be seen. They reached the building's rear door to find it neither locked nor guarded.

"Easier than I thought," Clay murmured.

"Don't lose your caution!" Ben warned softly. "There has to be a doctor or someone in there with the injured."

Clay opened the door a crack and peeked in. The large room had no doubt been used to store grain before the Union Army took it over. Stacks of plump burlap bags lined one wall while two kerosene lamps cast dim light over a row of cots on the other side.

"Don't see anybody but injured men in their beds," Clay said. "Come on."

With quiet steps they moved into the building. A musty odor of grain sacks and medicine hung in the air.

As they walked slowly down the line of cots Ben Colbert, with professional concern, noted each man's injury. He paused at the bedside of one soldier whose amputated leg oozed blood through the bandages.

Clay took Ben's arm. "Come on, Doc, we've got to find those supplies!"

"This man will bleed to death if he doesn't get attention!" Ben said irritably. "Where on earth is their doctor?!"

They turned as a voice came from the front doorway, "Who's there?"

Clay froze and saw a tall man with an impressive full beard walk up to them.

"Are you in charge of these men?" Ben asked the stranger.

"That's correct—I'm Doctor Charles Freeman. And just who are you?" He noticed Clay's gray uniform. "Why, you're Confederates!"

"I am Doctor Benson Colbert with the Tenth Confederate Artillery from across the river, and this is Sergeant Clay Allison."

Charles Freeman relaxed. "Well, I'm pleased to meet another doctor during this holocaust." He took Ben's hand in a friendly shake.

Clay looked on, astonished. The two men chatted as if they'd just met at a medical convention.

"Your patient here needs prompt attention, Doctor," Ben said.

Charles Freeman looked with tired concern at his wounded soldier. "You're right, I was just bringing more bandages. You see, I'm short of help."

"Then please let me assist."

Clay watched in disbelief as the Confederate and Union doctors worked together, stemming the blood flow and applying a new bandage.

"I know your regiment suffered a great number of casualties this morning," Doctor Freeman said. "You must have many more wounded than I have."

"Precisely why we are here," Ben replied. "I'm desperately in need of medical supplies."

Charles Freeman stood up with a knowing look. "And you

thought you might confiscate some from us? Well, we have ample. Come with me to the storeroom." He glanced at Clay's uniform. "But your sergeant friend had better wait here—if the guards see him, you'll both be arrested!"

Clay waited in the shadows, eyes darting cautiously into each corner of the warehouse. Soon, the two men returned with a couple of packages and Doctor Freeman handed one to Clay.

"I'm indebted to you for these supplies," Ben told the doctor.

Freeman's eyes softened with mutual concern. "Let's hope those are the last ones you'll need. I wish you luck." He looked around to be sure they were still alone. "If you'll go quietly the way you came, it should be all right."

The two doctors shook hands and Clay pulled Ben out the door.

So far, the mission had been a success, however more soldiers gathered at the street. Clay looked around for another route, but two of the men raised their rifles and began walking forward.

Clay handed his package to Ben. "Here, take the supplies, quick, and go to the boat. They'll think I'm the only one!"

"But you'll be taken prisoner!" Ben protested.

"And you'll have your medicine. Now run! Don't worry about me!"

Ben hesitated, then darted into the shadows. Behind him, he heard shouts from the soldiers and a short scuffle. He stopped to look back and saw Clay being led away, hands tied behind his back. Ben grumbled at the way things had turned out, but knew he must complete the mission he and Clay had started.

Ben made his way to the river bank and climbed into the wobbly little boat. He pushed himself away from shore, using his hands to paddle silently across the dark river. His fingers turned numb in the cold water, but his heart warmed with deep admiration for the courageous young man he'd met only that afternoon. Few would sacrifice themselves as Clay Allison had, for the sake of his fellow soldiers.

# Chapter Five

*T*he two Yankees forced Clay into a large barn and over to a horse stall. One of them untied his hands and shoved him into the stall where he fell onto a bed of straw. They closed a low slat door and locked it by shoving a wooden pin through the door's hasp.

Clay almost laughed, for he could easily climb over the small door. "Is this supposed to be a jail cell?" he asked.

"That's what we're usin' it for," the man snarled. "But we got a guard at the barn door watchin' your every move. You make one try to get outta that stall and you'll get a bullet in your head!"

The two soldiers turned and walked out, however an armed guard stood not far away leaning against the barn door. The man gave a menacing look and fingered the gun on his shoulder.

Clay relaxed on the crunchy floor with his back against a rough stone wall—at least he had straw to sleep on. Under the blanketing smell of dusty hay, oiled leather and sweating horses, he began to think.

Doctor Benson Colbert at least had his medicine, now, and the regiment would soon return to friendly territory. Clay wondered if he'd ever see Will Sykes or the doctor again.

"Here's your supper," the guard said with an ugly scowl, interrupting Clay's reverie.

Clay took the dirty tin plate, which held a piece of salt pork in watery gravy and a slab of stale bread. As he dawdled over the tasteless food he recalled his mother's cooking—roast squab, black-eyed peas, hot cornbread straight from the oven with freshly baked gooseberry pie. The thought made these meager scraps almost palatable.

The guard poured a tin cup full of water from a nearby barrel and handed it through the slatted door. "Reckon I won't have to be tendin' you scrubby Rebel for long."

"You mean they're going to move me?"

"No. They're gonna hang you!"

"Hang me? When?"

"Maybe tomorrow. I know they want to get it over with before the war ends."

The man returned to his post and Clay sat down with the plate. If he was going to die, anyway, there seemed no point in eating. But he was hungry.

After Clay had finished his dubious meal, the Union Doctor Charles Freeman appeared at the barn door. He spoke with the guard who nodded permission to enter.

Freeman came over to the horse stall and spoke in a low voice. "As a doctor of the Union Army, my obligation is to check on any prisoners. Are you all right, Sergeant?"

Clay got up and walked to the low slat door. "I won't be for long. The guard says they're gonna hang me!"

Freeman looked glum. "I'm afraid that's what they do with spies—it's what you're charged with, by the way."

"The guard says they want to get it over with before the war ends. What does he mean?"

"The Confederacy is losing fast and there's talk of surrender any day, now. The Union regiment here doesn't want to be cheated out of hanging you before a truce is signed!"

Clay shook his head in frustration. "If I could only get out of here—it'd be easy without that blamed guard!"

Freeman gave a quick look at the man relaxing against the barn doorway. "I'll go talk with the guard and try to divert his attention. If I can get him to turn his back, perhaps you can climb over this door and escape out the back way."

Clay still couldn't figure it out. "I'm not on your side—why do you want to help me?"

"Any man who did what you did should have another chance."

Clay found it hard to believe that one side didn't naturally hate the other. "It really doesn't matter to you if a man's a Rebel or a Yankee, does it?" he asked.

"I agree with your Doctor Colbert—we both deplore this needless killing and maiming. Thank goodness, it's all going to end soon."

"Well, I'm with you, Doc!"

Clay watched as Charles Freeman walked over to the guard and engaged the man in conversation. By some wily trick, Freeman got the Yankee to turn his back and look outside.

Clay took a breath and climbed silently over the stall door, edging his way toward the back area. His foot struck a bucket hidden in the straw and he cursed, praying the noise hadn't been heard, then crept onward.

He finally reached the opposite door and started to open it, but a rough hand grabbed his collar, yanking him back inside.

It was the guard, his face contorted in anger. "I oughta shoot you now and save 'em the trouble of hangin' you!"

Clay whirled, his fist striking the man's chin, and the rifle went flying. Clay thought of grabbing the gun and using it, but a gunshot would bring others.

He jumped behind the staggering guard and tightened an arm around his neck. With the other hand, Clay pulled his arm as hard as he could against the man's throat. It seemed to take forever, but the guard finally relaxed and Clay released his grip, dropping him to the floor. Clay wondered if he'd killed him, but he had no time to worry about that.

The dark of evening had fallen, a good time to escape among the shadows. Clay eased himself outside, picking his way across the back yard. Soon, he came to the river's edge. With a glance behind to be sure no one had seen him, he slipped into the water and began dog-paddling toward the other side. In a few minutes he had pulled himself up onto the opposite bank and lay on his back, gasping for breath.

With all his tension now washed away, the beauty of stars twinkling above came into bright focus. Somehow he felt they were smiling down, almost happy to fill the heavens with their bright sparkling. He felt a surge of freedom and wiped the water out of his eyes. If the war was coming to an end, to hell with the Army. He knew exactly where he would go, now—back home to his farm in Tennessee.

Although his uniform hung torn and dirty, Clay skirted the towns in case Union sympathizers would spot him as a Confederate soldier. Roots of young trees and creek water provided his only nourishment, until at last a farmer discovered him sleeping in a haystack.

"Ye a Rebel, ain't ye?" the elderly long-bearded man said.

"That's right," Clay answered with hesitation. "Which side you on?"

"Don't matter, now. The war's over."

Clay swelled with elation at first, then asked, "I reckon the South lost?"

"You reckon right. But like I said, it don't matter none. At least the shootin' and killin's over." The man squinted down. "You look mighty peaked, son. How long since you et?"

"Don't know if I can remember my last meal."

"Well, come on to the house. They took most ever'thin' we got, but the wife can fix you somethin' warm."

Clay followed the man to his dilapidated farmhouse where a thin, tired-looking woman smiled in welcome. She, too, wore clean but threadbare clothing.

"This feller's on his way north," the farmer told his wife, "but he's 'bout spent. Needs somethin' in his stomach to keep 'im goin'."

The woman's eyes moistened as she looked at Clay. Perhaps he reminded her of a loved one, a son or grandson who had been killed in the war. She spoke with tenderness. "Sit down, young man, and I'll fix you what I can."

Clay ate ravenously, hoping he wasn't taking their last bit of precious food. He told them of the escape from prison and his desire to get back to the little farm in Tennessee. "I've been gone so long, I can't wait to see my home again!"

The farmer gave him a sad look. "Troops have run up and down this country, lootin' and burnin'. Even if it's still there, boy, don't expect your home to be the same as it was when you left!"

The man wasn't just blowing in the wind, Clay soon discovered. As he approached the Tennessee Valley, war's havoc stared balefully from destroyed crops and ruined homes on each side of the road.

Finally, trudging into the little farm he had loved from childhood, his heart sank. The barn had disappeared and no green stalks of corn waved in the warm sun. But the big log house still sat there, waiting forlornly on the ravaged land.

He began walking at a quicker pace and his spirits rose at the sight of a lithe flaxen-haired woman approaching at a run, an apron flapping behind her. She could only be his sister Mary. Happy tears flowed as she threw her arms around him.

Close behind came Mary's husband Lewis and Clay's older brother Monroe, all with smiles of welcome.

Clay shook their hands eagerly, but his heart swelled at the sight of his younger brother, John, running from the house.

The years of growing up, working and playing together, discovering all the secrets hidden in cold streams and green forests that only two adventurous boys could understand, had formed a strong bond of love between them. Now, they greeted each other, not with just a handshake, but a warm hug. Clay thanked God that John, too, had not been shot down by a damned Yankee's bullet.

"Well, come on," Mary said, wiping her eyes with a corner of the apron. "I'll fix us all something to eat—why, it'll be the first time the whole family's sat down at the table since I can't remember when!"

After his sister put the scant servings of food on the table, Clay regarded it with sad eyes; it didn't come near to the meals he remembered before leaving home.

"It's not like how Mama used to fix," Mary apologized, "but we're lucky to still have some chickens and vegetables."

They all took seats and started passing the food around.

Clay held back on his appetite and took only one piece of fried chicken. "You wrote that the Yankees took our livestock, too," he said.

Mary's husband Lewis filled him in. "Everything but one of the mules. Monroe had it out in the field the day they came through."

John added, "and I got a good horse today. The man almost gave him away 'cause it's so wild." He winked at his older brother. "But I know you can tame him, Clay—you always had a way with horses!"

Clay's heart softened with happiness for the first time in years. "Well, it's really good for all of us to be together again. But it's gonna take a heap of work getting the farm back in shape."

Monroe, even more serious than John, didn't seem pleased. "If we could get another crop ready for market, there'd be nobody to sell to. The whole country's depressed."

Clay saw the shadow of despair on all their faces and he suddenly wanted to get away. The happy family life he knew as a child had been destroyed and sticking around here would just make him keep thinking about it. "Maybe we oughta move to someplace else," he suggested.

"It's not any better up north," Monroe told him, "and if we went west, it'd have to be mighty far west, maybe Texas."

Mary's expression became more pained. "I wish you'd all stop talking about leaving! This is our home, where we were born and raised. Papa and Mama worked hard to build up this farm and we can't just run off and leave it—what would they say?!"

Monroe gave her a grim smile. "They're in no position to say anything right now. But if they could, I know they'd want us to do what's best."

Near sundown, Clay and John walked out to their mother's grave. It lay in the family cemetery not far behind the house, nestled on a slight rise beneath large comforting oak trees. The two brothers stood with quiet reverence, looking down at the small weather-stained wooden markers for Nancy and John Allison and their four children who had died not too many years before Clay and John, Jr., were born.

John glanced at his brother's sad face. Ever since Clay had been kicked in the head by that mule, John had carried a nagging concern for the older brother he idolized. "You still havin' those head problems, Clay?"

"Nothin' I can't take care of."

"All that talk about us going someplace else—what do you want to do?"

"I'll go along with whatever the rest of you say."

John shrugged. "Well, there's nothin' left here. Maybe we oughta do like Monroe says—just pick up and go to Texas."

Clay's eyes remained on his mother's grave. "For me, I wonder if Texas will be far enough?"

# Chapter Six

*"I* might have talked Steve out of leaving," Hannah James said, "but he sneaked out during the night."

Ben Colbert made a grumbling sound as he sat at the familiar kitchen table. "I don't care what happens to Chunk, but I've got to find Steve and talk some sense into him." He looked up with one last hope. "There wasn't any hint of where they were going?"

Hannah shrugged. "Steve only told me he was going west with his Uncle Chunk—but I thought it was just another one of his lies to antagonize me."

Ben thought a moment. "Chunk's smart. He's seen all the others moving west, after being ruined by the blasted war. He'll go where the money is!"

Hannah had been overjoyed when the terrible fighting ended and she at last saw Ben Colbert trudging home. But, now, she felt a pang of despair.

"Ben, I'm so sorry—I feel like I've failed you!"

He relaxed in the kitchen chair and stirred a cup of coffee she poured for him. It was the thought of Hannah's sweet, gentle face that helped him survive all those nightmarish days on the battlefield, sewing up the mutilated bodies of young men.

"Don't say that, Hannah. If anybody's to blame, it's me. I shouldn't have asked you to take on such a difficult task."

She sat down with her own cup and rested sympathetic eyes on his worried face. It seemed even more tragic, now, with the loss of his son to a no-account brother.

She wanted to reach out with comforting arms, but said, "I reckon I ought to be looking for another place to live, now that you're home."

He looked surprised. "But you have no place to go, Hannah—your folks are gone and the family home's been destroyed! Without Steve, I'll be alone. You can just keep living here."

She uttered a small embarrassed laugh. "Ben, this is a small town, you know how people talk!"

A slight color brushed his cheeks and he glanced down at the coffee cup. "I've been thinking about that . . . if we were married, it wouldn't matter, would it?"

She sat up, dumbfounded.

He blinked in disappointment, thinking she had refused his offer. "I thought it showed in my face, Hannah, while you were here during Nora's illness. I knew it was wrong at the time because she was your sister. When I decided to join the Army after Nora died, I thought I'd change. But it didn't go away, Hannah. You've been in my heart all this time!"

Hannah's eyes filled with happy tears and she reached across the table, taking his hands. "Ben Colbert, that's just about the sweetest proposal any woman could ask for!"

He gave her a relieved but eager smile. "It's late now, so we'll have to get married in the morning." His face reddened again. "That means, of course, you'll be spending the night here."

It was her turn to blush. "I've loved you for a long time, Ben, and I want to be by your side as soon as possible . . . but we're still not husband and wife."

"I understand. I'll sleep in Steve's room." He graced her with a shy grin. "But do you think one kiss would be out of line?"

"I guess if a man and woman love each other, they do that at least once before they marry." She rose from the table and walked over to him, her eyes full of longing.

Ben stood up to open his arms and Hannah slid in next to his warm body. They held each other for a long moment before he bent down for a gentle kiss.

It was not Benson Colbert's style to waste time. The next morning, in his usual businesslike way, he took Hannah James in a buckboard to the local justice of the peace and they were quickly married.

On their way back to the house, Hannah's heart overflowed as she snuggled next to her husband. Wearing her Sunday best—white cotton dress with a yellow ribbon at the waist, and a matching straw hat—she seemed a different woman. Mrs. Hannah Colbert. She squeezed Ben's arm.

"Ben, we're both in our forties and a little old to be newlyweds, but I feel like a sixteen-year-old bride, starting a whole new life!"

He laughed and took her hand. "That's a good way to look at it, my dear, but we may have a rough time of it."

"How do you mean?"

"I'll hang out my shingle again, but the war has ruined the country's economy. The farms have been destroyed and food's scarce. All the states are starting over and everybody's pinching their pennies."

"But people still need a doctor."

He patted her hand. "We'll see."

As Ben had predicted, during the next two months he saw only a few patients. With income so small, the future did not look promising. While waiting for his evening coffee, he stood at the window, seeing nothing through the frosty panes while his mind tumbled in thought.

Hannah put water on the stove and gave him a worried look. "Ben, you're not sorry we got married, are you?"

He turned in surprise. "Of course not, Hannah. It's just that I'm concerned about our future. I don't see things getting better for some time, maybe years. Especially in this little town."

"You think we could go up north?" she wondered. "They must be living well on what they've taken from all of us here in the south."

"Prices are out of reason everywhere." He paused in thought. "Except in the western territories."

Hannah watched as her husband paced the room with hands behind his back.

"That's where we should go!" he finally said.

"The west? Oh, Ben!"

"It's a whole new, wide-open land with opportunity for everybody!"

"But Ben, California is so far away!"

"I don't mean across the whole continent. I read just the other day, they've found gold in the Territory of New Mexico. A place called Elizabethtown. The area is growing fast."

"Ben, I can't see you digging for gold!"

"No, no, my Dear. I'll let them bring their gold to me—in payment for my services, of course."

Hannah gave him a wondering look. "There's another reason you want to go to New Mexico, isn't there?"

He glanced aside without answering.

"You said Chunk will go where the money is. You're hoping you might find him and Steve in New Mexico, aren't you, Ben?"

His face reddened at her question. "I admit, that's part of it. But you've got to understand, Hannah—it's my fault I let Steve go wrong. I'll go to my grave under God's wrath if I don't do all I can to help my own boy!"

56

She went to him and put an arm around his waist. "I know how you feel, Ben. I pray that you *will* find him. Then your mind will be at rest and I'll have you all to my own again!"

She gave him a loving kiss, but a tiny dread stirred in her heart. She had kept a secret from him for the last few days. If she told him, now, it would ruin all his plans and he'd surely not take her west. It was better to wait until they were on their way before letting him know she was with child

# Chapter Seven

*C*lay felt proud of himself. He'd stayed out of trouble ever since the family decided to pack up and leave what was left of their little Tennessee farm. But it had been a struggle all the way.

From the Mississippi River's opposite bank, the Allisons pushed the wagon and livestock westward, eventually reaching the little settlement of Palo Pinto in the Texas Keechi Valley. After another day's travel, they chose an ideal place to make a new life for themselves.

For security, Fort Belknap sat nearby, with another military installation to the west. A verdant blanket of grass covered the valley floor and cool clear water ran down from the mountains, which would protect them from winter's cold winds.

They lost no time in building their modest sod home with a large room and fireplace, a bedroom for Mary and her husband, and a small adjoining area shared by the Allison brothers.

Next came the job of planting the surrounding fields. While the others busied themselves with the tilling, Clay and John got into their saddles and took Molly the mule for an overnight ride into town for supplies.

The little community of Palo Pinto rested quietly beneath a gold afternoon sky as the brothers pulled their horses to a stop in front of the general store. They purchased the few necessary items and began securing the packs on Molly's back.

Clay eyed the saloon next door and gave his brother a mischievous glance. "I got a little fly sittin' on the back of my tongue—says if I wash 'im down with some good whiskey, he'll take the soreness outta my backside!"

John only flashed a stern look. Clay's biggest problem had to be his taste for liquor—if he went a hair over the line, it was like the Devil took hold of him.

"Oh, come on, John. Just one little drink—I can control it!"

"You know what can happen if you start drinking . . . and if something gets you riled up, it's the same thing!"

Clay seemed determined. "Well, I've been in the saddle long enough. I'm gonna get me a drink!"

It had been a long ride and John was saddle sore, too. "All right," he agreed, "but we've got to get back to that lake and make camp before it gets dark."

The Allison brothers stepped into the saloon and hesitated in its shadowy cave-like atmosphere. Damp sawdust on the floor gave off a musty smell of spilled beer, wet tobacco and other ingredients they could only speculate on.

Two gray-bearded men, playing cards at a rickety table, glanced up, but deciding the newcomers wouldn't affect their day, resumed the game.

A man's rumbling voice broke the hollow quiet. "Afternoon, gentlemen. You look a mite dried out." The bartender had spoken from behind the counter. He stood wiping a glass, his wide black mustache raised in a friendly smile.

"Dry and glad to get out of the saddle!" Clay replied.

He and John crossed to the bar where a sign posted on the large mirror read, NO GUNS ALLOWED.

"You won't have any trouble with us," John told the bartender. "We don't have any guns."

The large man's eyes swept over them with a practiced look. "That tells me you're not from Charles Goodnight's ranch. You must be one of the new settlers. Those comin' from the east never carried a gun before. Out here, every man packs one!"

"You can give us a shot of whiskey," Clay said. "Who is this fellow Charles Goodnight?"

The bartender poured two glasses. "Everybody around here knows about Charlie. He started a place some time ago just north of here—calls it the Black River Ranch."

"That so?" Clay said. "Must be lots of ranches 'round here."

"Yes, but Goodnight's is different. After the war, he got restless and took two thousand head of maverick longhorns to New Mexico with his partner Oliver Loving. Turned out to be a good thing—ol' Charlie came back with his saddlebags full of money. Now, he's gettin' another herd together to do it again."

Two more customers entered the saloon and paused in the doorway to scan the room. One, tall and thin, wore a black hat and quality clothes, unlike the usual trail rider. The other, a boy of sixteen, had on well-worn pants and shirt. Hatless, his straight red hair matched a scattering of freckles on his cheeks. They walked to the bar, the older one's gun moving in a swaggering rhythm under his black coat.

The bartender pointed to his sign. "You'll have to leave your gun at the end of the bar, sir."

The man gave a patronizing look and pulled out his gun, thudding it onto the bar top. He spoke with a voice that reflected more schooling than most customers. "We'd like two glasses of your best whiskey."

"All my whiskey's the same, and it's the best you can find in these parts."

The strangers walked over to Clay and John as the drinks were

60

poured.

Clay gave the tall one a friendly smile. "Reckon you're new here, just like us. My name's Clay Allison and this here's my brother John."

The man shot Clay an annoyed look. As if obliged to answer, he said, "We're just passing through. My name's Chunk Colbert."

The name fired Clay's memory. "Colbert . . . would you be related to a Doctor Benson Colbert?"

Chunk Colbert turned a curious eye. "Where did you ever know my brother Ben?"

"When I was in the Army back east. He was the surgeon in my regiment. We got to be good friends—I even helped Doc Colbert steal some Yankee medical supplies." Clay looked at the young man beside Chunk. "Is this your boy?"

"No. He's my nephew Steve."

Clay's enthusiasm dimmed, recalling Ben Colbert's description of a rebellious son. This youth was obviously the doctor's boy Steve who had given his father so much trouble. Clay wondered what the boy was doing all the way out here in Texas with his uncle, but decided to change the subject. "The bartender's right, Mr. Colbert. This is good whiskey."

Chunk tossed down his drink with a scowl. "For what it is, you can give me another," he told the bartender, "and I'll take the bottle with me."

The bartender obliged. "Then you'll have to pay in advance. That'll be two dollars."

"Two dollars?! Why, this swill is hardly worth the bottle it's in!"

The bartender stiffened. "It's the going price and everybody pays it without an argument."

Chunk gave Clay and John a demeaning look. "Maybe some of your scurvy customers have never tasted high-class liquor before, but I have!"

The remark sent a familiar tingle up Clay's spine. He ignored the warning and said, "We think this is good whiskey, Mr. Colbert, and we also think the price is reasonable. Why don't you just pay the man?"

"And why don't you mind your own business, Mister . . . " Chunk searched for the name.

"Like I said, it's Allison—Clay Allison."

John put a nervous hand on his brother's arm. "We'd better go, Clay, it's gettin' late."

A sudden hush fell over the room and the two men at the table shifted their attention from the cards to the bar.

Clay shrugged John's hand away. "Wait a minute. If Mr. Colbert doesn't have the extra dollar, I can pay for him."

Chunk's left eye twitched at the insult. He drew an evil-looking knife from its leather sheath inside his coat pocket and held out the sharp curved point.

"I've had a hard day's ride, Mr. Allison, and I'm in no mood to argue. Your brother's right—why don't you just be on your way!"

Bolstered by the whiskey, Clay whipped out his own smaller hunting knife. "Not until the man here gets paid—*Mister* Chunk Colbert!"

The bartender raised his hands. "Look, gentlemen, we don't allow fighting in here!"

Chunk lunged forward and Clay jumped back, knocking over the card table. The two players rushed for the doorway.

"Go get the law!" the bartender called after them. "And hurry!"

Clay edged around, almost dancing. He slashed out with the knife but Chunk's arm proved quicker—the razor-like blade ripped through Clay's sleeve. The sight of blood only stoked his anger. He rushed forward with a side sweep that cut a nice red streak across his adversary's cheek.

Chunk paused to move a hand across the wound, frowning at the blood on his fingers.

His nephew Steve shouted in warning, "They've gone for the law, Uncle Chunk! We have to get outta here, fast!"

Chunk put the knife away and snatched his gun from the bar top.

"All right!" Menace shot like fire from the twitching eye. "But if we ever meet again, Mr. Allison, I'll see that this score is settled once and for all!" He turned and strode out of the room with his nephew close behind.

"Let me tie my kerchief around that cut," John said and began wrapping Clay's arm.

Soon, a deputy sheriff appeared in the doorway, giving the room swift appraisal before entering. "What's the trouble here?"

"It's all over," the relieved bartender said. "Just an argument over the price of whiskey."

"You want me to take them in?"

"Not them—it was two others. They're gone, now."

The deputy walked over to Clay and John. He looked at the red-stained knife in Clay's hand and the bloody kerchief on his arm. "I don't see a gun, but it's upstarts like you that cause trouble. Now, why don't you two just leave town peaceably?"

Clay flared again. "But we aren't to blame, I was just defendin' myself!"

The deputy's hand moved to the gun on his hip. "I'm givin' you five minutes to get out of my town!"

A bit of daylight still lingered as Clay and John arrived at the lake, which shimmered with clear cold water. They had passed it on the way in and decided to make camp there on their return home.

John dismounted first and started to help his brother down. "How's that arm, Clay?"

Clay brushed him aside and got down from the saddle. "It's my pride that's hurt!" He took off his shirt. "And look at this bloody mess—it's all over me!"

John studied him with exasperation. "Clay, you've got to try harder to control yourself. You might've got yourself killed back there!"

"I'm tired of fightin' it! When I told that Doctor Ben Colbert in the Army about my problem, he said the devil with it, that I'm just as good as any man. And he's right! From now on, I'll do whatever I damned well please!"

John flinched, since their mother had never allowed swearing.

"In fact," Clay grumbled, "I oughta go back there and teach that high-handed deputy a lesson!"

"You're not going anywhere except to the lake and wash off that blood. I don't want us to ride back to the house and let Mary see you looking like a stuck pig!"

Clay grumbled to himself while taking off his clothes, then walked down to the lake. He waded in slowly, adjusting his naked body to the cold water.

John began taking the load of supplies off their mule and glanced with troubled thought at his brother. With Clay still boiling, he might ride back into town and cause more trouble. Just in case, John rolled up his brother's clothing and hid them in some bushes.

Clay finished bathing and came back to the camp area, rubbing the cold water off his arms. He looked around. "Where the devil's my clothes?!"

"Where you can't find them till you sleep this thing off! Now, put a blanket over yourself and calm down."

Clay's face turned red and he sat down to put on his boots.

"Now, what are you doing?" John snapped.

"I'm gonna get even!"

John watched in disbelief as Clay, wearing only his boots, jumped into the saddle and checked his rifle to be sure he had ammunition.

"Clay, you can't go into town with no clothes on!"

"Watch me!" Clay kicked a heel against the horse and took off at a gallop.

"Come back here, you damned fool—they'll throw you in jail!"

John growled at himself for swearing and jumped onto his horse. He spurred it into a fast clip, hoping to stop Clay before he reached town.

The sun had edged behind the western mountains as Clay rode

in, but enough light remained for the local citizens to gape at a jaybird-naked horseman loping through their dusty street.

Clay raised the gun at a water barrel sitting in front of the general store. He let go a shot and two women ran in terror as a stream of water gushed out onto the board walk.

"Hey, Deputy!" he yelled. "I'll give you somethin' to blame me for!"

He kept riding, filling the air with shouts and gunfire while frightened citizens dashed for cover. Others stared in disbelief from their windows, until Clay reached the end of the short street. Not far behind came John on horseback, galloping in a frenzy. He grabbed the reins of Clay's horse and pulled hard. The horse reared in protest, but Clay stayed in the saddle, much to John's relief.

John led Clay's horse out of town and glanced back to see that a group of men and women had gathered to watch the spectacle disappear. Luckily, the deputy wasn't one of them.

Darkness had settled as they rode into their campsite and John pulled Clay down from the saddle in a not-so-gentle manner.

"Do I have to tie you down?!" John growled. "You're just lucky that deputy wasn't in town! It's dark, thank God, so he can't find out who was ridin' naked through his street!" He snatched a blanket from the back of Clay's saddle and threw it at his bare-skinned brother. "Now cover yourself and sleep it off!"

Clay wrapped the blanket around himself and lay down. He let out an angry breath and closed his eyes.

John got his own blanket and put it around his shoulders. Too worked up to sleep, he sat down against a tree and rested worried eyes on his older brother.

John wished they'd never grown up. Everything was perfect then, the two boys chasing possums through the Tennessee valley with its bright autumn leaves of maple, dogwood and oak that almost set the land afire. He leaned his head back, remembering the smell of honeysuckle lining a river bank where he and Clay used to hunt for salamanders.

A night breeze chilled his neck and he pulled the blanket tighter, waiting for sleep to drown out his troubles.

Mary cast a worried look at Clay's bandaged arm when they got off their horses at the sod house the next afternoon.

"Just a little accident," John covered up for his brother. "Clay cut himself, chopping up some wood for our campfire."

"Well, come on inside," Mary said. I've 'bout got supper ready. Reckon you oughta be starved by now."

They all gathered around the kitchen area table and Mary put on the plates. "Soon as the crops start taking on," she told them, "I'll be able to put more food on the table." She sat down and relaxed from her long day's chores. "But you know, I think I'm going to love it here. Why, the mountains are almost like the ones in Tennessee!"

"I wonder if they're full of deer like the Smokys?" Monroe ventured. "We might be able to get us some good meat."

John gave him a wry look. "Don't forget how Daddy used to preach against killin' any of God's creatures."

"Well, after you and Clay brought in a deer, I never saw Daddy object when Mama put venison on the table!"

Mary's eyes softened at the memory. "But Mama was no less religious. She always said a little prayer every time we planted a field. Mama loved the farm and every growing thing we put into its soil."

Clay swallowed a bit of food and set his water glass down with a thud. "Excuse me," he mumbled, "guess I'm not hungry." He got up from the table and walked to the door.

The others watched in surprise and John got up to follow his brother.

"If you two have to go outside," Mary called to them, "put on your coats—it's bitter cold out there!"

John grabbed two coats from the wall peg and followed Clay out the door, closing it behind them.

Clay trudged over to the corral shed, which they had worked a whole day putting together. He leaned against its cold wood siding.

John came over with Clay's coat. "Here, put this on or you'll take cold," he said.

"Thanks." Clay pushed his arms into the sleeves.

"It was all that talk about Mama and the farm, wasn't it?" John asked.

Clay banged his fist against the shed, bringing a small cascade of dirt down onto his shoulders. He brushed it off. "Every time they start it, I get so damned mad!" he sputtered.

John warmed his hands in the coat pockets. "We can't change the past, Clay. It's all over and done with. Can't you just try to forget about it?"

Clay shook his head. "I love Mary and the others, but they don't let me forget the past . . . maybe they can live with it, but I can't. I'm gonna have to get away from here."

John leaned against the shed next to him. "You have someplace in mind?"

"That fellow Charles Goodnight we heard about yesterday—if he's takin' another herd of cattle back to New Mexico, I'm gonna see if he'll take me with him."

John mulled over his brother's decision. "Well, with Lewis and Monroe here, I reckon Mary can get along without us."

Clay turned with astonishment. "What're you talkin' about?!"

John grinned and gave his brother's arm a punch. "You don't think I'd let you light out for New Mexico without me goin', along too, do you?"

After a short ride, Clay and John Allison arrived at Charles Goodnight's Black River ranch, only a few miles north of Palo Pinto.

They found the middle-aged cowman leaning over a corral rail, shouting orders to two men, one struggling to get a saddle on a protesting black horse while the other held a rope looped around its neck.

Goodnight's dark hair flew in the breeze and his short sturdy frame seemed hardened by an obvious lifetime on the open range. He turned with flinty eyes as Clay and John got off their horses and walked over to him.

"Good morning," Clay said. "I reckon you're Mr. Goodnight?"

"You got it right, boy."

"My name's Clay Allison and this is my brother John. We were wondering if you could use us on your next cattle drive back to New Mexico."

Goodnight ran skeptical eyes over the two. "I might be in need of some good men, but I got no use for slick-lookin' shorthorns!"

"Well, maybe we don't look like those cowboys yonder," Clay told him, "but we can ride."

"And we know horses and cattle," John cut in. "Been farmers all our lives in Tennessee."

"Farmers!" Goodnight spat into the dust. "What I need is a man who can sit in the saddle twenty hours a day and sleep with one eye open the rest o' the four!"

"We won't disappoint you," Clay said. "Just give us a chance!"

"Ride, you say?" The disgruntled man looked at the horse fighting its halter. "See that horse? He's an Indian pony—found 'im on the plains yesterday. He's still wild, not used to a saddle. Think you can ride 'im?"

Clay had been admiring the animal—a picture of carved ebony, kicking and rearing in stubborn defiance to the cowboy holding the rope. "I'd sure like to try."

John gave his brother a worried look. "Clay, I don't think this is the way to prove you're a cowboy!"

Without a word, Clay jumped into the corral and walked over to the young lanky cowboys. "I'm Clay Allison. Mr. Goodnight says he'd like to see me ride your horse."

The leathery face of one broke into a smile of relief. "I'm Wes Calley, and this here's my brother Jim. You can sure take this mustang off our hands, and with our compliments!"

"Yes *sir*!" Jim Calley added. His crooked grin exposed a missing front tooth. "We was afraid the old man was gonna make one of us ride 'im!"

The two boys had gotten a saddle on the horse, with a mouth rope instead of a bit. Wes Calley handed Clay the reins and the pony's large eyes appraised the newcomer. Clay placed a hand on its neck and the mustang flinched, rearing on hind legs.

"Come on, boy," Clay said. "I know what your thinkin' and I feel the same way."

The horse settled down, one shiny eye riveted on Clay who rubbed the black coat again. It whinnied, edging away.

"I ain't gonna hurt you—just wanna get up there so we'll be like one big animal, tellin' the whole world to go to hell!"

The Calley brothers had backed away while John Allison and Charles Goodnight watched. The older man's eyes narrowed in expectation.

Before the horse knew it, Clay had thrown himself up into the saddle and the animal erupted into kicking and bucking, trying to shake the man from its back. Clay stayed in the saddle like a magnet clinging to an iron bar. He uttered yelps of excitement while the horse jolted and tossed him around the corral.

After several rounds, the pony saw the futility of trying to dislodge its human cargo and came to a halt. Angry hot breath shot from its quivering nostrils while Clay used his knees to gently nudge it forward in a circle, all the while caressing its neck and talking in a soothing voice. He dismounted in front of his brother and Charles Goodnight while Wes Calley gratefully threw a rope over the horse's neck.

"I never seen a wild one give in so easy!" Goodnight said. "You got a magic touch, boy."

Clay showed both pride and embarrassment. "It'll take a while to train him."

"If you can turn that critter into a cow pony, then he's yours!"

"Does that mean you'll take us with you to New Mexico?"

Goodnight frowned. "Well, I reckon anybody who can ride like that can learn to drive cattle just as well." He looked at the brothers' waists. "But you two better get guns on those hips if you're gonna cross the Llano with me!"

Clay and John spent their days at the Goodnight ranch. While Clay let his new horse get used to a man on its back, the brothers learned how to handle large herds of cattle and helped the other cowboys prepare for the drive west. During a noon breather, the Calley brothers relaxed at the corral with Clay and John.

Jim Calley ran an appraising eye over Clay's shiny dark horse. "You 'bout got that pony eatin' outta your hand," Jim said. "You got a name for 'im yet, Clay?"

"I don't know," Clay said. "He's black as ebony. Maybe I'll just call him 'Ebon.'"

Wes put his foot on a lower rail. "What you and your brother plan on doin' after we get this herd to New Mexico, Clay?"

John answered for them. "Clay has the wild idea of maybe starting up a ranch of our own there. What about you and Jim?"

Wes spat to one side. "Heck, Jim and me, we've been hangin' loose ever since our folks died when we was just tads. Keep on wanderin', I guess."

"You both know that land in New Mexico and how to raise cattle," Clay said. "Why don't you two go in with us?"

Wes scratched his head of wild dusty hair. "That'll take money and a few head to start off with."

Clay went on with his plan. "After we get to New Mexico, we could use part of our pay to buy some cattle from Goodnight. Then we could split expenses while we get our feet on the ground. All profits would be divided equally."

Jim had been listening with growing interest. "I like the idea of bein' in business on our own—for once, we wouldn't be answerin' to no trail boss!"

Wes chuckled. "Well, let's see how things are goin' after we get to New Mexico. In the meantime, Clay, you and John better hurry and get yourselves guns, like Charlie Goodnight said!"

"Maybe you can tell us what kind," Clay said. "John and I never used a hand gun, only a rifle in the war."

"Then let's ride into town and get you and your brother fixed up!"

John Allison harbored doubts about showing up in town again since he and Clay had been run out by the law. But the deputy turned lenient on hearing they were leaving for New Mexico and the Allisons rode back to the farm with new thirty-two caliber six-shot pistols in sturdy leather gun belts strapped to their waists. Now, they felt like real cowboys.

Mary and the others had been told of Clay and John's plans to go to New Mexico and, now that the time had come, her sadness took hold. "It's more than just the family breaking up," she told Clay. "I know we'll never see each other again!"

"Now, we don't know that," he said. "John and me might get tired of New Mexico and come ridin' back with our tails between our legs!"

Mary knew better and shook her head. "I don't want you two to start out with nothing in your pockets," she said and pushed some money into his hand.

He looked at it in surprise. "But we're working cowboys, now—we'll get paid at the end of the trail. Here, you need this." He tried to give the money back.

"No, no," she objected. "The crops are coming along and by fall we'll be selling to everybody in the valley." She left the room before he could see the tears dimming her eyes.

The next morning, after farewell handshakes and goodbye hugs, Clay and John rode away to join Charles Goodnight.

The little sod house took on a dreadful silence that night, with only its three remaining occupants. While Lewis and Monroe talked in front of the fireplace, Mary cleaned up the kitchen and went with

71

sadness to her bedroom. She turned down the spread and had to catch her breath as tears spilled down her cheeks. Lying beside the pillow was the money she'd placed in Clay's hands the day before.

# Chapter Eight

*B*en Colbert wondered how he'd ever find Steve in the vast territory that lay ahead. He could only hope that by some miracle their paths would cross and he'd be able to talk the boy out of a life of crime.

But, now, he had a more urgent problem and Ben felt aggravated with himself. As a doctor, he should have noticed the signs earlier. Hannah had been careful to hide her morning sickness and it wasn't until they were well on their way that he realized the truth.

"Please don't be angry," Hannah pleaded, sitting beside him in the wagon filled with their belongings. "I knew if I told you earlier, you'd change your mind about going west."

Ben squinted in the dusty sun and tightened his grip on the mule's reins. "I'm not angry, my dear, just worried. The trip alone is hard enough, but this is your first child—and you're not a young woman!"

"Ben, please don't worry. Everything will be all right!"

Ben had taken them north to Kansas City where they would catch the route taken by settlers going west. Now, pulling into the large bustling city, Hannah stared in awe.

Tall buildings huddled together on either side of a wide, dusty main street that swarmed with carts, wagons and swarthy pioneers. Excited anticipation shone from every face.

"We'll find a room here," Ben said, stopping the wagon in front of one of the hotels. "I'll have to get supplies for the rest of the trip tomorrow."

Hannah looked forward to a comfortable bed, but she had doubts. "Ben, it looks awfully crowded . . . "

"I'll see." He handed her the reins. "You just sit here and rest a while."

Ben climbed down and pushed his way through the mass of people, finding it just as crowded in the hotel's lobby. He made his way to the front desk.

"My wife and I need a room for tonight and maybe the next," he said. "Can you oblige?"

The harried clerk gave an incredulous chuckle. "We're full up, mister. If you can find a room anywhere in Kansas City, I wish you luck!"

Ben growled under his breath. He'd just keep looking, anyway.

"You headin' west?" a man behind him asked.

Ben turned his agitated eyes to a young man dressed decidedly cleaner than the others milling about. A neatly trimmed beard graced his chin.

"Yes," Ben replied. "To New Mexico."

The man's eyes widened. "You ain't goin' alone, are you?!"

"That is my plan. But right now, my wife and I need a place for the night."

The man shook his head. "Takin' a wife all that way, just the two of you, you're askin' for trouble!"

Ben was in no mood for idle chitchat. "If you'll excuse me, my wife is waiting." He turned to leave, but the man took his arm.

"Maybe I can help," the stranger said. "I'm headin' a wagon train

74

goin' to California. That's the safest way to go—in numbers. Why don't you and your wife tag along, too? You could stop off at New Mexico."

Ben thought of Hannah. He certainly didn't want to place her in danger. And, in her condition, she would have the company of other women during the long trip.

"Perhaps you're right," he gave in. "Just where is this wagon train?"

"We're camped on the edge of town, right now. Leavin' in a couple of days." He put out a hand. "My name's Tom Briggs!"

Ben gave him a handshake. "I'm Doctor Ben Colbert and my wife's name is Hannah."

"You don't say? Why, that's even better, havin' a doctor along!"

Hannah delighted at the turn of events and forgot about the comfortable bed. They followed in their wagon as Tom Briggs rode his horse to the outskirts of town where ten covered wagons sat, grouped into a camp. Tom stopped beside one, which was large and comfortable looking.

"Orah!" he called. "Come down and meet some newcomers!"

A middle-aged woman in long skirt and a bonnet that shaded both sides of her kind face came down the wagon's wooden steps.

"Meet my wife Orah," Tom Briggs said to the Colberts. "Orah, this here's Doctor Ben Colbert and his wife Hannah. They're goin' with us as far as New Mexico."

"My, I'm so glad to meet you," Orah Briggs said and they all shook hands. "Mighty nice havin' another married couple along—and a *doctor* at that!" She turned to the nearest wagon. "Brighty! Come meet the newcomers that are gonna join us!"

A woman in her late fifties climbed down from the nearby wagon and walked over. Her tired eyes brightened with the prospect of having another woman for company.

"Brighty Elder, this is Hannah and Ben Colbert," Orah said. She added proudly, "Ben's a real doctor!"

Brighty Elder's wrinkled face smoothed into a wide grin. "I

swan, that's wonderful!" She took Ben and Hannah's hands in greeting. "My husband Jeb will sure be glad to meet you. He's in town right now, huntin' up some things for the trip."

Tom Briggs had been running doubtful eyes over Ben's wagon. "Speakin' of the trip, Ben, we better get a toppin' on that wagon of yours."

"A topping?"

"You know—a canvas stretched over supports, like all these other ones."

Ben finally had to laugh at himself. "Well, I have to admit this is all new to me. You might say Hannah and I are starting out blind!"

Tom put a reassuring hand on his shoulder. "Well, don't you two worry none. We'll go into town tomorrow and get you fixed up!"

The soreness in Hannah's back melted away, along with apprehension about the hard trip that lay ahead. Now, surrounded by such a friendly group of people, she could face any obstacle thrown in their path.

Ben's earlier comment turned prophetic. Indeed, the trip had become arduous but having the company of other women made it endurable for Hannah. The hardy little wagon train followed the Arkansas and Purgatory Rivers until at last they reached their greatest obstacle—crossing the Rocky Mountains at Raton Pass.

Hannah looked up at the steep rugged peaks soaring overhead. "Ben, how on earth are we going to get through here?!"

Tom Briggs gave the answer. "We'll take one wagon at a time," he told the group. "Take out everything you can carry, even if you have to make two trips takin' it over the mountain. Then, we put on extra horses and take the wagon to the top."

Thankfully, Hannah and Ben didn't have a great amount of belongings to empty from their wagon.

With agonizing effort, two teams of horses pulled the first wagon up the hazardous slope. The animals' hoofs slipped and Hannah gasped—surely the wagon would come crashing down, horses and all! But the men kept urging and they finally reached the top.

On the downhill side, ropes were attached to the wagon and wrapped around trees in order to gradually lower it to flat ground.

The slow and tedious process drained strength from both men and horses. Hannah saw that it would take days for the entire group of wagons to make just twenty miles over the forbidding Rockies.

At last, on reaching the crest of Raton Pass, Hannah and Ben climbed down from their wagon to gaze at the rugged mountains they had just crossed, all piled in masses one above the other.

"I've never seen anything so beautiful!" Hannah said, breathing in the crisp clean air.

Distant peaks lay sprinkled with snow and glistened in the sunlight like so many jewels. Beautiful flowers, wild plum, cherry trees and clematis vines with their white blossoms lined the lower slopes. It all reminded Hannah of her beloved Kentucky valley.

"A fitting end to the journey," Ben said and put a loving arm around Hannah's waist.

She turned in astonishment. "You mean we're almost there?"

He nodded. "It won't be much longer, so enjoy it while you can."

The rugged western peaks of Sangre de Cristo Mountains finally appeared in the distance as they reached the point Hannah had been dreading. Now they would have to leave the wagon train. She couldn't hide the tears as she gave Orah Briggs and Brighty Elder warm goodbye hugs.

"Have a safe journey to California," Hannah said. "I know we'll never see each other again, so I want to thank you both for your wonderful company!"

Orah put a handkerchief to her eyes. "Don't think of it that way, Hannah. Who knows—you and Ben might wanna come on out to California one of these days."

"And don't you worry 'bout that baby of yours," Brighty Elder said. "You're gonna have a healthy young 'un, I just know!"

Hannah climbed back into the wagon and watched the others move on for California. She prayed the hardships they faced would be minor.

Ben jiggled the reins and urged their own wagon forward. "We have just a few more miles to go," he assured her.

Hannah took a deep breath, for she knew an exciting, new life awaited them in Elizabethtown where gold had been discovered. Her eyes moved up to the obstinate Mount Baldy that towered nearby. It seemed to glare back in mocking silence.

# Chapter Nine

*C*harles Goodnight's second cattle drive moved out onto the Llano Estacado, a vast, arid flat land that stretched to the horizon with nothing in between. It gave a sense of hopelessness to any hardy soul who would attempt crossing it.

"Just go easy on your water," Wes Calley told Clay and John Allison. "And pray we don't run into Comanches!"

Clay hadn't thought about Indians. He recalled the wild tales he'd heard about their savagery and said, "Well, I have my gun, now, so I won't worry."

"That ain't the only thing we could run into," Jim Calley added. "This time of year, the buffalo start migratin' to the southeast. We'd be in a heap o' trouble if we ran into a sizeable herd!"

Surely as Jim had predicted, two days later a dark silhouette appeared on the horizon. It seemed to stretch for miles.

"Damn, if it ain't buffalo!" Wes said.

"They've seen us, but they're holdin' still, tryin' to make up their minds," Jim surmised.

Charles Goodnight rode past the men and shouted orders. "Keep 'em movin—maybe those critters will go around us!"

Clay and John worked with the others, moving the herd west in a line. All the while, Clay kept an eye on the black horde waiting just to the northwest.

Suddenly, as if by a phantom signal, the buffalo moved forward and gathered speed, determined to let nothing stand in their path. Like an onrushing storm, their thundering hoofs shook the ground. The huge beasts cut into the line of cattle, sending the front half stampeding forward and the last half racing back the way they had come. Goodnight's men rode alongside with angry shouts, trying to keep the herd from scattering.

It seemed to Clay that the strange-looking animals roared through for nearly an hour before they finally passed on their way to whatever destination the shaggy creatures had in mind. He and John worked with the other men, riding line for miles weeding out younger disoriented buffalo from the herd of cattle. It took them until sundown to get their cattle back together. With the herd finally calm and at rest, the tired cowboys made camp for the night.

Charles Goodnight walked through the men rolled up in their blankets on the ground. "I got a feelin' we're bein' watched," he told them. "Indians like to take horses during the night, so hobble yours and keep an eye on 'em."

As Goodnight walked away, one of the men asked, "How can he have a feelin' there's Indians around?"

Wes chuckled. "Ol' Charlie was livin' on these plains before you was a baby suckin' tit. I don't know. Maybe he can smell 'em. But I'll tell you one thing—if he says an Indian's around, you don't ask no questions!"

Clay and John took the sage man's advice and joined the Calleys in hobbling their horses. Although they slept light, they heard nothing during the night. Four of the men, however, were foolhardy by not following Goodnight's orders. In the early morning hours, they realized their mistake.

"Our horses are gone!" one shouted. "Them Indians must've took 'em last night!"

Goodnight was furious. "Now, maybe you'll wipe that dew from behind your ears and listen to somebody who knows better. Get on another horse and follow me—I'll get yer horses back!"

Clay and John joined the group and they rode out just as the sun rose on the horizon. In the morning light they found the Indians' trail.

Goodnight studied the hoof prints. "Looks like there's only four of 'em," he said. "Come on, we can ambush 'em."

They soon discovered the four stolen horses tied to mesquite bushes in the distance. Goodnight put a finger to his lips and motioned the others to follow in silence.

The Indians heard their approach, but too late and rose from their blankets, trying to load their rifles.

Goodnight let go a blast from his six-shooter and one Indian fell.

Clay raised his gun at one of the Indians and pulled the trigger. The shot missed, giving the red man time to load and take aim at Clay. Goodnight fired, sending the Indian onto his back.

Clay cursed himself for not being familiar with his gun. He took aim at the last remaining savage and was lucky this time. The Indian dropped from a shot in the head.

With the stolen horses recovered, the group moved their herd out again toward Horsehead Crossing. It would be hazardous getting the cattle across, but Goodnight had done it before, so Clay and John didn't worry.

As the Allisons and Calleys rode along together, Clay wondered if he'd ever soak up a tenth of what Charles Goodnight had learned during all his years. But, one thing Clay had decided on, for sure—out here in this raw wild country, a man's best friend was his gun.

# Chapter Ten

*H*annah quickly forgot about her pregnancy as they pulled into the busy community of Elizabethtown. Buildings had been hastily put up to form a dusty main street, teeming with horses, mules, wagons and people of all descriptions. Other structures mushroomed on a rising slope in the distance.

Ben wondered if he would be the only doctor in town until he noticed a sign reading, DR. FREDERICK HAAS. He stopped the wagon. "You wait here," he said to Hannah. "I'll see if the doctor can give me a perspective on this place."

Ben entered the office to find a slender young man of German extraction, no doubt the doctor, bandaging the arm of a rough-looking miner.

Doctor Haas looked up through horn-rimmed glasses. "Be with you in a moment, mister."

Ben watched with approval while the doctor finished his job and accepted cash.

After the patient left, Dr. Haas looked Ben up and down,

searching for an ailment. "Now, sir, just what seems to be your problem?"

Ben gave a rueful smile. "I'm afraid I have no problem— medically speaking, that is. My name is Benson Colbert. I'm a doctor, also. Just arrived in town."

Haas' dark eyes sparkled. "A fellow practitioner!" He took Ben's hand in a warm shake. "What can I do for you, Doctor Colbert?"

"I'd hoped to set up a business here, but I don't want to intrude on your grounds."

Haas laughed. "No intrusion! Believe me, I have more than I can handle—it'll be a relief to have someone else helping with all these injuries!"

"My wife is waiting outside and we were wondering if you could give us some pointers on getting settled."

"My word, don't leave the poor woman sitting out there in all that rabble!" Haas walked to the door and Ben followed.

"This is Doctor Frederick Haas," Ben said to Hannah, raising his voice against the street clamor. He helped her down from the wagon. "Doctor, my wife Hannah."

Haas took her hand. "Do come in, Mrs. Colbert, so we can talk."

They went into the office where Haas closed the door and offered them crude wooden chairs. "I take it you haven't a place to stay yet?" he said.

"My, no," Hannah told him, "and from the looks of the town, I wonder if there's an empty room anywhere!"

"Then you must be my guests. I live in the back, here. It's too big for one person, but it was the only place available and came with the building. You're welcome to share it with me."

"That's very kind of you, Doctor," Ben said. "It'll be only temporary till we can find other arrangements."

Haas gave an ironic smile. "The way people are filling up E-Town, that might be quite a while."

"E-Town?"

"That's what they call this place—seems like everybody's too busy to call it Elizabethtown!"

Ben and Hannah gratefully accepted Frederick Haas' offer and he helped them move their belongings into a small clean room in the wooden building at the rear of his office.

"So, you say your hands are full here?" Ben said.

"You won't believe the number of accidents taking place in those mines on Mount Baldy," Haas told him. "Sometimes I have to make a special trip up there to take care of a man's broken leg—or maybe both legs! Then, there are the ones in town who have all kinds of medical problems." A sudden idea hit him. "Doctor Colbert, you're not going to find it easy getting an office in E-Town. What would you say if we worked together as a team—you could use my office here."

It came as a tempting offer to someone who had just stumbled into a strange environment. "That sounds good, but I do feel as though I'm taking away some of your business!"

"There's plenty for both of us—or any other doctor, should he care to step into the fire!"

Hannah Colbert's life changed abruptly. Elizabethtown proved to be vastly different from the quiet little Kentucky home that now seemed a continent away. Cooking, washing and taking care of the house for both her husband and Fred, as they now called Doctor Frederick Haas, kept her busy. Bustling activity in the dirt street meant dusting the front office twice a day. On one such occasion an excited young boy stuck his head through the door.

"Been shootin' at the Black Whip Saloon!" the lad yelped. "They need a doctor right away!"

Hannah frowned. The only thing marring her happiness was the violence in Elizabethtown. "All right," she told the boy. "I'll get the doctor."

She didn't have to bother, for Ben had heard the announcement and came from the back room, clutching his black bag.

Hannah stopped him. "Ben, do be careful, they might shoot you, too!"

He patted her arm. "I'm sure it's all over with by now. I'll be right back—don't you worry."

She followed him to the door and watched as he made his way through the crowd of people, horses and wagons in the street. Four scrubby men on horseback suddenly appeared, yelling obscenities and waving pistols in the air. Their guns roared as the group galloped past the office and Hannah stepped back in terror. She slammed the door closed, leaning against it to catch her breath.

Long minutes passed before Ben returned to the office. As soon as he stepped inside, Hannah threw her arms around him as if he might slip away.

He rubbed her back. "There, there, dear, everything's all right."

"I'm sorry, Ben," she sniffed. "I guess it's just the baby making me so edgy."

He admired her with adoring eyes. "You're a brave woman, Hannah. If it'll make you feel better, I've heard that the women here in E-Town are demanding more law enforcement. Things will get better."

But, as her stomach swelled, Hannah worried about the future of her child coming into such a violent world. Finally, on a warm afternoon while Ben and Fred were up at one of the mines, her first contractions began.

Hannah stopped her ironing and grabbed a chair back at the first assault. Ben had told her when labor pains occur every five minutes or less, it was a signal to make preparations.

The second contraction came ten minutes later. Her heart quickened at the prospect of giving birth all by herself before the men returned. But it was late and they should be home soon. She put the iron to cool and sat on the bed. With an eye on the bedside clock, she felt the contractions coming at faster intervals. Perspiration dotted her face. She berated herself for not contacting one of the wives in town, but now walking the bustling streets was out of the question. Another strong twinge made her realize it had been only six minutes since the last one.

On the verge of panic, Hannah at last heard Ben and Fred open the office door.

"Ben, I need you!" she called, hoping they could hear her in the back bedroom.

Ben appeared in a moment.

"It's the baby . . . " she moaned.

"Now, don't worry, dear," he said. "Just try to relax." He helped her lie back on the pillow.

Fred lit a kerosene lamp, for evening had settled in.

"I'll have to raise your dress," Ben said.

She looked up in horror.

He smiled. "Don't worry, Fred has seen many women during childbirth."

Ben got his black bag and equipment, then made an examination while Fred held the lamp closer.

"Dilation has begun," Ben said and checked the clock with the next contraction. They came at one-minute intervals, now, and Hannah moaned. Ben knew the baby had moved into the pelvic area. "You'd better pull the dress up around her breasts, Fred."

Fred set the lamp as close as possible and got behind Hannah. She swallowed her pride as he pulled up the dress and put a gentle arm around her neck.

"Just hold onto me, Hannah," he said, "and do what Ben tells you to. Everything's going to be all right."

Pain wrenched through Hannah's lower body and she cried out.

"I'd give you chloroform, my dear," Ben said, "but it's better if you can do without it. You'll have to work with us."

Her mind clouded and it seemed ages before she heard Fred's voice again.

"It's all over, now, Hannah. You're doing fine."

She tried to look up. "Ben . . . is the baby all right?"

His reply seemed to come out of a fog. "It was a little girl,

Hannah."

"It *was*? What do you mean?"

Ben smoothed her hair with a loving hand. "It's been a difficult birth and the baby was stillborn. I'm as devastated as you, my dearest Hannah, at losing our baby."

She closed her eyes in pain and exhaustion. "I just thank God it's over!"

He kissed her forehead. "But I must tell you, darling, it's fairly certain you won't be able to have more children . . . I'm so sorry."

She whispered softly, "Oh, Ben, I don't *want* to have another baby!"

Hannah regained her strength quickly, happy to get back to the household chores. A few days later, Ben and Fred came in as she set the table for their evening meal.

Fred held up a large bottle. "About time we celebrated your recovery!" he announced.

"Fred, what's that?"

"Just the most expensive wine in all of Elizabethtown!" He began working at the cork.

Hannah put a hand to her face. "Fred, you can't afford such a thing!"

"Don't worry. Ben and I had four fracture cases up on Baldy today—all paid in cash!"

They sat at the little table while Hannah put the roast and vegetables in the center.

Fred poured them all a glass of the blushing-pink wine and raised his glass. "Here's to Hannah Colbert!" he proclaimed.

After they had taken a pleasing sip, Ben turned serious. "Hannah, I'm beginning to think I should never have brought you here. It's really not the kind of town for you to live in."

She patted his hand. "I love you for that, Ben, but please don't worry about me."

Fred leaned back with interest. "Maybe we should all get out before the whole place turns into a ghost town!"

Hannah looked aghast. "This busy place—a ghost town?!"

"Some of the miners say they're finding less gold up on Mount Baldy. You know it'll have to give out some time."

The thought of leaving Elizabethtown gave Hannah a surge of relief. "But where would we go, Fred?"

"We could take our practice to Santa Fe."

Ben shook his head. "That's fine for a young, single man like you, Fred, but I'd prefer a smaller, quieter town—for Hannah's sake."

"You know of a place?"

"I was talking the other day with John Turner. He's the sheriff here in Colfax County. He shares his duties with Deputy Case Gordon in Cimarron. The way John describes it, Cimarron would be just right."

Fred laughed. "You won't make a fortune there, Ben. It's too small. Santa Fe's the capital city and can only get bigger!"

"I don't aspire to be a rich man, Fred. I just want enough income for Hannah and me to be comfortable. John Turner tells me Cimarron doesn't have a doctor, so I wouldn't have any competition."

Hannah loved the idea. "Oh, Ben, I know I'd be happy there!"

He chuckled. "You'll never get away from violence in this Territory, my dear, but I'd guess there's less of it in Cimarron. If you're agreeable, I'll drive over there tomorrow and have a look around."

"You'll have to deal with Lucien Maxwell," Fred advised. "He and his friend Kit Carson settled this area. Maxwell's a powerful man—he bought up so many land grants, he owns a third of this Territory and even part of Colorado!"

"I'm sure Deputy Case Gordon must know Lucien Maxwell," Ben said. "I'll ask Case to open the doors for me."

Fred Haas sighed with resignation. "Well, it seems you've made up your mind, Ben." He poured them all more wine and raised his glass. "Here's to the Colberts, happy and comfortable in Cimarron, and Frederick Haas, happy and rich in Santa Fe!"

# Chapter Eleven

Cimarron snuggled like a quail's nest in the long afternoon shadows of Sangre de Cristo Mountains. Their rugged peaks rose majestically in the west while the sun gave them the deep orange-red glow, from which they got the Spanish name, *Blood of Christ*.

But not all lay serene in the little community. A small group of Mexicans had gathered in the forecourt of Lucien Maxwell's big Cimarron home and waited in fearful silence. Each held his breath as one of their fellow men was pulled up a flight of wooden steps. The bright New Mexico sun hit the man's eyes like a hammer and he cringed, half dead after two days in a cellar without food or water. To make things worse, a forty-pound chain wrapped about his neck dug into an open bleeding sore.

Unable to stand, the man was dragged by his arms over to Lucien Bonaparte Maxwell, a short but powerful-looking man who stood holding a cowhide whip in one of his big hands.

"Strip off his clothes and tie him up," Maxwell ordered.

Lucien Maxwell presented a threatening figure, his ebony hair waving in the warm afternoon breeze while he waited with legs apart, clad in rough-weave blue trousers and fine half-boots. His red woolen shirt, open at the neck, revealed a hairy grizzled chest and his dark-blue eyes glowered at the proceedings as he chewed impatiently on the dark-brown cigar stuck under a generous black mustache.

Luz Maxwell, who seldom made an appearance, rushed out of the large adobe home and rounded up their four young daughters playing nearby. "Come quickly, *hijas*," she said in a hushed voice, "you are not to see this!" Skirt billowing over her ample body, she herded the girls into the house.

Maxwell took the cigar from his mouth and walked over to the pitiful man hanging limp from the ropes.

"I should beat you myself for stealing from me!" Maxwell said. "But instead, I'll let one of your friends administer the punishment!" He turned to the group of onlookers. "Ramon, come do the honors!"

A meek little man stepped forward and with hesitance took the whip.

"Twenty-five lashes," Maxwell growled, "and make them worthwhile!" He stood back to watch.

The man called Ramon gritted his teeth and struck the whip against his friend's naked back.

"Harder!" Maxwell shouted.

More lashes were given and the prisoner moaned.

Maxwell threw down his cigar in disgust. "Hold on! I'll show you how to whip a man—strip off your clothes, Ramon, and take the other post!"

With his clothing removed, Ramon was bound to another pole.

Maxwell raised the whip and struck it forward with a crashing blow, lacerating the smooth brown skin. The Mexican screamed as Maxwell beat him again and again. Ramon's body soon became a mass of raw bleeding flesh. On the fourteenth blow, he fainted.

Maxwell stood panting, his ruddy square face dotted with sweat. "Throw some water on him!"

Water was sloshed over the man and he raised a half-conscious face.

Maxwell scowled over him. "Now, the next time I tell you to whip a man, you'll know how to do it!"

Across the way, Charles Morris, a guest of the household, and Maxwell's thirteen-year-old son Peter had been watching from the shade of a large tree. Morris wondered what the boy must be thinking of his father's wrath. He shuddered and said, "Well, I could certainly use a strong drink right now!"

Young Peter looked up at the fading sunset. "If you can wait a bit, Father will soon be pouring his good whiskey before dinner."

"Thank you, but I think I'd like to get away—please tell Lucien I'll be here for dinner."

Inside his Red Brick Saloon, Sam Aikens wiped out a clean shot glass and wondered if he should even bother; darkness had begun to fall and he'd seen only a few customers the entire day. His prospects rose as a man, dressed in expensive eastern clothes, entered.

"Good afternoon," Charles Morris said and stepped up to the bar. He had a perturbed look on his face and a nervous catch in his voice. "I'd like a shot of your good whiskey."

"Sure thing." Sam poured the glass full of cheap whiskey, his only kind, and studied the man's custom-tailored suit. "I'd guess you're stayin' at the Maxwell place."

"That's right. My name is Charles Morris. I'm here negotiating the possible sale of Lucien Maxwell's land grant to a group of Santa Fe businessmen."

"Don't tell me ol' L. B. ran out of liquor and you had to come to my place for a drink!"

"No, not at all." Morris took out a handkerchief to pat on his damp forehead. "But I've just seen a terrible thing there and needed to get away."

Sam Aikens grinned. "Then you must've seen ol' L. B.'s mean side." He wiped the splintered bar top with a dirty rag. "Maxwell treats the Mexicans like you people treated Negro slaves back east."

"I never thought of Lucien Maxwell as a tyrant, although I know he owns a great deal of this Territory."

Sam laughed. "Two million acres is a great deal, all right! Why, the town of Cimarron wouldn't exist without Lucien Bonaparte Maxwell. You put that much power into a man's hands, he can do anything he wants, and nobody gets in his way!"

"But for such a rich man, he's really quite generous. Last night, some of the guests had bad luck at poker and this morning, Maxwell returned all their losses—and he won't even accept payment for our rooms and all the wonderful food and liquor!"

Sam uttered a heartier laugh. "Old L. B. knows how to butter his bread. If he plays nice to the big boys, he knows they'll play nice to him. Same with the Indians. As long as he gives 'em their rations, they won't steal his cattle or raid the farmers developing his land." Sam gave a knowing wink. "And don't forget—the government's payin' Maxwell to feed those Indians!"

"If he owns all the land around here, how does he treat you and the other businessmen in Cimarron?"

"Oh, we get along fine. If we don't bother him, he don't bother us." Sam noticed the barely touched glass. "I'll leave the bottle here if you want any more of my good whiskey."

Morris shook his head, realizing the liquor had burned his throat. "No, thank you, I'll just nurse this one. What's the charge?"

"A dollar a shot."

Morris raised an eyebrow and placed a dollar on the bar.

As Sam took the money, he looked through the doorway and grinned. Two horsemen had just ridden up. "Well, looks like I might make a profit today, after all!"

The strangers entered, a taller one swaggering in the lead as if he owned the place, with a young cowboy close behind. The boy wore a cocky look to go with his auburn hair and freckles.

The older one pushed a black hat from his dark red hair as they walked to the bar. "We're passing through and need a room for the night," he said.

Sam's smile faded. If that's all they wanted, he wouldn't turn a profit for sure. "This little place ain't got a hotel yet, mister."

The man scowled. "Then we'll sleep down by the river. In the meantime, give us a shot of your good whiskey—none of that under-the-counter swill!"

Charles Morris had been studying the two men's faces. "You're Chunk and Steve Colbert, aren't you? I'm Charles Morris. I believe I saw you two in Santa Fe a week ago—at a horse race."

While the two whiskeys were being poured, Chunk Colbert looked thoughtfully into his glass before turning to Charles Morris. "I don't recollect seeing you there."

"I showed up at the end of the race. There was an argument about your winning. Something about your nephew Steve jumping the gun in order to get your horse across the finish line first."

Chunk tossed down his whiskey with a grimace. "We won that race fair and square!"

Morris chuckled. "The sheriff didn't seem to think so. I heard he asked you to leave town."

Chunk shoved his glass forward for a refill. His left eye danced wickedly. "I think you ought to know, Mr. Morris, that no one's ever called me a cheat without an apology."

Sam Aikens started to pour the drink, but paused as Chunk took a gun out of his holster.

"See that little lady up there?" Chunk nodded at a picture of a scantily-clad woman, hanging above the bar. He took aim and with two quick shots blasted out the woman's eyes. "That's what happens to anybody who doesn't apologize for calling me a cheat!"

Sam recovered himself. "Mister Colbert, I think you oughta know—the sheriff's office is just down the street. He probably heard the shootin'!"

Chunk's mouth twisted in a smirk. "Well, then he knows there's some life in this town. Now, give me that drink!"

Sam poured the whiskey and moved the bottle over to Steve Colbert.

Steve shook his head. "One will do me," he said and turned to his uncle. "If the sheriff's comin', Uncle Chunk, you oughta put that gun away!"

Chunk ignored his nephew. He gulped down the whiskey and took aim at one of the bottles lined up on a shelf. With another shot, he blasted away the cork. Turning his gun on Charles Morris, he said, "Now, about that apology, Mister Morris!"

Morris backed away, fresh beads of sweat dotting his forehead. "I'd challenge you, Colbert, but you can see I'm not armed!"

Sam Aikens held his breath. There had never been a killing in his saloon, but now it appeared the record was going to be broken. He breathed in relief at the sight of Cimarron's lawman standing in the doorway.

Just in his thirties, Deputy Case Gordon's handsome face sported a well-trimmed mustache while his eyes, usually a languid soft brown, now shone hard and alert. His right hand rested on a holstered gun and his low steady voice made it clear who was in charge. "I heard shooting, Sam. You got any trouble here?"

"Just a little disagreement, Case," Sam replied.

Case stepped inside and paused, ready to draw if necessary. "I'm Deputy Case Gordon," he said to Chunk Colbert. "Since we don't use guns to settle arguments here, I'll ask you to put that gun away."

Chunk had heard of Casey Gordon, a man of cold steel, fast on the draw and a dead shot. As sheriff in another county, he had cleaned up several other towns with his cool daring. Some men found out the hard way they couldn't out draw Case Gordon, and Chunk Colbert didn't plan to join the ranks of the dead. He slipped his gun back into its holster.

With the tension eased, Case walked over to the gunman. "What's your name, mister?"

"Chunk Colbert."

Case eyed his companion. "And your friend, here?"

Steve answered, with a glare of defiance. "I'm his nephew, Steve Colbert!"

Case's eyes went back to Chunk. "What's your business in Cimarron, Mr. Colbert?"

"Just passing through."

"Well, I think we'd all be happier if you and your nephew kept moving on."

Chunk sneered and walked to the door. "Come on," he growled at Steve. "This is a one-horse town, anyway!"

Steve flashed a vengeful look at the deputy and followed Chunk out the door.

"Hey!" Sam Aikens called after them. "You owe me three dollars." But the men had vanished into the dark evening.

Case Gordon dug a hand into his pocket and slapped three dollars onto the bar.

Sam looked at him in surprise. "You don't have to do that, Case!"

"It's worth it to get those mongrels out of town."

Charles Morris moved the handkerchief across his forehead once again. "I feel I should be the one to pay!" he said in relief.

Case turned to him. "You might be safer back at Lucien Maxwell's place, Mr. Morris. You want me to go with you?"

"Thank you, Deputy, but that won't be necessary." Morris gave a nervous laugh. "I do believe, however, that if I weren't leaving for Santa Fe tomorrow, I'd start wearing a gun!" He nodded a goodnight and left the saloon.

Sam Aikens waved an arm at the empty room. "Well, Case, the place is all yours! I owe you a drink on the house!"

"Thanks, but I never drink on duty."

"Everybody's glad you joined up with the sheriff. John Turner sure needed another man, what with E-Town gettin' so rowdy."

"Well, he has his hands full. I'm glad to help John out by splitting our time between E-Town and Cimarron."

"With old John gettin' up in years, maybe you'll be the Colfax sheriff one of these days, Case."

"Something I wouldn't wish on a dead dog!"

Suddenly two muffled gunshots came from the outside, followed by an urgent shout. Case Gordon strode to the door and peered into the dark street; several yards away, a man stood beside his horse. Case went quickly to investigate.

"They shot 'im in the back!" the man said, holding the reins of his horse. He pointed to a man lying face-down in the dirt. "I was just leavin' for E-Town and saw 'em do it!"

Case knelt down and rolled the body over. In the pale moonlight, he recognized the face of Charles Morris. "Did you get a look at them?"

"No, but they was on horseback—a big feller and a young one."

Case uttered a low oath for not taking in Chunk and Steve Colbert back at the saloon, but he had no reason then to make an arrest. "Did you see which way they went?"

"To the north, across the river."

After crossing the narrow Cimarron River on the edge of town they could have gone anywhere, probably north to the border and into Colorado Territory. But it was too dark, now, to go after them.

"This man was staying at Lucien Maxwell's place," Case said. "Help me get him over to the house—it's just over there."

They took the body by the shoulders and dragged it across the street to the large Maxwell home.

"My name's Ed Eakins, if you need me for a witness or anything," the man said. "Is it all right if I get on my way to E-Town, now?"

"Kind of dangerous traveling at night, isn't it?"

"Cooler that way, and I got a rifle with me."

"Then go ahead, and be careful." Case looked down at the unfortunate Charles Morris. "I'll tell Lucien Maxwell that his business friend's been killed. He can take it from there."

The man left for Elizabethtown and Case knocked on the big front door. Sounds of an obvious poker game came from inside and Case pictured the room clouded with heavy tobacco smoke, plus the usual array of liquor bottles. He knocked again, louder.

Apparently the Mexican servants had the night off, for Lucien Maxwell opened the door. "Case Gordon!" he exclaimed. "What brings you here, Deputy?"

"Bad news." Case nodded at the body lying beside the door. "One of your guests, Charles Morris, has just been killed!"

"Charlie Morris?!" Maxwell roared and looked down at his dead friend. "What the hell happened?!"

"Shot in the back—no doubt by a man named Chunk Colbert. He and his nephew Steve got away before I found Mr. Morris."

Maxwell rumbled like an erupting volcano. "Nobody kills a friend of mine and gets away with it! You're a good deputy, Case—when you find that son-of-the-Devil, bring him to me so I can carve his heart out!"

Case gave an assuring smile. "I know you want to see justice done, Mr. Maxwell, but I'm sure you realize this is something the law has to take care of!"

# Chapter Twelve

*J*ohn Allison had to smile at his older brother. "I don't think our own Mama would recognize you, now, Clay!"

Clay flashed a grin of white teeth through the heavy black beard that nearly hid his face. "Well, you sure don't look like the little brother I used to know!"

Along with Clay's transformation, John had acquired a clean short beard and mustache during the cattle drive west.

After Horsehead Crossing, Charles Goodnight's group moved north along the treacherous Pecos River to a place just east of the lower Rocky Mountains in eastern New Mexico Territory. With Wes and Jim Calley's help, the Allison brothers soaked up a lifetime of cowboy skills along the way.

As they straggled into Goodnight's Bosque Grande ranch, Clay surveyed it in surprise. For housing, dugouts had been carved out of the Pecos River bluffs with dirt and straw used as roof extensions. In contrast, the cattle pens and sheds appeared well constructed.

"Cattle must be more important here than a nice place to live in!"

Clay said to John.

A short middle-aged man had emerged from a lean-to, and stood watching while the large group of dusty cowboys rode up. He walked over as Charles Goodnight dismounted and took his hand in a warm shake. "Good to see you again, Charlie!"

"Well, we made it, Oliver," Goodnight said in greeting to his partner Oliver Loving. "Pretty easy trip, considerin' everything, and we brought most of the herd through. How're things here on the Bosque?"

"Good enough, Charlie," Loving told his old friend. "Sure glad to see some more cowboys! We've got over three thousand head to get ready for market—the Fort Sumner Indian reservation and everybody in Santa Fe are waiting for deliveries!"

Later in the day, things settled down and word spread that all cowboys who had brought the herd to New Mexico were to be paid off that afternoon.

"I'm itching to start that ranch," Clay said to the Calley brothers. "Do you two still wanna go in with John and me and buy some cattle?"

Wes considered the proposition. "I reckon between the four of us we might be able to get a few," he said. "But just where are we goin' to put up this ranch?"

Jim had been looking forward to the opportunity. "Wes, remember when we drove a herd up here the last time? That land south of Mount Baldy 'round Ponil and Cimarron Creeks is perfect. Full of grassy meadows."

Wes, the older and wiser, looked doubtful. "It still seems like we're gamblin' on the future," he said.

"Heck fire, Wes!" Jim countered. "We always took life the way we found it. If one thing don't work out, we just move on to the next. I say we go for it!"

The four brothers went to pick up their pay from Goodnight and Clay broached the subject.

"We appreciate your lettin' us help drive your herd to New

Mexico," Clay told the older man, "but now, me, John and the Calleys have decided to go in together and start our own ranch."

Surprised, Charles Goodnight scratched his head. "Well, now, I hate to lose four good men," he said, "but I gotta admire you. Most cowboys just live from job to job." He squinted at them. "Where and how are you plannin' on startin' this here ranch?"

"South of Mount Baldy, 'round Ponil and Cimarron Creeks," Wes Calley told him.

"But we need to buy a few head of cattle for starters," Clay added. "We thought maybe you could sell us some."

Goodnight had to chuckle. "Well, I reckon it'll be some time before you'll be my competitors. How many head you want to start with?"

Clay rubbed fingers through his dense beard. "It's more like how many we can afford."

"Seems to me," Jim put in, "with just the four of us, two or three hundred is all we could handle."

"Well, I won't rob you," Goodnight said. "Why don't you cut out a couple hundred head and we'll make a fair deal!"

With hearts full of bright expectation, the Allisons and Calleys began their drive north. Wes and Jim swung their horses around to ride alongside Clay and John as they supervised the herd.

Jim, tall and thin as his older brother, spoke through the missing front tooth, a souvenir from many hard years on the plains. "Reckon you two don't need me and Wes lookin' after you, now. Y'all turned out to be real cowboys!"

"If I was a real cowboy like you," Clay replied with a tease, "I'd chase that steer back in line over there!"

Jim saw with chagrin that one of the steers had wandered away from the others. He gave Clay a shame-faced look and spurred his horse after the varmint.

"Since we used most of our money buyin' this herd from Charlie Goodnight," Wes said with a worried expression, "reckon we'll have to watch our pennies for a spell!"

Clay stifled a laugh, thinking how much alike his brother John and Wes Calley were, always looking at the heavy side of things. But he wasn't about to let them dampen his carefree mood.

However, as they moved past the huge establishment of Fort Union, Clay's mind began to stir with old memories of the war and the Union Army that had destroyed his beloved Tennessee home. It was the damned Yankees that had caused his mother to die of heartbreak. Now, in a somber mood, he hunched down in the saddle as Ebon carried him onward in silence.

John saw the storm clouds gathering on Clay's face—the same look that usually preceded an outburst of some kind. But it was nothing new, for John was always there to take care of the situation. Nevertheless, he put himself on guard.

Lucien B. Maxwell's grist mill at Cimarron, NM, in the late 1860s, showing Indians receiving their rations. The two-story white building, center background, is Maxwell's large double-wing home.

*Courtesy Museum of New Mexico, Neg. 8957*

# Chapter Thirteen

*W*ord of Charles Morris' senseless killing by Chunk Colbert in Cimarron spread quickly to Elizabethtown. Sheriff John Turner had the sad duty of passing the news to Ben Colbert.

"After your brother and his nephew killed that man in Cimarron," Turner said, "Deputy Case Gordon thinks they went up into Colorado Territory."

Ben's heart flew in two directions. Steve had been so close, but now he was mixed up in another killing. "I'm still trying to find my boy Steve, but if he and my brother are on the run, they'd surely not come back to Cimarron."

John Turner shrugged. "If Chunk Colbert has a mind to come back, he will. I don't imagine he's afraid of anything."

"Well, Hannah and I are moving to Cimarron tomorrow. I don't look for any more violence, but I do hope maybe I'll see Steve there one of these days."

Ben and Hannah bade Frederick Haas a sad farewell and packed their few belongings into the little buggy.

The early afternoon sun spread its welcome mat of golden shafts over a small bridge as Ben urged the mule across Cimarron River and into the sleepy town. A few houses hugged the riverbank while the center of activity waited a short distance away. Hannah could make out a dry goods store, church, post office and the essential saloons.

She gazed with wonder at a fat three-story tower of stone that dominated the whole town. "What is that large building across the way, Ben?"

"It's a grist mill," he said. "Lucien Maxwell had it built. The government pays him to give grain to the Indians and he sells what's left to everybody for miles around."

"He must be a wealthy man!"

Ben chuckled. "He has what you might call a mansion not far from here!"

Ben halted the mule at a medium-sized house, third from the bridge. "Well, Mrs. Colbert, here's your new home. Mr. Maxwell let me have it for a very reasonable price."

Hannah appraised the modest abode with delight. "It's lovely, Ben—and with a river at our doorstep!"

"I even have a room for an office." He got down to tether the mule. "But come see the rest of it."

Hannah followed him throughout the four rooms, mentally placing her bits of furniture here and there.

"Oh, it's beautiful, Ben . . . and I have my own kitchen!"

A man's voice called through the open front door, "Ben Colbert, I see you've finally arrived!"

Ben turned to see Case Gordon. "Come in, Case, and meet my wife Hannah."

Case Gordon stepped inside and took a hat from his wavy brown hair. An engaging smile matched his soft melting eyes.

"Hannah," Ben said, "this is Deputy Sheriff Casey Gordon. Case helped arrange the sale of our house with Lucien Maxwell."

Hannah took Case's hand for a brief shake. "You certainly did

105

us a favor, Deputy, I love my new home!"

His eyes twinkled. "I saw your wagon come across the bridge and thought you might need some help moving in."

"That's mighty kind of you," Ben said. "My back isn't what it used to be!"

Case took off his coat, revealing a six-gun strapped to his waist. "Reckon I won't need this," he said and undid the gun belt, laying it down next to the door. "As soon as you're settled, Hannah, I'll take you into town for introductions." With a wink, he added, "Our womenfolk are just itching to meet the new lady in town!"

While unloading the wagon, Ben said to Case, "I guess you were surprised to know the new doctor in town has a brother who killed a man here!"

"At first, yes. But I know you're not anything like Chunk Colbert."

"It was a dirty trick of fate that I just missed running into my boy Steve. I don't suppose you've heard anything more about him?"

"Sorry I have to say 'No,' but I'll sure let you know if I do."

Ben shook his head. "Steve's mixed up in another murder, now, thanks to my brother Chunk. If I could find Steve and talk him into giving himself up, do you think they'd go easy on him?"

"I reckon that'd have to be up to a judge—and a jury!"

Ben glanced over his shoulder. "Please don't say anything to Hannah. I don't want her to worry."

By late afternoon, Hannah finished putting things away and plopped down into Ben's large stuffed armchair. "I'd ask you to stay for supper, Case," she sighed, "but I don't have a bite of food in the house!"

He looked with amusement through the doorway. "Well, I don't think you have to worry about that!"

Hannah turned to see three women at the open door. One, probably in her fifties, stood imperiously in the lead while two younger girls waited respectfully behind. They all wore smart-looking dresses, which Hannah would call "shopping clothes." Each carried a box or basket.

The older one sported a black hat with a large feather, which went well with her hawkish face and beady eyes. She spoke, unsmiling, in a businesslike voice. "Doctor and Mrs. Colbert, on behalf of the ladies of Cimarron, we've come to bid you welcome."

Hannah and Ben stared in surprise while Case Gordon smoothed his mustache, trying to hide a smile.

"My name's Alma Fries," the woman said, "and these young ladies are Dora and Bettie McCullough, daughters of our Postmaster John McCullough."

The girls nodded with bright pleasant faces.

Hannah recovered quickly. "Come in, ladies, come in! How nice of you to welcome us! This is my husband, Doctor Benson Colbert . . . and I'm sure you know Deputy Case Gordon."

Alma Fries ignored Case. "We're very glad to have a doctor in town," she told Hannah and walked over to the kitchen table, setting down her container.

Dora and Bettie McCullough placed their baskets alongside and took turns shaking the Colberts' hands.

"We've brought a little something for your supper," Dora said.

Bettie added, "We thought it'd tide you over till you can do your own shopping."

"Why, that's very thoughtful of all of you!" Hannah replied. "Won't you stay and join us?"

Alma Fries' stern look had not changed. "Thank you, but we must be on our way. I have a husband to feed and the girls must prepare supper for their father." She finally gave Case Gordon a glance. "And for the deputy, also, I presume."

The three women disappeared as quickly as they had arrived and Hannah gave Case a puzzled look.

"I'm afraid Mrs. Fries doesn't approve," he explained with a sheepish grin, "but I rent a room at the McCullough house . . . and take my meals there."

Hannah started to giggle and they all burst out laughing.

# Chapter Fourteen

$\mathcal{A}$t last, grassy plains of northeastern New Mexico spread before them in soft afternoon light as the Allison and Calley brothers drove their small herd of longhorns into the area. For Wes and Jim Calley, it was familiar territory, but Clay and John Allison had never seen such beautiful flat land. It could hardly be called a prairie. Rich grass stretched for miles in a cool green carpet. It sloped gently upwards to meet rounded purple hills, forerunners of the Sangre de Cristo Mountains to the west. Runoffs provided clear cold water to the region's many rivers.

Early evening had crept in by the time they reached the outskirts of Cimarron and Clay looked with disfavor at a small military establishment squatting in the distance. Next to it sat a large pen holding a number of Army mules.

"The Army has a few men here to keep order when Lucien Maxwell gives the Indians their rations," Wes explained to Clay and John.

Clay glared at the Army headquarters and the grudge, simmering ever since Fort Union, finally boiled over. He broke from the line of cattle and raced Ebon toward the pen.

"Clay!" John shouted. "What're you up to?"

He watched as Clay threw his rope around a corral slat, yanking it free. The startled mules began moving out through the opening.

John turned to the Calleys. "You all stay with the herd!" He galloped in fury over to the corral, shouting, "Clay! Close that pen back up!"

Clay had become alive with angry excitement. "They're not movin' fast enough!" he yelled and pulled his gun, firing a shot into the air.

John uttered an oath as fear-crazed mules raced out into open country. Making things worse, the gunfire and commotion had excited their herd of cattle. Wes and Jim worked frantically to keep them in a circle.

"Clay, put that damned gun away," John raged, "and get outta here before the Army comes runnin'!"

Clay started to holster the pistol but it caught on the reins and fired downward. Clay yelled again, but this time in pain—the bullet had torn through the instep of his boot.

"Now, look what you've done!" John screamed at him.

Clay gripped his right ankle in agony as John dismounted to examine the injury. He tugged off Clay's boot and rolled off the sock. The foot was a bloody mess with shattered bones protruding from the nasty wound.

"You need a doctor, Clay! Maybe that Army place has one, I'll take you over there."

"No, you won't! No Yankee doctor's gonna touch my foot!"

John saw two soldiers come out to investigate the ruckus. "They'd arrest us, anyway—come on, let's get outta here!"

Clay gave Ebon a nudge and rode back to the herd.

John got onto his horse and looked back to see if the Army had taken after him and Clay, but the soldiers were too busy on their horses, trying to round up the mules scattering over the plain.

Their longhorns had quieted down and were moving again as Clay rode up to lope alongside the Calleys.

Wes glanced down at Clay's bloody foot. "I saw what you did back there. You hurt bad?"

Clay didn't want to look at him. "It's not bad, but John says I oughta see a doctor."

"Maybe there's one in town."

Jim gave a wry grin. "Well, if I was you, Clay, I'd start learnin' how to use that gun!"

The men got their cattle settled down for the night, but John kept a worried eye on Clay who rode in the saddle with teeth grinding against the pain crawling up his leg.

"Come on," John finally said, "I'm gonna find you a doctor!"

Clay didn't answer. Both the embarrassment of shooting himself in the foot, and the mounting pain kept him quiet. He clenched his jaw and rode with John toward the small town's flickering lights that beckoned not far away.

Soon, they trotted their horses into the dusty street of Cimarron, a pleasant sprawl of houses and stores sitting in the still night along a small river.

John stopped a man who was about to enter one of the saloons. "You got a doctor here? My brother hurt his foot and needs attention."

The man glanced at Clay's wounded foot and nodded. "You're in luck, mister. We got a new doctor here last month." He pointed to the north. "His place is just this side of the river, third house east of the bridge."

"What would his name be?"

"Colbert."

Clay forgot the throbbing pain in his foot. "Benson Colbert?"

"Yes, that's it—Doctor Ben Colbert."

Clay turned his eager face to John. "Quick, let's go find him!"

They pulled up in front of the house and John dismounted to help his brother down from the saddle. Clay waved him aside, but as he touched the ground he started to fall. John helped him over to the door and gave it a hard knock.

A kind-faced woman, holding a lamp above her head, cautiously opened the door a crack.

"My brother here needs help," John said. "He's hurt his foot and can't walk. Is this the doctor's place?"

A short bearded man came to the door. "I'm the doctor, bring him in."

John helped his brother inside while the woman turned up her lamp wick, brightening the room.

Clay smiled through the pain at his old friend from the past. Ben Colbert, although a bit older, had changed very little, but with a short-cropped beard and a streak of gray in his hair.

"Doc Colbert, remember me?" Clay said eagerly. "I'm Clay Allison—we stole all that durned Yankee medicine together!"

Ben Colbert squinted with disbelief through his wire-rimmed glasses. "Clay Allison! It's hard to tell through all those whiskers, but it really is you! Why, I thought after you were captured, they must've hanged you!"

"Those Yankees couldn't hold me—I escaped before they had a chance!"

"Please meet my wife Hannah," Ben said. "What brings you to Cimarron, Clay?"

"This is my brother John. We came out with a cattle drive. Decided to put down here and start a place of our own."

John, still holding his brother, shifted with impatience. "Clay, did you forget why we're here?! Let the doctor look at that durned foot!"

"Come over here and sit down," Ben said and they assisted Clay into a large chair. "Hannah, move the lamp a little closer, if you will." Ben adjusted his glasses to look at the foot and frowned. "This is a gunshot wound—how the devil did it happen?"

Clay's thick beard hid his embarrassment. "It was an accident, Doc . . . I shot myself in the foot!" He grimaced as Ben poked a finger around the wound.

"This might call for amputation," Ben surmised.

"Doc! You're not gonna cut off my foot, are you?!" Clay had visions of Ben sawing off a leg during the war and throwing it onto a pile of other amputated limbs.

"No, no. Maybe a toe, but I can't say for sure till I do some cutting. I have a table in the back room where I do surgery."

They helped Clay into the other room where Ben dropped his razor-sharp knives into a tray containing a strange-looking solution.

"You washin' your knives, now?" Clay asked. "I don't remember you doin' that before."

"It's carbolic acid," Ben told him. "Joseph Lister in Europe has proved that wounds can be infected by germs, not only in the air, but on surgical instruments and even the surgeon's hands. Using this makes a wound heal like magic." He wiped the knives dry with a clean towel. "I only regret that the discovery came so late—I could have saved many a life and limb during the war!"

Ben had Clay lie down on the operating table and gave him enough chloroform for partial sedation. Hannah held a lamp close while Ben gently cut away the flesh around Clay's foot, then removed bone fragments and readjusted the toes. He sewed up the wound, washed it with more carbolic acid solution and applied a neat bandage, wrapping it firmly almost to Clay's knee.

"Your brother will be off his feet for a while," Ben said to John. "In the meantime, I recommend that he stay here so I can keep an eye on him."

Clay listened through his groggy half-sleep. "I can't stay here," he mumbled. "Gotta help John start up the ranch."

Ben put a hand on Clay's shoulder. "You're not going anywhere just now, young man. We have plenty of room and you'll be taken good care of till you can get around by yourself."

Clay shook his head in resignation. "Sorry 'bout all this, John. You sure you can get along without me?"

John gripped his brother's hand. "It'll be good havin' you out of my hair for a spell!"

"Before you go, John, don't forget to pay the doctor."

Ben chuckled. "That would be an outrage! I owe you for risking your life to help me and your fellow soldiers."

Before leaving, John Allison thanked Ben and Hannah for their generosity. "Least I could do," he told them, "is pay for letting Clay board here—he'll eat you out of house and home!"

"Keep your money," Ben replied. "You're going to need it!"

Clay Allison in 1868, soon after shooting himself
in the right foot. Photo shows left foot wounded,
since this was a reversed-image tintype.
*Courtesy Barney Hubbs Collection*

# Chapter Fifteen

*B*en removed the bandage. There had been no pus to drain off, as in nearly all previous operations, and the wound seemed to be healing nicely, thanks to the carbolic acid treatment.

"How does it look, Doc?" Clay asked with concern.

"Good, very good. But you'll have to keep a tight bandage on it a little longer." Ben began applying another large strip of cloth that had been sterilized in boiling water and dried in the clean hot sun.

"I think I owe you an apology," Clay said. "Back in Texas, I ran into your brother Chunk Colbert. Your son Steve was with him. Chunk and I had a disagreement and got into a knife fight . . . guess I cut his face a little."

Ben frowned. "I'm sure he must have asked for it. Sheriff John Turner told me that Chunk killed a man right here in Cimarron. You can imagine Deputy Gordon's shock when he found out Chunk Colbert's brother was the new doctor in town!"

"He doesn't hold that against you, does he?"

"Oh, no. Case and I are good friends, although I'm sure he'd hate having to arrest my son. I really wish he would, though. Maybe then I'd have a chance to get Steve away from that no-good brother of mine!"

"I take it you don't care much what happens to your brother."

"Chunk's a hopeless scoundrel—beyond saving. But Steve's young and doesn't know any better. I failed him as a father and now I've got to make up for it. It's my duty to find Steve and help him before it's too late."

Hannah came into the room, wiping her hands on an apron. "I've got food on the table, if you can break away."

Clay gave her a tender smile. He'd grown fond of the doctor's wife while she tended him with such loving care during his recuperation. She reminded him of his mother, who worked so hard raising all the children after Clay's father had died.

"You two go ahead," Ben told her and picked up his little black bag. "I promised the Adleys I'd ride out today and check on their little girl. They're afraid it may be smallpox . . . let's pray to God it isn't!"

Hannah's brow wrinkled with concern as she helped him into his coat. "You ought to eat a little something before you go, Ben."

He kissed her on the cheek. "Your cooking is too good. If I started now, I couldn't stop!"

Ben rode away in his little buggy and Clay sat down at the table with Hannah. She had prepared, with little effort, a tempting midday meal.

"Clay, I'm so glad you're here," Hannah said as they began to eat. "It gets lonely whenever Ben's off on a call like this. Sometimes he doesn't get home till early morning."

"Ben was just telling me his brother Chunk's in bad with the law."

"It's a shame about those two! Ben and Chunk never got along, even when growing up. Chunk was always jealous of his older brother and Ben tried to mend fences, but it was no good. Now, the two despise each other." Hannah shrugged. "Ben couldn't care less about Chunk—the most important thing in Ben's life, now, is finding his boy Steve and getting him away from Chunk's influence."

Clay pushed away his cleaned plate with a satisfied grin. "Well, I do think, Mrs. Colbert, that you're trying to fatten me up just so I can't walk out of here and you can keep me around for company!"

They heard a knock on the open door and John Allison stuck his head in. "Is that lazy, no-account brother of mine still here?"

"Come on in," Clay answered, "but stomp the dirt off your boots first!"

With chagrin, John checked his clean boots, then entered, stopping at the table. "I warned you, Hannah—keep feeding Clay like this, you'll never get rid of him!"

Hannah got up to fetch another plate. "Sit down, John, you came just in time for dinner."

He waved a hand. "Thanks, but I've already eaten."

"Well, can you sit down and visit a spell?"

John took a seat. "I just wanted to say that we found a nice place for the ranch, a few miles northeast of here. Started on a little house to use till we can afford to buy more lumber for a bigger one."

Hannah gave him a wary look. "Maybe you should wait till you know you're on that land legally, John. Lucien Maxwell owns all the land around here. So far, he doesn't seem to care who settles where, but he's selling his land grant to those men in Santa Fe. Who knows what they'll do?!"

"We'll play it by ear," John said, "but our main worry, now, is that we're running out of money! Wes Calley was right—we didn't plan far enough ahead. It's gonna be a spell before we have any cattle ready for market."

"Maybe we can get a loan," Clay said and looked at Hannah. "Does this town have a bank?"

Hannah shook her head. "Only person in Cimarron with enough money to need a bank is Lucien Maxwell—and he keeps it all hidden somewhere in that big house of his."

Clay's blue eyes narrowed with calculation. "Maybe we can get

Maxwell to shake loose some of that money. We could pay him back when the ranch starts showing a profit."

Hannah looked dubious. "Lucien Maxwell's a strange man—I can't say I've ever heard of him loaning money to anybody!"

"Well," Clay said, "when I can get on my feet, I'll go have a talk with Mr. Maxwell."

John got up from the table. "Hope that'll be soon. The Calleys and me got our hands full!" He shook his head at Clay. "Don't it bother you none, sittin' around here all day?"

Clay pointed to his gun belt nearby. "I've taken Jim's advice, learning how to use that gun."

Hannah laughed. "Land sakes, I hear him shooting out there by the river 'most every morning!"

After John left, Clay strapped on the gun belt, put a crutch under his arm and hobbled to the river's edge in front of the house. The Cimarron River, though more of a stream, ran deep and wide enough to require a bridge for travelers coming from Elizabethtown and other parts north.

Clay leaned on the crutch and loaded his gun, then took aim at a rock; with one shot, he blasted it into splinters. He holstered the gun and eyed another rock, whipping out the gun to fire immediately. Again, rocky shards flew into the water.

A female voice behind him said, "That's very good, are you expecting trouble?"

He turned to see an attractive young girl smiling at him. She wore a long beige skirt with a yellow blouse cut low enough to reveal her graceful porcelain-white neck; a neatly braided pony tail of light brown hair rested on the nape. Her matching brown eyes sparkled in the morning sun and the hint of a mischievous smile danced on soft pink lips.

"A man never knows when he might run into trouble," Clay said. His white teeth gleamed in a shy grin and he wished he'd trimmed the scraggly beard that morning.

"I'm Dora McCullough. I was just visiting Hannah Colbert and heard the shooting. She told me you were practicing."

"Then I assume she told you who I am . . . Clay Allison." He did a slight bow, the best he could on the crutch. "They're letting me stay with them till I can get along without this thing."

She walked to his side and gazed into the bubbling stream. "That's why we haven't seen you in town. You've been hiding out here till you can help your brother John build your ranch."

Clay's eyes danced in surprise. "You remind me of the brown-eyed owl we have back in Tennessee."

She turned with a puzzled smile. "What do you mean?"

"He's a right pretty bird. Soft tan feathers speckled with white—and big brown eyes that don't miss a thing. He sits in a barn window, or maybe a tree branch, watchin' your every move. People say if the brown-eyed owl could talk, he could tell what a man in the next county had for dinner, or even the name of the little gal he was sparkin' the night before."

She gave him a rueful look. "In other words, you're telling me I'm being nosy. Well, you see, I've already met your brother—the first time he came to the post office to mail a letter to your sister in Texas. My father is postmaster and my sister Bettie and I help him out."

"Sounds like John's been doin' a lot of talking!"

"Not really. When he told us you were recuperating at the Colbert's place, I just had to come and see if you're as nice as your brother."

Clay loved her teasing. "And what's the verdict?"

"I'll hold on that. But so far, I think you're ahead."

During a moment of silence the two studied each other. Clay couldn't remember ever seeing such a beautiful girl and Dora McCullough's boldness made her even more appealing.

"Maybe you'll be able to dance in another week," she finally said.

"With this?" He wiggled the crutch. "I don't think so. Never was much of a dancer, anyway."

"Bettie and I are trying to arrange one. Mr. Maxwell's letting us use his grist mill. Bettie and John will be there—you'll come, too, won't you?"

"John always liked to dance. Guess I oughta be there to see he doesn't get too carried away!"

# Chapter Sixteen

*B*en Colbert seemed pleased as he removed the final bandage from Clay's foot. "Let's see if you can stand on it." He helped Clay to his feet.

Clay winced as he tried a step. "Still can't put it down too hard."

"Then try this cane." Ben took a walking stick from the closet.

Clay forced himself to walk, using the cane to keep his balance.

"That's good!" Ben said. "I think you'll be able to attend the dance tomorrow—but on a social basis. I wouldn't recommend dancing!"

The next evening Clay ran a comb through his hair, trimmed the beard, and put on the fresh clothes Hannah had washed and ironed. A quick study of the mirror told him he hadn't looked this good since leaving Tennessee. With expectation, he joined the Colberts going to the grist mill dance.

They walked the short distance, Clay using his cane with dexterity, and found a sea of horses, buggies and wagons parked in front of the mill.

"It looks like everybody from Cimarron to Santa Fe is here tonight!" Hannah said eagerly.

People from every farm and ranch in the area congregated at the mill, even a few citizens from Elizabethtown. The first floor of the huge three-story building, cleared of all but the heaviest equipment, now had its gray stone walls draped with colorful bunting. The large room echoed with the sounds of happy dancers' stomping feet and lively music from two bewhiskered fiddlers. Alma Fries sat prim and straight-backed, plunking out a tune on a piano her husband had moved in.

Clay and the Colberts made their way through a crowd of farmers, ranchers and miners—some clad in their Sunday best, some in clean work clothes—toward a long table spread with cakes and cookies furnished by the hard-working wives.

Hannah grabbed her husband's hand. "Ben, come on, it's been too long since I've danced!"

Ben looked ruffled. "Hannah, you know I'm no good at that sort of thing."

"Just try, Ben, we're here to have fun!" She turned to Clay. "You don't mind us leaving you alone, do you Clay?"

"Of course not," he said. "Go ahead, enjoy yourselves."

Hannah dragged Ben onto the floor and they blended in with the throng of happy revelers.

Clay searched the crowd for a familiar face and spotted John swirling with a pretty brown-haired girl in a long maroon dress; Bettie McCullough, no doubt, who was much like her sister Dora. Unable to find Dora's delightful face among the dancers, he took a cookie and munched it with disappointment.

"There you are!" Dora's voice came from nowhere.

He turned to see her walking toward him, leading a tall handsome man by the hand.

"I'm so glad you came!" She looked at the walking stick. "I suppose that means I won't get a dance with you tonight?"

Clay swallowed the bite of cookie to answer, but she beat him to it.

"Clay Allison, I want you to meet Case Gordon. He's our deputy sheriff."

Clay shook Case's hand.

"Sorry about your accident," Case said, "but Dora tells me you'll be running around soon."

Clay forced a smile; the whole durned town knew all about him by now. He shrugged. "I'm lookin' forward to that."

The music ended and John came over with Bettie McCullough in hand. He introduced Bettie to Clay and said, "I'm glad to see Dora talked you into coming, Clay. How's the foot?"

Clay wished they'd all stop talking about his blamed foot. He cursed it and the cane, too; if it weren't for that, he might have a chance to feel Dora McCullough in his arms out there on the dance floor. That is, if Deputy Case Gordon didn't object.

The music started again and Dora turned to John Allison. "You don't mind if Case dances with Bettie, do you John? I'd like to sit this one out and visit with Clay."

"Whatever suits Bettie," John said.

Case Gordon took Bettie's hand with pleasure and they disappeared into the crowd. John selected a cookie from the table and took it over to sit on a grain sack.

Dora led Clay by the hand to two other sacks where they seated themselves.

"I need to rest before someone asks me for another dance," she said, waving a breeze to her face.

Clay leaned the cane against his leg. "Wish I could be the one to do the asking."

"There'll be another time." She glanced at John. "Your brother is a good dancer, isn't he?"

"He's always been the serious one. I'm glad to see him having fun for a change."

She turned to watch the laughing couples stepping to the catchy music. "I think that's why everybody came west, to escape all the

123

trouble in the east and be happy again." She looked back at Clay. "John says you lost your farm in Tennessee. I suppose you're starting over again, too."

It had all been out of Clay's mind for some time and he didn't want to drag it back again. "What did you and Bettie leave behind?" he asked, changing the subject.

"You might say Bettie and I were city girls. Daddy was a lawyer in Knoxville. His business just seemed to vanish when the war came. When it was all over, he decided to move west. Mama didn't like it out here and went back east. Daddy didn't know anything about ranching or farming, so it was pure luck that Lucien Maxwell give him the postmaster job here in Cimarron."

"Now, I guess the next step is for you and Bettie to find husbands and settle down to raise a family."

She laughed again in that light way, as if she'd take life as it came. He liked that; it was the same way he looked at things.

"If the right man comes along," she answered.

"I thought maybe the deputy was the right one." He watched Case Gordon waltzing smoothly with Bettie McCullough.

Dora's mouth opened in surprise. "Why, don't be silly—Case and I are just good friends! He rents a room at our house."

Clay's spirits shot up a degree. "If it weren't for this durned foot, I'd have you out on that dance floor in a minute, Miss Dora!"

# Chapter Seventeen

*B*en frowned with concern. "I should have done a better job," he said to Clay, "but with a few less bones in that foot, you're bound to have a limp."

Clay laughed. "But I can *walk*! That's what's important. I'm grateful for what you did, Doc." He took Ben's hand in a farewell shake.

Hannah walked over to them and put her arms around Clay. "You don't mind if I give you a motherly hug, do you?" she cooed. "We've all been just like family . . . I'm going to miss you, Clay!"

He placed a quick kiss on her cheek. "Thanks for being a mother hen, Hannah . . . and for all those good meals!" He put on his hat and walked to the door, favoring his right foot. "You two'll have to come out and see the ranch, soon's we get it built up."

"I've already put the saddle on Ebon for you," Ben told him. "That horse is going to be glad to have you on his back again."

"I'm obliged to you for riding him while I was laid up, Doc." Clay gave them a wave. "Thanks for everything. I'll stop by when

125

I'm in town."

Ben put an arm around Hannah's waist as they watched Clay hobble out to their small stable in back of the house.

"There goes a fine young man," Hannah said with pride.

Ben squinted with a tiny worry. "Yes, he's a good boy. I just hope he can stay out of trouble."

She turned with curiosity. "What do you mean?"

"He just has to control that touch of epilepsy."

She gaped in stunned surprise.

Ben growled at himself for thinking out loud. "Now, don't you go saying anything, Hannah. This is just between you and me—and Clay Allison! If Clay has too much liquor or loses his temper, he's apt to have a partial seizure. Trouble is, he likes whiskey and he has a fragile temper."

Hannah's face turned to sympathy. "The poor boy. One would never guess!"

Clay tried flexing his right toes in the boot and wondered if the foot would ever limber up. As he walked into the Colberts' stable, Ebon whinnied with a nod of greeting.

"Missed me, did you, old boy?!" Clay laughed and rubbed Ebon's neck.

The beautiful black horse snorted with pleasure while his master got into the saddle once more and guided him out of the stable.

Clay looked forward to seeing the new ranch, but first he had important business to take care of. He trotted Ebon down the street and stopped in front of Lucien Maxwell's large home.

As usual, Clay didn't tether his faithful horse. Ebon had been found in the wild and Clay let him be as free as he could. If the horse wasn't where he'd left him, Clay had only to whistle through his fingers and Ebon came running.

Clay knocked on the big front door and a beautiful Mexican girl opened it. He took off his hat.

"I'd like to see Mr. Maxwell, if he's to home."

"*Sí, Señor.*" Her smile was almost intimate. "Come, I take you to him."

Clay followed the girl through a cavernous living room to an open doorway. He saw the bulky frame of Lucien Maxwell sitting at a table, poring over a scattering of papers.

"*Perdón, Señor,*" the girl said. "A visitor to see you." She hurried away as Maxwell looked up.

"Good morning, Mr. Maxwell," Clay said. "I'm Clay Allison, but if you're busy, I can come back at a better time."

"No, no," Maxwell replied with a look of agitation. "Come in. Glad to take a break from all this legal mess!"

With hat in hand, Clay entered the smaller room. He quickly felt a sense of intimidation under the stocky man's piercing eyes.

"So you're one of the Allison brothers," Maxwell said. "You got run out of Tennessee by the Yankees and you're starting up a ranch here in Cimarron." He glanced down at Clay's foot. "And how's that foot you nearly shot off?"

Clay stifled his irritation. "My foot's coming along fine and I find it interesting that you know all about me."

"I have to know everything about newcomers coming into my territory—whether they plan to steal from me or shoot me while my back's turned!"

Clay had to grin. "If my brother and I planned to do either one, you'd have known about it before now."

Maxwell rarely smiled, but his dark-blue eyes twinkled at Clay's straight manner. "Then just what *do* you have in mind?"

"Like you said, my brother John and I are trying to start a ranch here. We've already got our cattle paid for, but we have to build a house soon. Cold weather's not far away."

"You don't have to tell me it gets cold in Cimarron."

"But we're running out of cash. The way I look at it, we'll start having cattle to sell maybe by spring. I was wondering if we could make some kind of deal for you to buy our beef for the Indian rations that the government is paying you to give out."

Maxwell gave it a quick thought. "Not too many cattle ranches in the area. I can always take on some more beef besides what I raise."

"The only trouble is, we need the money now—for somebody to make us a loan till we're ready to sell our beef."

Maxwell nodded. "And you're asking me to give you a leg up?"

"That's what I had in mind, yes. You can take it all off from your first order of beef, as soon as the ranch gets on its feet."

Maxwell leaned back in the large chair, his hard blue eyes riveted on Clay. "I might've given money away for a good cause, but I've never found a man I could trust to loan it to. What kind of collateral can you put up?"

"Collateral?"

"Yes . . . security."

Clay's shoulders drooped. He'd never thought about having to put up a security. Between them, the Allisons and Calleys had nothing. There was only one thing he valued most. He took a deep breath before answering. "What about my horse Ebon?"

Maxwell's eyes widened, their dark blue turning almost cobalt. "You'd give me your horse if you can't make the payment?"

"Yes. If you're a horseman, you'd know that Ebon's the best you'll find anywhere in the Territory."

"I've seen Ben Colbert ride your horse a time or two while you were staying with him. I'm not a horseman, but I'm a businessman, and I know I could sell that horse of yours for a fistful of money—maybe *two* fistsful!"

"Then you'll use him as collateral?"

"You must be pretty damned sure of yourself, Clay Allison. I like that in a man!" He pulled a clean sheet of paper from a drawer and dipped a pen in ink. "I'll make it due and payable one year from now. That should give you some extra time. How much do you need?"

Clay swallowed and wanted to knock himself in the head for not thinking of an amount. He didn't even expect to get the loan. "Well, the first thing is building a house. I've been laid up with this foot and John's been busy, so we don't have a dollar amount on that."

"I've put up buildings ever since stepping foot on this territory, so I can approximate what you'll need. Then, there's the cattle and living expenses. I'm experienced in that, too. I think fifteen hundred ought to get you through the year."

"Yes, sir, that sounds good," Clay gulped. "And what kind of interest?"

"No interest. I've got my eye on that horse! You just pay me back on the due date with your beef or the money . . . if you can."

Maxwell wrote out the contract and pushed it across the table for Clay to sign, then turned around to an old cabinet behind him.

Clay signed the document and watched Maxwell open a bottom drawer to pull out a stack of bills.

"Is it safe to keep your money in a drawer like that, Mr. Maxwell?"

Lucien Maxwell's face came close to a smile. "I never lock my doors. Everybody in Cimarron knows the price they'd pay for stealing from me!"

After a heartfelt thank-you, Clay walked outside where Ebon greeted him with a nicker of reproach.

Clay laughed and rubbed a hand over the sleek animal's nose. "Dammit, Ebon, don't look at me like that—we're never gonna part company!"

He grinned with satisfaction and climbed into the saddle, pointing Ebon in the direction of the Allison ranch.

# Chapter Eighteen

"*G*lad to have you back!" Wes Calley hollered as Clay reined Ebon to a halt in front of the sad little frame structure they called a house.

"Glad to *be* back!" Clay sat in the saddle and looked around at the wide flat land spread with green grass reaching toward the northwest mountains.

John Allison and the Calleys galloped in from the herd of grazing cattle.

"Well, Clay, what do you think?" John asked with pride, pulling up next to Ebon.

"You picked a nice spot. Looks like you've all been kind of busy, too."

Jim Calley shook his head in disgust. "But I hate to think of four of us, now, sleepin' in this little shack—three's been bad enough!"

"Well, I've got news for you," Clay said. "It won't be long before we have a bigger place. I just got a fifteen-hundred-dollar loan from Lucien Maxwell!"

John's mouth opened in surprise. "Maxwell?! How did you swing that?"

Clay rubbed Ebon's ear. "Just my good looks, I reckon!"

"Boy howdy, that's somethin'," Wes said. "But gettin' lumber is gonna be the hard part."

"How do you mean?"

John waved his arm toward the mountains. "Nearest timber is over there, but with all the building at E-Town, wood's kind of scarce. We'll have to go over there and dicker for some."

Clay glanced down at his foot. "I still can't walk too good, so I won't be much help around the ranch. Why don't I go to E-Town and handle the business part. If I get the wood, you think we can all build the house?"

Jim snorted with pleasure. "I'd break my back for a decent place to sleep!"

With the day still young and Elizabethtown just over twenty miles to the northwest, Clay decided to ride over, make a deal and return to the ranch next morning.

The raw mining town's non-stop activity greeted him on arrival in late afternoon. Horse-drawn carts and wagons rumbled toward their own important destinations down the main dirt street, lined on both sides with wooden buildings. Signs touted everything from hardware and clothing to fresh bread and professional undertaking. Every third building seemed to be a saloon.

The town hall, a large two-story building made of smoothed stone, sat proudly on a rise at the south edge of town. Stretched across its beautifully arched windows hung a banner, which announced in bold letters, TONIGHT ONLY! KITTY LYNNE IN CONCERT.

Clay had no trouble following the smell of sawdust and rode to a sawmill behind the town.

"You came at a good time," the owner told him. "Got a pack of lumber somebody backed out on."

"I'm surprised you don't have a waiting list," Clay said.

The man looked around to be sure no one else could hear. "Just between you and me, some people are beginning to hold back on their plans. Rumor has it the gold up on Mount Baldy is just about played out. Else, why would Lucien Maxwell be selling off his land? I hear he's got all the gold he could outta his Aztec Mine."

"Well, I'm not into gold. I'm a rancher and need some wood to build a house. Can you give me a good price on that pack you're holding?"

The man was glad to unload it. "I think we can come up with a deal you'll like. Of course, there'll be an extra charge if you want it delivered."

"My place is four miles northeast of Cimarron."

"Why, that's like down the road a piece—won't cost you much at all!"

Clay made arrangements for the lumber to be delivered next day, but insisted on paying half now and the remainder on delivery. He then rode back into the busy town and found a hotel room for the night.

After enjoying a fine dinner in the hotel dining room, and with the evening still young, Clay decided to visit one of the saloons before retiring. He stepped out into the warm night air and heard a delightful singing voice drifting over the hubbub of street noise. Realizing it was Kitty Lynne performing at the town hall, he paused to listen. In the distance, the building's windows glowed with the warm yellow light of kerosene lamps while the song ended to the clamorous applause of a packed house. He smiled and walked with a slight limp to the nearest saloon.

Inside the hazy room, Clay met the familiar smell of stale beer, liquor and tobacco smoke. He worked his way through a swarm of loud-talking miners, cowboys and men in traveling clothes and ordered a whiskey at the bar.

"What's your thinking about old Charlie Kennedy?" the man standing next to him said.

Clay glanced at his drinking companion. He was probably one of the local businessmen, not wearing expensive clothes like the transients, but also not dressed like the miners.

"Can't say," Clay replied. "I don't know the man."

"Then you're new in town. Well, you ought to know about Charles Kennedy—that's what everybody here's talking about!" He nodded at the other customers. "And they're gettin' up a head of steam."

Clay had planned on only one drink and then return to the hotel, but he wanted to hear the story. He swallowed the whiskey and ordered another. "What about Charles Kennedy?"

"He's got a place on the mountain road to Santa Fe. Well, two nights ago, his poor wife crawled all the way to E-Town and came busting in here, screaming about Charlie beating her up. She looked it, too, her face all bloody and covered with bruises."

Clay frowned. "He oughta be horsewhipped! I was brought up to show a woman respect, no matter who she is!"

"But that's only the beginning," the man continued. "Said she saw Charlie kill at least five traveling men during the last year, take their money and bury them under the house. The sheriff went up there, tore up the floor boards and sure enough, found some human bones! Well, they arrested old Charlie Kennedy, brought him back to E-Town and put him in jail."

Clay simmered at the thought of a poor woman in the hands of a brutal husband. He downed his drink in anger. "So that's it. Charles Kennedy is where he belongs—in jail."

The man shook his head with dark foreboding. "It's not over yet. Most folks here think since his wife's the only witness, he'll get a quick trial and be set free." He looked around at the other men in the room and moved closer. "They want Charlie Kennedy hanged!"

A man at one of the tables jumped up, obviously well saturated. "I say we oughta go lynch the bastard!" he shouted. "Who all's with me?"

Another customer with liquor-inflamed eyes rose from the next table. "You can count me in!"

"The sheriff's not in town," came another shout. "Probably nobody's watching Kennedy—he'll escape and kill somebody else!"

"Yes, maybe that poor wife of his, this time!"

"Let's go hang 'im and save the law the trouble!"

Like a grass fire, flames racing from one dry patch to another, the whole room burst into conflagration.

"You comin' along?" growled the man beside Clay.

Clay hesitated. The liquor had whetted his fury—maybe the lowly cur should be hanged. The old tingle in his spine ignited a strong urge to join the vengeful crowd. He clenched his jaw and managed to control himself. "This isn't my town," he said.

"Well, I'm goin' with them!"

Clay watched as nearly every man in the saloon blended into an angry mob and stormed out the doorway, into the street.

"No man should beat up a woman!" he said to the bartender. "I oughta go, too!"

The little bartender reached over and put a hand on Clay's arm. "This man, he could be innocent!" he said with a French accent. His sparse hair was neatly slicked down and a thin mustache streaked his upper lip. Wide liquid eyes held a touch of pity. "Who can really know without a trial?"

Clay stood for a moment, trying to rid the devil from his brain. He took a deep breath. "Well, it's really not my concern," he finally convinced himself. "I'm leaving this town tomorrow, anyway. In the meantime, you can give me another drink!"

The bartender filled the glass and looked at the almost empty room. "My wife and I, we are leaving this town, also. It will soon be dead, anyway."

"Where will you go?"

"Lucien Maxwell has sold me a bit of land in Cimarron. I plan to build a fine hotel there—with a first-class restaurant." His chest swelled with pride. "I am not only a bartender, but I am a great chef, also! I even cooked for President Abraham Lincoln in

Washington." His eyes drooped. "But then someone killed him and I come west." He put a hand over the bar to Clay. "My name is Henri Lambert, but everyone calls me Henry."

Clay shook the hand politely. "I'm Clay Allison. I have a place just outside of Cimarron. When you get your hotel built, I'll drop in. What you plan on callin' it?"

"I already have a name. The Saint James Hotel, with saloon and dining room!"

The mob evidently wasted no time. Soon a number of the men came rumbling back into the saloon.

One carried a bloody burlap bag and announced, "We strung 'im up at the slaughterhouse!" He held out the bag. "Here, take his head, Henry, and put it over the bar—it'll be a warning to anybody who'd murder a man and beat up his wife!"

Henri Lambert cringed and wouldn't touch the thing offered to him. "Please, no—not in my saloon!"

Clay looked at the bag dripping with blood and thought of the poor woman being beaten to a pulp. With the liquor's help his suppressed anger finally boiled to the surface.

"I'm glad you did it!" he told the man. "If you hadn't cut off that scoundrel's head, I would've done it for you!"

He grabbed the gunny sack from the man and pulled out the gruesome head by its tangled black hair. The eyes bulged out in the last moments of terror while blood ran down Clay's wrist. "You don't have to put it over your bar, Henry—I'll stick it on the fence outside for you!"

Clay stomped out and plunked the severed neck down onto a pike at the saloon entrance. He wiped a bloody hand on his trousers and staggered in drunken rage back to the hotel where he fell asleep in the tiny room.

# Chapter Nineteen

*B*en Colbert guided his mule and small black buggy off the road that led from Cimarron to Elizabethtown. Since the day was still young, he followed the directions Clay Allison had given and soon found their little shack squatting in the distance.

Two wagonloads of lumber had just arrived, with Clay supervising the unloading. Ben drove over to a stop.

"Doc Colbert!" Clay walked up to the buggy, taking Ben's hand in a hearty shake.

Ben leaned back in the seat. "I'm on my way back from the Adley place and thought I'd take a detour to see your ranch."

Clay laughed. "Ain't much to see right now. I just got this lumber from E-Town—we're gonna replace that durned thing!" He waved his hand at the shack.

Ben gave the pitiful structure a dour look. "I really can't say that I blame you!"

John Allison and the Calley brothers had seen Ben's arrival and John rode in from the field, leaving the Calleys to watch the cattle.

"Good to see you again, Doctor Colbert," John said.

"The Doc's on his way back to Cimarron and stopped to see our place," Clay told him.

"You can tell we have a ways to go, Doctor," John said and dismounted, holding the reins. "Well, Clay, looks like you got enough lumber here."

Clay swelled with pride. "Should be enough to give us a room for Wes and Jim and one for you and me. Maybe some left over to build a storage shed and corral."

After the last wagon had been emptied, Clay gave the remaining payment to the driver and the wagons started back to Elizabethtown.

A man on horseback passed them and rode over to the Allisons and Ben Colbert, reigning to a stop. "Good morning, Doc," he said, "and John Allison."

"Well, Sheriff Turner," John greeted the man, "what brings you out here?"

John Turner's tired but determined face showed the hard lines of a man who had spent twenty of his sixty years dealing with drunks, gunmen and horse thieves. He nursed a stiff leg getting down from the horse. "Just came from E-Town and need a little information, is all."

John Allison held out his hand for a friendly shake. "If it has to do with the law, I don't see how we can help."

The sheriff looked at Clay. "Is this your brother?"

John ducked his head with embarrassment. "I'm sorry, Sheriff, this is Clay Allison. I thought everybody 'round here knew my big brother by now."

Clay grasped Turner's hand. "Pleased to meet you, Sheriff."

"I understand you were at E-Town last night," Turner said, as if thinking aloud.

"That's right. I was getting this here lumber."

"Did you know that a man named Charles Kennedy, was dragged out of jail and lynched at the slaughterhouse there?"

John Allison's eyes widened in surprise while Ben sat up with interest in the buggy seat.

"Yes, sir, I did," Clay told the sheriff.

"I couldn't find out the names of the men who did it."

"They were a bunch, I guess."

"But somebody else from Cimarron was there, too. Said he saw you, Clay Allison, walk out of a saloon with Charles Kennedy's severed head in your hand. Said you stuck it on a fence pike in front of the saloon, then walk away."

"That's right, Sheriff. But I didn't have anything to do with takin' off that man's head!"

"Did you know any of the men that lynched Charles Kennedy and cut off his head?"

"No! I was new in town, didn't know anybody . . . but it was the mob that did it! I was in the saloon all the time." Clay thought a moment. "You can ask the bartender, Henry Lambert. He owns the place."

Sheriff Turner finally smiled, but wryly. "I already did, and he backs up your story. I can't arrest you for murder—I was just tryin' to find out some names, is all." He carefully got back onto his horse and wheeled it around to leave. "You're gonna have a nice place, here, John." He glanced back at Clay. "And Clay Allison . . . try to stay out of trouble!" He touched his hat brim in goodbye and rode off.

Ben Colbert could see an explosion ready to go off between the Allison brothers. He suppressed a laugh. "Well, I'd better get back before Hannah begins to worry. Stop by when you can, both of you!" He flicked the reins and drove off.

John stood speechless while Clay avoided his brother's eyes. Finally, the words tumbled out of John's mouth. "What the devil, Clay!?"

"Nothin' really happened, John. It's all over with, now, so let's just forget about it! Come on, we've got a house to build!"

It wasn't all over with, Clay soon found out, when he went to town a week later to buy a keg of nails. While loading the wagon, he spotted Dora McCullough walking over to him.

He felt a soft glow while drinking in the sight of her slim figure dressed in a pretty, full-length brown dress to match her shining hair, the first time he'd seen it done into a bob. She held a small yellow parasol over her head.

"Clay Allison! How have you been?"

He tipped his hat and smiled broadly. "Just fine, Miss Dora. You're lookin' well. I hope your father and sister Bettie are the same."

"They're fine. We haven't seen you and your brother for some time."

"Well, we've been kind of busy, putting the ranch together. Already got our house almost finished. You'll have to come out and see it!"

She flashed a teasing smile. "But you haven't been too busy to avoid E-Town. I've heard rather shocking rumors about your visit there!"

He looked down, abashed. "It wasn't anything. You shouldn't listen to what people say."

She shuddered. "Everybody says you cut off a man's head! Of course, I know it isn't true—you'd never do such a thing!"

"No, ma'am, I sure wouldn't."

"Ben and Hannah Colbert were asking about you the other day. You really ought to see them before you go back."

"I'd planned on doin' just that."

She furled the parasol. "Well, let us know when the house is finished. Bettie and I would love to drive out and give it our approval!"

"I look forward to that." He tipped his hat again and she vanished into a store.

Clay got into the wagon and jiggled the reins, wishing he wasn't so tongue-tied; he could have said more. Arriving at the Colbert house, he tethered the horse and Hannah met him at the door.

"Clay Allison! I've been worrying about you!" She put her arms around him for a warm hug. "How's your foot?"

"Almost like new, only a limp."

"Come on in. Ben's holed up in his work room, but he'll want to see you."

Clay followed her inside and Hannah knocked on the study door. "Ben, Clay Allison's here!"

Ben came out with a medical book in his hands and beamed with pleasure. "Well, well, just how is my rambunctious patient?" He put the book down and shook Clay's hand.

"Still have to limp to keep it from hurting."

"Come into my office, I want to look at it."

"You two go ahead," Hannah said. "I'll round up some coffee."

Ben and Clay went into the office where Clay sat down and removed his boot and sock.

Ben Colbert studied the scar tissue, pressing at various points of the instep. "Tell me where it hurts."

Clay winced. "There . . . and there!"

Ben sighed with concern. "The foot has more bones in it than a Pecos River catfish! I could cut it open again and see if something more could be done . . . "

"Oh, no, Doc! I don't want another operation, I can get by with just a limp." Clay put on the sock and boot.

Ben leaned back in his large reading chair. "Well, give it a year or two. If it doesn't clear up, you'll just have to get used to it."

"I'm not going to worry about it."

Ben's eyes twinkled. "Dora McCullough has been asking about you. Maybe you ought to drop by the post office and say hello."

"I already saw her, in town."

Ben gave him a knowing look. "I think she rather likes you. Ever think about developing the situation?"

Clay leaned forward in frustration. "Doc, remember back in the Army when I told you why I got my first discharge?"

Ben nodded. "Yes, I do. Epilepsy, wasn't it?"

"That's right. I was always gettin' into a fight."

"But I thought you had it under control."

"That's just it. I still have these flare-ups and something makes me do things I know I shouldn't be doin'."

Ben chuckled. "The whole town's talking about that episode in E-Town."

"I didn't do what they're sayin'!" Clay blurted out. "But, Doc, the thing that bothers me is that I *wanted* to do it! I'd had a few drinks—that's when it's the worst." His face turned baleful. "You see, Doc, a woman's not going to put up with that kind of man. That's why I'm not pushing things with Dora. If anything developed, she'd only end up gettin' hurt."

Ben gave a sly look. "Maybe you just need a little help. Sometimes, you know, it takes a woman to tame a man!"

Hannah came in holding a tray with cups of steaming coffee and freshly-baked cookies.

"Enough business for now, you two. Let's go into the parlor, I want to hear all about Clay's ranch!"

# Chapter Twenty

 $Y$ oung Steve Colbert felt edgy as he climbed up onto the sleek brown horse. His uncle had won the fine animal in a poker game, but he'd cheated, of course. The poor cowboy, devastated over losing both his poke and his faithful companion, went on a drunk and shot his brains out in grief.

Steve couldn't shake the jittery feeling while trotting the horse up to the starting gate. This race would be against the ranch owner's horse, and Jake Wagner was a smart man, a lot keener than any rancher around. How else could he have acquired this large spread and impressive home north of Trinidad, Colorado?

Visiting ranchers from miles around had brought their best horses for today's racing and were keyed up. This would be the last race and each man bristled in an all-or-nothing mood.

Chunk walked over to Steve for a quick word of encouragement.

"Don't forget, I've got a bundle tied to this race!" Chunk said. He gave Steve's leg a squeeze and looked up with a hard smile.

Steve had sometimes caught Chunk giving him a kindly, almost proud, look. But he'd learned that his uncle's smiles were never for pleasure; they always carried something grim. Even so, it made Steve feel good. When they had started out together, Steve felt like he was extra baggage until he'd learned how to jump the starting gun at the races. Now, he'd won several times and felt appreciated.

"Don't worry, Uncle Chunk. I'll do just what you taught me!"

Chunk left to join the spectators and a seasoned rider on Wagner's horse moved up alongside Steve. The crowd held its breath while a cowhand raised his starting pistol. As usual, out of the corner of his eye, Steve watched the trigger finger. Just as it moved, Steve gigged his horse and the shot rang out.

With a fraction lead, Steve whipped his horse forward, Jake Wagner's steed close in the rear. Bettors shouted and waved their hats as the two horses rounded a turn, then came thundering back, neck-and-neck. It looked like it'd be a dead heat, but Steve brought his horse across the line a nose ahead of the Wagner horse and the spectators roared.

Bets were paid off and the visitors rode away, either in good spirits or grumbling over losses.

Steve trotted the panting brown horse over to Chunk and dismounted. He'd have to ride his own, now, while Chunk took the swift one.

"You did all right," Chunk said. "I'm proud of you, Boy!"

Steve felt good that he'd pleased his uncle. "Reckon you can collect that bundle, now, Uncle Chunk!"

Chunk threw his saddlebags over the horse. "All ready got it, right in here!"

He tightened his gun belt and the two prepared to leave, but halted as Jake Wagner approached. The wealthy rancher, a stocky little man, carried an authoritative look with his gray hair, neat beard and mustache. A widower, he lived alone in the big house with only hired hands for company.

"Before you leave," Wagner said, "how about a drink to celebrate your win?"

Chunk eyed him with suspicion. He wanted to get away with the money as soon as possible, but after all, Wagner was the host.

"Thank you, Mr. Wagner, but only one drink."

Steve and Chunk followed the aging rancher inside to a large room with a big floor-to-ceiling window that overlooked the racing area. Jake Wagner opened an ample liquor cabinet and poured three drinks of expensive whiskey.

Steve looked around the cavernous room and figured they were the only ones in the house. As the man handed over the drinks, something in Wagner's slate-colored eyes added to Steve's discomfort.

They settled into large leather chairs and sipped the excellent whiskey.

Wagner said, "You've got a right good horse, Mr. Colbert—but I still think I could beat you if we ever get around to running a fair race."

Chunk threw him a sharp look. "We ran a fair race and you lost!"

"I didn't want to stir up trouble with the others about your nephew jumping the gun like that, but I want you to realize that I know what you did. So, let's just say it wasn't a fair race and we can try it again sometime—on a different basis."

Chunk reddened with anger and the corner of his eye began to jump. "Nobody calls me a cheat, so I'll ask you to kindly retract that statement!"

"Sorry, but there's nothing to retract!"

Chunk pulled the forty-five from his holster. "I say there is!"

Steve gulped his drink, knowing there'd be hell to pay.

Wagner's face paled. He set the glass down and got to his feet. "Put that thing away. I don't want the money. Why don't you just admit it was an unfair race and then be off!"

"I'll admit nothing!" Chunk snarled and pulled the trigger.

The gun roared and Jake Wagner clutched his chest. He staggered against a wall.

"Hold him up!" Chunk shouted to Steve.

Steve rose quickly, grabbing the little man by his hair. Chunk walked over and pushed the gun barrel into Wagner's chest. The sound of gunfire was muffled this time, as four more bullets thudded into the man's body.

Steve let Jake Wagner slide to the floor, the wall behind him impacted with hot lead and streaked with blood.

"Thanks for the drink!" Chunk said to his dead host. He holstered the gun and glanced at Steve. "Let's get out of this mausoleum!"

The two ran outside and jumped onto their horses. As they galloped off, Steve looked back with a curse. Two of Wagner's ranch hands had seen them leave the house and stood watching as Chunk and Steve rode away from the ranch.

# Chapter Twenty-One

*C*lay rubbed a loving hand over Ebon's nose. "With me hangin' around the house, old pardner, you're not gettin' much exercise. How about a little run?"

The sleek black horse whinnied with pleasure and Clay climbed into the saddle. He trotted the horse out into the pasture, then gave Ebon a little gig. The horse leaped forward, speeding across the stretch of grass like a zephyr around the grazing cattle. After circling twice, Clay pulled Ebon to a halt beside John and the Calley brothers who rested in their own saddles, watching the herd.

"You ride that horse like the two of you was growed together!" Wes said.

Clay gave Ebon's neck an affectionate pat. "He likes to run, all right." He turned to John. "Think we'll have any calves soon? About time we started making a profit."

John shook his head with the usual serious expression. "It'll be a while before we have any to sell, and that money you borrowed from Lucien Maxwell is running low."

A tinge of dread ran through Clay at the thought of losing Ebon.

Wes grinned at Clay's horse. "That there Ebon is mighty fast, Clay. Maybe you could win some races at the big track up at Raton. They have racin' there every weekend."

John shook his head again. "I never was for gambling."

"Wouldn't take much to try," Jim told him. "You could put just a little down. If Clay didn't win the first time or two, he could come on back home."

"At least I'd be doing something," Clay said. "I'm not helping out here like I want to."

The idea received another discussion that night with John being outnumbered. They decided on a sum of money for Clay to take with him and he prepared to leave the following morning.

After Clay tightened the saddlebags and got into the saddle, John reached up for a goodbye handshake.

"Now you behave yourself, Clay!"

Clay looked down, confident. "Don't worry, I'll be back Monday with these saddlebags stuffed with money!"

As John watched his brother gallop off on the handsome black horse, something told him he should be going along, too.

"Oh, what the heck," he muttered to himself, then turned to Wes Calley. "I haven't been to town for a spell, Wes. How 'bout me getting the supplies today, while you and Jim see to the herd."

Ben Colbert had just driven his buggy across the bridge and saw John Allison down the street, tossing a bag into his wagon in front of the general store. Ben turned the mule and drove over. "Good afternoon, John. I haven't seen any of you boys for some time. How are you getting along?"

John leaned against the wagon for a breath. "Could be better. Our cash is gettin' kind of low."

Ben shook his head. "I was afraid that loan from Maxwell wouldn't last till spring."

"Well, don't you worry, Doc. Clay got the harebrained idea of running his horse in a race up at Raton. Thinks he'll win enough money to get us through." He shrugged. "But that horse of his is fast—he just might come back with something!"

"Let's hope so," Ben said. "Nice seeing you again, John. Let me know how Clay makes out."

Ben turned the buggy and went on to the house where Hannah greeted him with a hug, but minus the usual loving smile.

"You feeling all right, dear?" he asked. "Your color seems a bit off."

"Case Gordon stopped by while you were out," she told him. "He had some news about Steve."

Ben's face came alive. "He's found Steve? Where?"

"He hasn't found him, but he's looking for Steve and your brother." She clutched her hands together. "I hate to tell you this, Ben . . . the sheriff in Trinidad, Colorado, sent a report to Sheriff John Turner that Chunk and Steve killed a wealthy rancher up there."

Ben's hopes plunged and he cursed under his breath.

Hannah continued. "Everybody knows that Chunk has won lots of money at horse racing. They seem to think that with Raton so close, he'll show up there, since they have the biggest races in the Territory."

"Is that where Case has gone—to Raton?"

"Yes. If he finds them, he'll bring them back for trial."

Ben shook his head. "Clay Allison is in Raton, now, too. There's bad feeling between Chunk and Clay. If those two meet up, there'll be another killing for sure!" He gritted his teeth. "And Steve is right in the middle!"

Hannah put a hand on his shoulder. "Ben, there isn't anything we can do—let Case Gordon handle it."

Ben could only stare into space, his mind in turmoil.

"Now, sit down and relax," she consoled him. "I'll finish getting your supper on the table."

Hannah went back to the kitchen and minutes later realized Ben had disappeared. She rushed to the bedroom to find him putting clothes into a small bag.

"Ben! What are you doing?"

He kept packing. "Hannah, I know Steve isn't to blame. If I can get to him first, maybe I can save him from getting hanged!"

Hannah gasped. "Ben, you're not going to Raton?!"

His eyes brimmed with both love and concern as he turned to her. "It's something I have to do, Hannah—probably my last chance!" He put his arms around her. "I want you to stay with the McCulloughs while I'm away. Case Gordon has moved out and taken a room at Henry Lambert's new hotel, so the McCullough's will have a place for you."

# Chapter Twenty-Two

"*H*ere's an extra helpin' of oats," Clay said to Ebon in the hotel stables. "I want you rarin' to go tomorrow!"

He had taken a room at The Clifton House. The three-story hotel with fine dining facilities was the centerpiece of Raton, New Mexico, nestled at a mountain pass thirty miles northeast of Cimarron near a branch of the Santa Fe Trail. Behind the large building lay a quarter-mile racetrack that catered to ranchers who brought their fastest horses to compete in matched races.

Clay went back to the hotel desk. "I'd like to register for the next available race tomorrow," he told the clerk.

"We're pretty full up," the man said and ran down a list of entrants. "The next opening is this one here." He showed the paper to Clay.

Clay saw that he'd be racing against a horse owned by Chunk Colbert and ridden by his nephew Steve. "Well, I'll be a three-legged horned toad," he muttered. "You can put my name on that one, for sure!"

150

The next afternoon arrived crisp and sparkling clear, a great day for racing. Clay rode Ebon over to the starting line where Chunk Colbert stood talking to his nephew who sat on a beautiful brown steed.

Clay pushed back his hat. "Nice meetin' you again, Mr. Colbert. Looks like we'll be ridin' against each other today."

Chunk studied Clay's face and large beard. "Are you that Clay Allison I ran into somewhere back in Texas?"

Clay rubbed his dark whiskers. "That's right. And I'm sorry we didn't hit it off so good the last time."

Chunk touched a finger to the slight scar on his cheek. "I've still got your calling card, Clay Allison. I told you then, we'd settle our disagreement later—maybe this race will take care of that!"

"I just might have to disappoint you."

Chunk flashed one of his dark smiles and went to join the other spectators.

Chunk and Clay had each put up a hundred dollars, with a percentage of crowd bets to be given to the winner. If Clay could win the first race, he planned to go back to Cimarron the next day with his saddlebags full of money.

Ebon snorted in anticipation. Clay gave him a good-luck pat on the neck and noticed Steve watching the man who held up the starter pistol. Just before it cracked, Steve spurred his horse forward, getting a split-second lead, and the crowd began to roar. Clay dug his heel into Ebon's side, but the feisty horse didn't need encouragement; it dashed forward eagerly, kicking up large clumps of turf to close the distance quickly.

Spectators had been strung out along the racetrack, but now gathered at the finish line, waving and cheering for their favorite steed.

Clay gave Ebon the reins and let the horse surge forward, like they were back at the ranch flying over an expanse of green pasture. Just before the finish line, Ebon passed Steve's horse and the crowd went wild.

151

Clay let out a "Yahoo!" of victory. He trotted Ebon back to tell Chunk Colbert that his nephew ran a good race, even though the boy cheated. But Chunk had vanished in a cloud of anger.

"Well, let's get our money," Clay said to Ebon, "then I'm takin' you back to the stables for all the oats you can eat!"

As purple shadows of evening crept over Raton, Chunk and Steve Colbert entered a saloon next to the Clifton House. Chunk's losing a race only added to his overbearing attitude and the two pushed their way to the bar.

"Give us two of your best whiskey!" Chunk ordered. As soon as the drinks were poured, he tossed his down and motioned for another.

Steve only sipped his drink and eyed the room warily to see if anybody showed a badge. "Uncle Chunk, I still think we oughta get outta this town right away. Everybody knows you like horse racin', and that Colorado sheriff's bound to figure you'd come to Raton!"

Chunk finished his second shot. "You may be right, but I'm getting my money back from Clay Allison, first!"

"How you figure on doin' that?"

"He's probably at the hotel, now, gloating over that prize horse of his. Let's go over there and play nice, for a change. We'll catch him with his guard down!"

A few minutes after Chunk and Steve had left the saloon, Ben Colbert pushed his way through the swinging doors. He stopped at the entrance and took his time, studying each face in the large smoky room; with Steve so close, he didn't want to miss this last chance. But here, again, he found disappointment and turned in determination to check the saloon two doors away.

Ebon munched his victory feed while Clay finished brushing down the beautiful animal, then rubbed its nose.

"Enjoy yourself, Old Pal!" He patted the wad of bills tucked in his coat pocket. "John and the boys are gonna be proud of you when we get back with all this money!"

He had left his gun belt at the stable during the race and now strapped it around his waist before going to the hotel. At the entrance he ran into Chunk and Steve Colbert.

"I don't want you to think I'm a sore loser, Clay," Chunk said with unctuous good will. "Just to show you I hold no animosity, let me buy you supper."

Clay looked with surprise at the pair. "That's mighty nice of you, Chunk. I was just about to go to the dining room."

"Not the hotel, it's too busy. Why don't we go across the street to that chili restaurant? It's early and we'd have the place to ourselves so we can talk."

Steve Colbert was not wearing a gun, but Clay felt uneasy when he saw the one on Chunk's hip. He shrugged. "All right with me."

A warm smell of hot chili peppers and fried beef greeted them as they entered the small establishment. It was empty, except for the owner, busy behind a steamy counter.

"Bring us some chili and coffee," Chunk told the man and then picked a long table in the corner. He sat down opposite Clay while Steve took a seat at the end.

"I'd enjoy the meal a lot better if we kept our guns on the table," Clay said and slowly took his from its holster. He hesitated until Chunk smiled and withdrew his own pistol. Each warily laid his weapon on the table.

The owner appeared with a tray holding the chili, coffee, cream and sugar. Noting the deadly hardware lying on the table he gulped and set the food down, then scurried away.

Chunk poured some cream into his cup. The spoon was already in the bowl of chili, so he started to pick up his gun. Clay made a move for his six-shooter and Chunk froze with a taunting grin.

"Just stirring my coffee," Chunk said and put the muzzle of his gun into the cup for a quick swirl, then placed it down beside his bowl of chili.

Clay relaxed, but each kept an eye on the other while they ate.

"Your brother and I are good friends," Clay said. "Did you know he's living in Cimarron, now?"

"I heard."

"Don't you care to see him?"

"Why should I? The only thing we have in common is our last name!"

"Well, I think he'd be glad to meet you on equal terms."

Chunk's left eye did its little dance. "Ben and I were the only children. He was older and got all the special treatment. Our father spent a fortune to put Ben through medical school and told me to go into banking. You might say I got the left-overs." He scowled. "I have no use for Benson Colbert!"

Clay thought it best to change the subject and turned to Steve. "Your father always talks about you, Steve. Ben sure wishes you'd stop all this wanderin' and come live with him."

Steve didn't look up from his bowl. "He's the same as Chunk's pa. He don't care 'bout me, neither."

"That's not true. He's worried about you. Why don't you come over to Cimarron and pay him a visit? You'd see how much he thinks of you."

As Clay talked, Chunk slipped his hand beneath the table and pulled a smaller firearm from an ankle strap. Clay didn't notice until Chunk raised the gun quickly, but it struck the table edge and went off, the bullet missing Clay by a hair.

Clay grabbed his own pistol and jumped to his feet, letting go a blast at the same time.

The walls shuddered under a roar as the bullet hit Chunk square between the eyes, bits of brain matter tearing out the back of his head before he crumpled to the floor.

The restaurant owner, paralyzed with fear, stood trembling behind the counter.

"Uncle Chunk!" Steve cried in disbelief. He rushed to kneel beside his uncle and put a hand on the dead man's cheek. Through a flood of tears, Steve looked up at Clay. "You killed him, you bastard! You killed my uncle!"

"He drew on me, you're a witness." With an air of calmness, Clay put his gun back into its holster and turned to the restaurant owner. "You saw it, too, didn't you, mister?"

The poor man couldn't stop shaking. "N-No sir, I didn't see a thing!"

"Well, you'd better get the law. Is there a sheriff in this town?"

"I'll go find somebody!" The owner ran out of the place.

With the Colorado sheriff looking for him and his uncle, Steve knew he had to get away fast. He stood up and glared at Clay. "I ain't hangin' around for the law!"

"They won't arrest you. You're just a witness."

Steve wiped the tears from his cheeks. "Now there's two names on my list—you and Case Gordon. First, it was that deputy who tried to make a fool outta my uncle Chunk, and now *you* went and killed him!" His face turned to a nasty snarl. "You're gonna pay for this, Clay Allison! I'll see to that!" He ran out of the restaurant.

Clay stood for a moment, alone in the room that now reeked with the ugly smell of gun smoke. With a sigh, he dropped into a chair and waited for the law to come arrest him. It didn't take long. Soon, a familiar voice made him turn around.

"Clay Allison! I didn't expect to find you here."

Deputy Case Gordon stood in the doorway, hand on his gun, while the shaken restaurant owner cowered behind.

"Come on in, Case," Clay said over his shoulder. "I'll buy supper if you haven't eaten."

Case relaxed and walked over to the table. He looked down at Colbert's head lying in a pool of blood. "Thanks, but I'm not hungry." He took a chair beside Clay. "It looks like you saved me the trouble of taking Chunk Colbert in."

"For killing that man in Cimarron?"

"That and another one up in Colorado. Sheriff in Trinidad told John Turner that Chunk and his nephew Steve might come to Raton and I just got here. Where's Steve Colbert?"

"He heard the law was coming and took off."

"That's not the only one looking for him. His father Ben Colbert's in town, too. I hear he's hitting every hotel and saloon, asking about his boy." Case laid his gentle but firm eyes on Clay. "Did you and Chunk Colbert have a beef?"

"Just a little misunderstanding, a long time ago in Texas."

"Bad enough to kill him?"

Clay held his anger. "Of course not! Look, he drew on me first—even fired a shot! I had to shoot quick or he'd have gotten me with the next round!"

"You got a witness to that?"

Clay leaned back with a frown. "The restaurant owner says he didn't see anything. Steve Colbert saw it, but he's run off."

"Well, I'll have to take you back to Cimarron for trial."

"You don't believe me?"

"That's irrelevant. I've got to do it, Clay, it's just the law. Since the restaurant owner was the only other one here at the time, he'll have to testify—but if he didn't see anything, it doesn't look good."

As Case and Clay walked across the street to the hotel they saw Ben Colbert approach, the distraught man's eyes filled with concern.

"Oh, no!" Clay muttered. "We've got to tell him I've just killed his brother!"

"That's right," Case said and called to the doctor. "Hold up, Ben, I have something to tell you."

Ben stopped, relieved to see his two friends. Case and Clay walked over to him.

"Have you found Steve and Chunk?" Ben asked with new hope in his eyes.

"In a way, yes," Case said. "But it isn't good. Chunk pulled a gun on Clay and Clay had to shoot him. Ben, your brother's dead."

The terrible news seemed to go over Ben's head. "But what about Steve? Is he all right?"

Clay finally spoke up. "He's all right, Ben, but he ran off since the law's after him." He put a hand on Ben's shoulder. "I'm sorry I had to kill your brother—but it was him or me!"

Ben looked relieved. "Don't feel you're to blame, Clay. I hold no grudge. If you hadn't gotten him, somebody else would have." With a touch of anger he added, "At least he'll do no more killing, now."

Case Gordon felt sorry for the doctor. "I'll be taking Clay back to Cimarron tomorrow for trial, Ben. You want to come along with us?"

Ben took a deep breath. "Thanks, Case, but I ought to stay here and see that Chunk gets a proper burial." He gave an ironic smile. "I wonder if he'd thank me for that?"

Clay and Case Gordon left Raton in the dark hours of early morning, riding southwest to Cimarron.

"I sure wouldn't want a job like yours," Clay said as they rode side-by-side. "How come you got to be a lawman, anyhow?"

Case kept looking ahead. "Just want to give people a chance to live a peaceful life."

"Kind of risky, isn't it?"

"Everybody's put on this earth for a purpose. I figure if I can stop men like Chunk Colbert from killing innocent people, I've paid my dues for being here."

Clay thought for a moment, trying to figure out what purpose he'd been put on this earth for. He couldn't come up with a good reason and rode on in silence.

Henri Lambert's Saint James Hotel, Cimarron, NM, in photo taken during 1920. With renovation, the upstairs railing and balcony have been removed.
*Courtesy Museum of New Mexico, Neg. 49157*

# Chapter Twenty-Three

*T*he morning sun had already stirred Cimarron awake as Clay and Case rode past Henri Lambert's recently-opened Saint James Hotel. The beautiful, white two-story building sported large windows with a railed balcony surrounding the upper floor.

"I wonder how Henry's business is going?" Clay mused.

"Not bad," Case said. "I've even got a room there." He laughed. "I reckon Mrs. Fries is disappointed that I moved out of the McCulloughs—she won't have anything to talk about, now!"

Case showed Clay into the little stone-walled jail, a dark and musty closet-like cell with an iron bed and chamber pot.

After Case locked the metal door, Clay peered at him through the tiny iron-grilled window. "It's sure not like home! How long do I have to stay in this rat hole?"

"Circuit Judge comes in tomorrow," Case said. "I'll try to get you out as soon as I can."

"Would you let John know I'm here? He's gonna be mad as a bull caught in a barbed wire fence!"

"I'll tell him," Case said. He added with a grin, "You just stay snug, now."

Case Gordon sent a rider out to the Allison ranch with word of Clay's arrest, then went to the sheriff's office to write his report. The judge would be arriving next morning and he didn't want any delay.

By late afternoon Case had finished the paper and looked up in surprise as Ben Colbert walked in.

"Ben! I didn't expect you back till tomorrow at least."

Ben lowered himself carefully into a chair by the desk. "There were no services," he said, "so the burial went fast, and I wanted to get back to Hannah. Guess I pushed my mule more than I should have." He laid concerned eyes on Case. "How is Clay—you've got him in jail, I suppose?"

Case only nodded.

"Will the judge go easy on him?"

Case gave a yes-and-no shrug.

"Case, I know Clay Allison. He wouldn't shoot a man unless he had to. Why, he risked his life for his regiment during the war when we stole medical supplies together. He let himself be taken prisoner so I could get away—I thought he'd been hanged!"

Case clenched his jaw. He hadn't wanted to arrest Clay Allison, but now, he regretted it even more. "Maybe I can re-word my report to say that the restaurant owner swears Clay shot in self-defense. We'll just hope the judge won't question the man."

Ben's face lightened. "But that might get you in trouble!"

Case winked. "We'll see."

It didn't take long for John Allison to ride into town. He went first to see Case Gordon, then to the jail and tapped on the door.

Clay's face appeared at the small window. "Now, before you say anything, John, I got us a lot of money while I was in Raton. Case Gordon's holding it for us."

John's face showed no recrimination; only his eyes reflected discontent. "Case already gave it to me. He's finished his report for the circuit judge."

"How does it look?"

"I don't know, you'll just have to wait. I'll stick around and let you know anything."

Clay gave the door a frustrated kick. "In the meantime, I reckon they'll let me starve to death—I haven't eaten anything since this mornin' in Raton!"

"Don't worry—Henry Lambert's having meals brought over." John's eyes glinted with amusement. "I guess you'll be the first prisoner in Cimarron to be fed gourmet dinners!"

Clay uttered a dry laugh. "Good old Henry! I guess everybody in town knows I killed a man." He thought of Dora McCullough and wondered what she must be thinking.

"Well, you can't stop people from talking," John said and turned to go. "Henry's given me a room at the hotel. I'll see you tomorrow morning."

Later in the evening, Clay finished a tray of Henri Lambert's specialty of the house and felt much better. But his well-being vanished as Ben Colbert came up to the cell door.

"I really feel bad about all this, Doc," Clay said through the grilled window.

Ben shook his head as if waving away a bad thought. "I know what my brother was like, that's why I believe you. I came to ask . . . did Steve give any indication—say anything—that might tell me where he was going?"

Clay shook his head. "It's anybody's guess."

Ben took off his glasses and wiped them with a handkerchief. "If I ever do see him again, I imagine it'll be in a jail cell like this one."

"And I wouldn't wish this place on a mangy coyote! Have you heard anything about gettin' me out of here?"

"I think Case Gordon's going to tell the judge that the restaurant owner swears it was self-defense."

Clay gaped. "Why does Case want to stand up for me?"

161

Ben finally smiled. "Case believes in justice being served— for the guilty as well as the innocent."

News of the Raton incident reached Lucien B. Maxwell's ears and he exploded into action. The burly man rarely stuck his nose into Cimarron's business, but this morning was different. With a full head of steam, he made his boisterous way out of the big house, down the dusty street and burst into the sheriff's office where Case Gordon, sitting at his desk, looked up in startled surprise.

Maxwell jerked the trade-mark cigar from his mouth. "I hear you're holding Clay Allison for killing Chunk Colbert. What's the decision going to be for Allison?"

Case felt like he was being questioned by an angry general. "The circuit judge is going over it, now," he replied.

Maxwell took a fast puff from the cigar. "You know how I feel about Colbert killing my friend Charlie Morris. I want you to do everything you can to absolve Clay Allison for getting rid of that horn-headed snake!"

"I've already told the judge there's a witness to back up Clay's self-defense. If you want to talk with the judge, he's in the back room right now."

Without another word, Maxwell brushed past Case into the other room.

A pudgy little man with gray hair and skinny-rimmed glasses sat at a desk, going over his report. He looked up in surprise at the intruder, who spoke first.

"I understand you're determining the fate of Clay Allison for killing Chunk Colbert," Maxwell said. "My name is Lucien Maxwell and I want to see that justice is done!"

The judge stiffened in dismay. "Why, yes, Mr. Maxwell, I've heard of you—everybody has! My name is Judge William Clark, and I'm handling the case."

"Clay Allison fired in self-defense and Chunk Colbert deserved what he got!"

"So Deputy Gordon tells me," the judge said in a hedging voice. "But I may have to talk with that owner of the restaurant in Raton before a decision is made."

"A ruthless killer has been eliminated from our society, Mr. Clark." Maxwell clamped the cigar between his teeth and put both hands on the table, leaning forward with his nose only an inch from the judge's. "If necessary, I'll contact my associates in the governor's office at Santa Fe to obtain Clay Allison's immediate release—even if it means replacing a circuit judge who might think otherwise!"

The judge, unable to answer through the gagging cigar smoke, could only swallow his words.

Maxwell turned and left the room, stomping past Case Gordon and out the office door. Case broke into a wide grin. He put hands behind his head and leaned back with gleeful satisfaction.

Evening came early in Cimarron, with the sun easing behind the western Sangre de Cristo Mountains. Clay slumped in dejection against a hard cold wall of the wretched cell, wondering if he could hold onto his sanity through another night in the dirty hole.

Soon, his brother, John, appeared with Case Gordon.

"Judge wants to see you," Case said and unlocked the door.

Clay jumped to his feet in a gush of hope. "What's the verdict?"

"Let him tell you."

Clay saw John's smile and knew it must be good. But no one said a word as they walked to the sheriff's office. Ben Colbert waited in a chair beside the sheriff's desk where Judge Clark sat.

The judge wore a nervous expression as he signed a paper and looked up at Clay. "You Clay Allison?"

Clay ground his teeth in irritation. *Who else was he expecting?* "Yes, sir, that's me."

"It's the judgement of the court that you, Robert Clay Allison, shot the outlaw Chunk Colbert in self-defense. If you'll sign this document, you're free to go."

Clay signed the paper, then shook Case Gordon's hand. "I sure want to thank you for helping me, Case."

Case put a hand on Clay's shoulder. "All in a day's work. Now go enjoy your freedom!" He gave Clay a friendly little shove toward the door.

Clay stepped outside with his brother and Ben Colbert. He breathed in the fresh pine-scented air. "Dang, if that don't smell good!"

"Come on, Clay," John said. "Let's go home, now. I've been seeing to Ebon—he's with my horse at the hotel."

Clay looked at the elegant Saint James Hotel across the street where the horses were tethered. "Wait, this calls for a celebration —and what better place than Henry Lambert's new hotel! Besides, I want to thank him for all that good food he sent me while I was in jail!"

John felt Clay had earned it. "All right, Big Brother." He turned to Ben Colbert. "You joining us, Doc?"

Ben smiled. "I wouldn't miss it! Hannah will just have to wait for me."

They crossed the dirt street and entered the hotel's spacious, well-decorated lobby.

Henri Lambert's pretty French wife stood behind a registration desk while a door to the right opened onto a large saloon and dining room full of happy customers.

Henri Lambert, wearing an expensive suit and tie, moved among the tables, seeing to the diners' satisfaction. He noticed the three men enter and his eyes sparkled as he rushed over. "Welcome to the Saint James! Seeing you here, Clay Allison, I know you must have been exonerated from that terrible incident!"

"We're here to celebrate!" Clay said happily. "And I have to thank you for all that food you sent me while I was locked up." He looked around the room. "I sure do like your new hotel, Henry."

"Let me present you with a celebration dinner. 'On the house,' I think you call it. I'll find a table!"

Two diners had just finished and Lambert chased them away,

then clicked his fingers for a Mexican helper to clear the table.

"Sit down and enjoy yourselves," Lambert said proudly. "Tonight I have only one entree, roast venison vinaigrette, prepared by myself. But later I will have an extensive menu." He pulled out chairs for the men to sit. "You may order anything from the bar, compliments of the Saint James Hotel!"

They all ordered whiskey and John watched with concern as Clay tossed down his drink, then asked for another. After the superb meal, Clay ordered another round of drinks while the table was being cleared.

"Clay, it's late," John said. "I think we oughta get back to the ranch."

"Just one more," Clay told him. "It's not every day I get out of jail!"

John gave him a serious look; as long as he was with Doctor Colbert, maybe it would be all right. "Well, I want to get back," he said. "Ben, if you promise to take care of my wayward brother, I'll go on. If Clay can't ride, would you see that he gets a room for the night here at the hotel?"

"I'll watch him," Ben said. "We'll be leaving soon, anyway. I don't want Hannah to worry."

John got up from the table. "Then, I'll see you at the ranch, Clay. Goodnight gentlemen."

A half hour later, Clay and Ben Colbert left the saloon with Clay in a congenial mood. They said goodnight in front of the hotel where John had left Clay's horse Ebon.

"You sure you'll be able to make it back to the ranch all right?" Ben asked.

"Fine, fine," Clay replied and put a foot into the stirrup.

Ben waved goodbye and walked down the street toward his house.

As Clay got into the saddle, he saw Case Gordon approach the hotel entrance.

"Case," Clay called. "Hold on a minute!" He dismounted and

walked over. "I have to thank you again for what you did."

"Don't thank me," Case replied. "You have a few other friends in Cimarron. I think it was Lucien Maxwell who swung the verdict."

"Maxwell?! Well, that was mighty nice of him. But Case, I oughta buy my best friend a drink. Come on into the bar, it's the least I can do!"

"Thanks, Clay, but it's late. I was just going to my room."

"Case, don't let the air outta my bag!" Clay took the deputy's arm and led him into the hotel.

It had grown very late with only two other men left in the saloon. Clay and Case finished off two drinks at the bar and Clay ordered another round.

Case stopped him. "I don't want to go to bed drunk!"

Clay's speech had become thick. "I can see you're not used to drinkin', but that's the way a deputy sheriff oughta be, I guess."

Case set down his empty glass. "Then, I'll say goodnight and go to my room." He looked at Clay's bleary eyes. "Maybe you'd better call it a night, yourself. Think you can make it back to the ranch all right?"

"No problem!"

As Case left the saloon, the man next to Clay said, "That Case Gordon's a mighty fine lawman. Fastest draw in the Territory, I hear tell!"

"I don't know about that," Clay boasted. "I've been doing a lot of practicin'. I'll bet I could out draw Case Gordon any day!" A thought struck him and he got Henri Lambert's attention behind the bar. "Henry, can you tell me which room Case Gordon has here?"

Lambert raised a suspicious eyebrow at his tipsy friend and replied, "He stays in number three."

Clay finished his drink and went to the now-deserted lobby. Mrs. Lambert had closed the desk and gone to bed. He walked to the stairway and up to the second floor where two kerosene lamps cast a soft light in the long hallway. Clay found the door marked with a numeral three and knocked.

"You in there, Case?"

"Who is it?"

"Clay Allison. I want to prove something."

The door opened slightly and Case Gordon appeared in his under shorts. "I thought we'd said goodnight. What do you have to prove?"

"That I can out draw you!"

Case chuckled. "You've had too much to drink, Clay. Go back to your ranch."

"Not before I prove I can out draw you!"

"Clay, I'm ready for bed."

"Let's go downstairs, out front of the hotel, and see who's the fastest draw in the Territory. Then you can go to bed."

"I'm in my underwear!"

"Well, I never challenge a man unfairly!" Clay took off his boots, pants and shirt, dropping them in a pile beside the door. He stood in only his under shorts.

Case watched in amusement. He knew there'd be no sleep till he humored his friend. "If it weren't for that whiskey you forced down my throat, I'd close this door in your face! All right, a couple of draws—but I'm putting on my pants!"

They strapped on their guns and went downstairs, Case in only his trousers and Clay still in his under shorts. Both were barefoot.

The lobby sat empty and quiet, except for voices coming from the saloon doorway. Clay and Case walked outside and stopped, facing each other twelve feet apart in the crisp cool night.

"I'm ready any time you are!" Clay said with drunken cockiness.

Taught silence hung in the air as each man kept an eye on the other's gun hand; then both men whipped out their pistols and fired. Dirt sprayed at Clay's feet, while his shot, a fraction of a second late, kicked the dust around Case.

"Again!" Clay ordered and they holstered their guns.

The sound of gunfire brought Henri Lambert and the two bar customers running to the hotel entrance.

"Stop!" Lambert called. "You're disturbing my guests!"

Clay and Case drew again. In the wink of an eye, two more shots broke the quiet and dirt again spewed around their feet. Curious faces peered through curtains of the upstairs windows.

"Enough!" Lambert shouted and walked over to them. "What are you trying to prove?"

Clay looked chagrined. "That Case Gordon is really the fastest draw in the Territory!"

"I'll accept that," Case said. "Now, will you let me get some sleep?" He strode back into the hotel and up to his room.

Henri Lambert gave Clay an imploring look. "Do you not think, also, it is time to go to bed? I have an available room."

"All right—but another drink, first."

"I am about to close the bar." Lambert glanced at Clay's near nakedness. "And bedsides, your attire is hardly proper for a public saloon."

"Heck fire, Henry, it's just us four men. Come on, one more before you close!"

The rest of the night was only a blur. Clay tried to remember, but his throbbing head wouldn't cooperate. A blinding ray of sunlight through the window made him sit up in the hotel room bed and he heard a loud knock.

"Clay Allison, are you awake?" Henri Lambert's voice called through the door.

Clay crawled out of bed and staggered to the door, but looked down to see that he was naked. He looked around for his clothes. "I don't have anything on, Henry!"

"I know—I have your clothing with me, just open the door."

Clay opened it a crack to see the little Frenchman holding a napkin-covered tray in one hand and Clay's clothes in the other.

"I knew you would be unable to come to the dining room," Lambert said. "I have brought your clothing and something to eat."

"Much obliged," Clay mumbled. "Come on in."

Lambert entered, closed the door and set the tray on a table. He put the clothing on the bed and cast a reproachful look at his disheveled hotel guest struggling into underwear and trousers.

"Mmm, that smells good!" Clay said. Without waiting to put on his shirt, he dropped into a chair, attacking the toast and eggs like a starved animal. Between bites, he glanced with guilt at the Frenchman's expression. "Hope I didn't cause too much trouble last night, Henry."

Lambert shook his head. "It was quite a show!"

"What do you mean?" Clay gulped some coffee.

"You do not recall?" Lambert raised his eyes to the ceiling, enumerating the events. "Let me see . . . you argued with two gentlemen customers . . . you danced on top of my bar in a complete state of undress . . . you fired your pistol into my ceiling . . . and we were forced to drag you upstairs to the room!"

Clay stared in disbelief. "Come on, Henry—I didn't really shoot up your barroom!"

"For proof, I have three new bullet holes in my ceiling and two broken kerosene lamps!"

Clay swallowed another bite and shook his head. "I'm sorry, Henry. Just give me a bill for damages and I'll see that you get paid."

Lambert softened. "The Territory is indebted to you. It is not every day a loathsome murderer such as Chunk Colbert is eradicated. On behalf of all of Cimarron, there will be no charge!"

"Mighty nice of you, Henry, but I know one person who might not agree with 'all of Cimarron.' When John hears about this, I'm gonna have some high explainin' to do!"

# Chapter Twenty-Four

*T*owering mountains in the west stood heavy under a mantel of powdery snow, a silent reminder to everyone in Cimarron that Christmas lingered not far away.

Ben Colbert slipped into his big coat and headed for the door, but Hannah's voice stopped him.

"Where are you going so early in the day, Ben?" She had taken a tray of holiday cookies from the oven and the house swirled with spicy aromas.

"Just to the post office, dear. I need to check on a medicine shipment."

It was a little white lie, for Ben had to find something at the store for Hannah's Christmas present. He stepped outside and saw that Clay Allison had pulled his wagon to a stop in front of the Indian Agency. Two men came out to unload freshly-prepared beef that would be Lucien Maxwell's rations to the Indians. Ben walked up the street to say hello.

"Good morning, Clay. Business appears to be good!"

Clay's face held a satisfied look. He pulled his coat collar tighter against the cold air and said, "Good morning, Doc. Now that the ranch is paying off Maxwell's loan, we oughta be debt free by July and showing a profit."

Dora and Bettie McCullough, about to enter a store not far away, gave a little wave and made their way over to the men.

Clay took off his hat, admiring the girls who looked like one of those pictures he'd seen in a mail order catalogue, all done up in long warm coats and furry hats.

As they walked up, Dora rested playful eyes on Clay, her face turning to an enticing glow.

"Good morning, ladies," Ben Colbert said. "I'd think you two would be home by a warm fire on a day like this!"

Bettie shivered and replied, "Dora pulled me away from the fire. We're out to buy a Christmas present for Daddy."

"Mind if I join you?" Ben asked. "Maybe you can help me find something for Hannah."

Bettie warmed her hands in a muff. "You're welcome, Doctor, but when I get back home, I'm not going out again until the Christmas church services!"

Dora finally spoke. "We're having a little Christmas dinner after the services, Clay. Ben and Hannah will be there. Why don't you and John bring the Calleys and join us?"

"It might be hard for all of us to get away at the same time," Clay said. "But maybe John could ride in with me—just for the services."

Dora looked surprised. "I didn't know you were a religious man, Clay."

"In a way. Our father was a Presbyterian preacher back in Tennessee. He died when I was just a tad, but Mama kept reading the Bible to us kids."

"Then do come to the church on Christmas morning. Henry Lambert and the other saloon owners are closing for the day, and Reverend Tolby will be reading the service."

171

Clay warmed at the chance of seeing Dora again, especially on Christmas. "I'll have to talk to John and the Calleys. I don't know what they'll say, but at least you can count on me being there." He put on his hat. "Now, if you all will excuse me, I've gotta pick up my sales receipt."

Ben and the two girls watched as Clay disappeared into the agency building.

"I wonder how handsome he is under that dark beard?" Bettie mused aloud.

Dora gave an impish smile. "And just look at those nice long legs!"

Ben Colbert couldn't help laughing.

"Dora!" Bettie said in mock surprise. "A lady doesn't say such things!"

"When I look at Clay Allison, sometimes I forget I'm a lady!"

Dora took her sister's arm and the two walked with Ben Colbert to the general store.

Clay rode back to the ranch with news of the holiday invitation, only to be met with resistance by the Calleys.

"That's mighty nice of the McCulloughs to ask us," Wes said, "but Christmas is just another day to Jim and me."

"It ain't that we're not religious," Jim added. "But our church is the big outdoors. 'Sides, we'd rather stay here and see that them heifers don't get froze to death!"

John didn't agree. "Well, it's high time I saw a church again," he told them. "If you two don't mind, I ought to run into town with Clay. We won't be gone too long."

Clay had to smile. With his little brother tied up for weeks at the ranch, Clay knew it wasn't a church John wanted to see. It was Bettie McCullough.

Cold weather still hovered over the Territory on Christmas morning, turning Clay and John's breath into clouds of white vapor

172

as they rode into town. They left their horses at the Saint James Hotel and walked to the church location, but were greeted by a tragic surprise.

Around the smoldering remains of their beloved house of worship, the devout townspeople huddled like a small flock of lost pigeons.

Ben and Hannah Colbert, with the McCullough sisters, stood beside the preacher, a short man wearing a long black coat and matching wide-brimmed hat. Every face held the gray look of devastation.

"Oh, Clay!" Dora said. "You and John did come!" She took Clay's arm. "I want you and John to meet Reverend Tolby."

The little man gave them a pitiful smile as he shook their hands. "I regret we have to meet under such circumstances."

"How did it happen?" John asked, putting a warming arm around Bettie.

"Nobody knows, really," Tolby said.

Alma Fries hovered nearby in a big coat with a shawl tied over her head. Her nose, red with cold, seemed even larger. "It was one of them from the saloon!" she replied sourly.

The reverend turned a kind face to her. "We must have only forgiveness in our hearts and not cast blame."

Alma snorted. "All the saloons in town agreed to close on Christmas, 'cept one—the Red Brick Saloon. You can't tell me Sam Aikens didn't care about losing some business!"

Clay pitied the cold dejected citizens, gripping their hymnals and family Bibles. He remembered his father bundling up to ride through swirling snow just so people in the Tennessee valley could worship their Lord.

He looked across the street at the Red Brick Saloon and fumed in anger. "Come with me, Reverend, I'll find a place for your services!"

Everyone watched in puzzlement as he started toward the saloon. Reverend Tolby hesitated, then followed and the group moved along behind.

An icy breeze swept the room as Clay threw open the door of the Red Brick Saloon. Men at the bar and those at the card tables turned with startled eyes. With his bristling beard and heavy coat wrapped around his six-foot-two frame, Clay resembled a riled-up grizzly bear. He pulled a pistol from his shoulder holster and fired a shot into the ceiling, sending a few customers diving for safety under tables. The others stood shaking in their boots.

"We can't hold our Christmas service because somebody burned down the church last night!" Clay roared in a commanding voice and moved his pistol over the men. "So I know you'll be kind enough to let Reverend Tolby hold his service here."

Hannah Colbert clutched Ben's arm while Reverend Tolby hesitantly stepped in beside Clay. John Allison could only sigh and let his brother continue.

Sam Aikens gaped from behind the bar, his face as white as the others who stared in fear.

"Now move those chairs into rows facing the back wall," Clay ordered, still holding his pistol on the men. "That's where the reverend will do his preachin'!"

The men began to move under Clay's watchful eyes and threatening gun. With the arrangements quickly made, Clay motioned for the townspeople to come in. He put away his gun and everyone took a seat, with Clay, John, the Colberts and the McCullough sisters in the front row.

Reverend Tolby coughed politely and asked the congregation to please turn to page thirty-two in their hymnals; they would sing the first hymn.

Alma Fries sat down at the saloon's rickety out-of-tune piano and frowned with disfavor as she began thumping the worn keys. For the first time in its history, The Red Brick Saloon echoed with joyful voices praising the Lord.

At the end of the services, Clay and John prepared for their ride back to the ranch, but Dora stopped them.

"Clay, can't you and John have Christmas dinner with us before you go? Daddy would love to see you again—he couldn't make it to the services because of his rheumatism."

Clay felt tempted, but said, "It wouldn't be right to leave Wes and Jim all alone on Christmas while we stay in town, fillin' our bellies."

"We have plenty," Bettie told him. "Why don't you take some back with you and all have Christmas dinner together?"

It was agreed and they went to the McCullough house where the girls prepared two large baskets packed with delicious food.

After a short visit with John McCullough, Clay said, "We oughta be getting back. I'll go get the horses." He put on his hat and walked out the door.

"Clay, wait!" Dora called and threw a shawl around her shoulders.

Clay stopped on the porch as Dora went to him, her face aglow with admiration. She wrapped her arms around his body, giving him a big hug.

"What's that for?" he asked in astonishment.

"For what you did today—you were magnificent!"

He reddened with embarrassment. "Well, I don't like to see good people get stomped on."

"I agree with you." Then teasingly, "But I must say, your methods are rather severe!" She reached up and pulled the coat collar snugly around his neck, her eyes filled with loving expectation.

Clay held his breath. She was asking him—no, begging him—to kiss her. But he couldn't allow it to happen. He was determined not to let her get hurt.

John and the Colberts appeared in the doorway with the baskets of food.

"You gettin' those horses, Clay?" John asked.

Clay's face still glowed with mixed emotions as he pulled away from Dora. "Be right with you!"

175

He made long strides to the hitching post, muttering quiet oaths with every step. He wondered if he'd ever be able to get rid of the dark thing in his head that had become a barrier between him and Dora McCullough.

# Chapter Twenty-Five

*E*ach new spring brought harsh winds racing across New Mexico and Ben Colbert accepted them in two ways. Making calls on the scattered farms in his buggy was a nuisance, squinting in the blinding dust and spitting out the grit, but the various pollens carried through the air brought with them sneezing, snuffles and wheezing coughs. It only increased his business.

On this particular day, however, he could walk to his appointment. Lucien Maxwell's wife Luz had requested him to come to the large house and work his magical cures.

A polite young Mexican girl showed Ben up the big staircase and they entered the master bedroom. The girl nodded shyly, closing the door behind her.

Luz Maxwell lay fretfully on a spacious bed, her large body propped up against a big fluffy pillow. Her dark eyes came to life at the sight of the doctor and she raised a hand.

"I'm indebted to you for coming, Doctor. I have this same trouble each year."

Ben took her hand briefly. "Well, let's see what we can do to make you feel better." He took a stethoscope from his black bag and put it to his ears, listening to her breathing. "There is some congestion, but I have something that might clear it up."

"My oldest daughter, Virginia, is downstairs preparing some hot tea. I thought that might help."

"Oh, is Virginia in Cimarron again?"

Luz finally smiled. "Just for vacation, from that school in the Midwest."

Ben rummaged through his bag for the correct medicine. "That must be a fine university. I'm sure you and Lucien are very proud of her."

"Oh, yes. Now that she's turned twenty, Virginia has become quite a lady." Luz chuckled, bringing forth a little cough. "Being our first child, Virginia is Lucien's favorite, you know. He's spent a fortune on her." She frowned. "Not only for education, but to see that Virginia marries the right man."

"Would that be the handsome Captain Alexander Keyes who saw her so often the last time Virginia was here?" Ben took a glass of water from the bedside table and poured a dark mixture into it.

"Goodness, no!" Luz coughed again. "Lucien absolutely forbids Virginia from having anything to do with an Army man! He's already selected her future husband—a wealthy landowner who lives on the Rio Grande."

Ben felt sorry for the girl. It was obvious to everyone that Virginia Maxwell and Captain Alexander Keyes were very much in love. He wondered how it would all turn out. But it wasn't his concern. "Now just swallow this medicine," he said.

Ben gently lifted Luz Maxwell's head and she took the medicine with a little frown of distaste, then lay back again.

"I'll leave the bottle here," Ben told her. "You're to take a tablespoon each evening. If you don't improve in two days, just send word and we'll try something else."

"Thank you again for coming, Doctor. I'll see that your fee is paid by tomorrow, earliest. I'd pay you myself, but Lucien is out of town and I don't dare touch his money!"

"I'll not worry about that." Ben snapped his bag closed. "Your health is what we must think about right now."

He made his way back down the staircase and stopped at the front door as Maxwell's daughter Virginia appeared carrying a small teapot. She walked over to him.

"Oh, Doctor Colbert—how is my mother?"

"Doing fine. Just be sure she takes the medicine I left. It might taste better with a little apple cider or honey."

Virginia Maxwell flashed a melting smile, her beauty and charm accented by a strong independence inherited from her father. "You'd think living in New Mexico all her life, Mama would be used to the spring miasmas. I'm away most of the time at school in the Midwest, and when I come home to visit, it doesn't bother me at all!"

"Is your stay this time for very long?" Ben asked.

Virginia's forehead wrinkled. "It all depends on how well things go."

"I'm sorry, I don't understand."

She looked around to be sure they were alone. "While Daddy's been away, Captain Alexander Keyes and I were free to see each other." Her eyes filled with intrigue. "Last night, we decided to be married as soon as possible!"

Ben looked startled. "Then you've convinced your father?"

"Oh, no. Daddy will never change his mind. But he'll be back tomorrow, sooner than expected—that's why Alexander and I have to do it quickly and in secret. I was hoping you could help us, Doctor Colbert!"

"Surely you know I couldn't do such a thing—and I'm afraid you'll not find another person in Cimarron who'd go against Lucien Bonaparte Maxwell!"

Her face turned downcast. "Yes, I know. Reverend Tolby has already refused . . . but we've found a traveling preacher who'll perform the ceremony at a friend's house. We've worked out a plan.

179

All we need, now, is for someone to keep Daddy occupied at the time. I thought maybe you . . . "

"That sounds dangerous, Virginia. This is a small town. Everybody would know your friend's house was being used!"

She gave him a despairing look. "Can you think of anything better?"

"I'll have no part of it!" he replied, then smiled with connivance. "But I imagine the grist mill will be overrun with Indians and soldiers tomorrow while rations are being handed out. Lucien doesn't bother himself with that activity—and even if he did, there would be no reason for him to climb to the *top floor.*"

"Oh, Doctor Colbert!" she cried with delight. Balancing the teapot in one hand, she gave him a kiss on the cheek. "I love you!"

He straightened his coat and opened the front door. "This conversation never existed! In fact, I haven't seen Miss Virginia Maxwell since she returned from the Midwest!" He gave her a wink and departed.

However, Ben chastised himself after leaving the big house. Perhaps he'd done the wrong thing. If Virginia Maxwell's plan didn't work out and she got into trouble with her father, Ben would never forgive himself.

The handsome young Captain Alexander Keyes appeared as usual the next day to oversee Indian rations handed out at the grist mill. At exactly four o'clock in the afternoon, Virginia Maxwell arrived, supposedly to weigh herself on the mill scales.

Lost in the crowd, the two lovers made their way to the top floor of Lucien's huge stone mill where the miller and his wife, Mr. and Mrs. Rinehart, waited as the only witnesses. Reverend Harwood, the traveling minister, slipped in unnoticed and climbed silently up the stairway. In a few moments, Virginia Maxwell and Alexander Keyes were pronounced man and wife.

However, the marriage still had to be kept under wraps. The couple needed to wait for Captain Keyes' transfer papers before they left Cimarron. Two days later, as the happy newlyweds passed through Trinidad, Colorado, on the northbound stage, they sent Lucien Maxwell a copy of the marriage certificate.

Lucien clutched the foul paper and marched to his wife's bedroom, flinging the document onto the bed.

"Luz, I demand to know—did you have any knowledge of this marriage between our daughter and that Army captain?!"

Luz Maxwell scanned the certificate and suppressed a smile. "Of course not, Lucien. But remember, Virginia has your blood. She's as headstrong as you and no one could have stopped her!"

In fury, Maxwell grabbed an expensive bottle of perfume from his wife's vanity and smashed it into the mirror. "If that Reverend Harwood ever sets foot in Cimarron again, I'll personally hang him from the top floor of the grist mill!"

Luz finally had to smile. "Why, Lucien, I think that would be a most fitting place!"

"Mark my words, Luz—from this moment on, my daughter's name will never be mentioned in this household again!" He stormed out of the bedroom on his way to the liquor cellar to get drunk.

Luz Maxwell lay back on her large soft pillow and sighed in relief. It was just another crisis in the complicated life of Lucien B. Maxwell. She had weathered all the ones before and she would survive this one, as well.

# Chapter Twenty-Six

*H*annah stood before a large mirror, adjusting the stylish bonnet Ben had given her last Christmas. She smiled at his reflection while he got into his Sunday best and her heart grew tender, wondering if he had resigned himself to the fact that he'd never see his son Steve again. Maybe today's festivities would get his mind off it.

This being the fourth of July, Cimarron bustled with excitement over the prospects of Lucien Maxwell's lavish barbecue party. Dora and Bettie McCullough had come over in their bright dresses and the three women bided their time in nervous anticipation, waiting for the Allisons and Calleys to arrive.

"They're here!" Dora finally announced from the front room.

Hannah joined the girls and they all rushed outside.

Clay and John Allison, handsome in dressy suits, sat in their buggy, with the Calley brothers on horses alongside.

"Now, that's the prettiest covey of little quail I've ever seen!" Clay greeted them.

Bettie giggled. "Who's riding with whom?"

182

Ben Colbert came out, looking as if he'd dressed for either a wedding or a funeral in his dark suit and tie. "It's not that far," he told the group. "We can walk to Lucien's place!"

"We want to arrive in style," Clay told him. "In a buggy like everybody else!"

Ben snorted. "All right, three to a buggy. John, why don't you ride with Hannah and me—let the girls go with Clay."

John frowned at the arrangement, but helped Bettie and Dora into the buggy with Clay, then climbed into the Colbert buckboard.

Throngs of citizens had come from miles around to gather in and around the grounds of the large Maxwell estate for barbecued beef and venison, all to be washed down with the wealthy landowner's best liquor.

Even Maxwell's old fur-trapping crony Kit Carson, although in poor health, had come down from Colorado to help his friend celebrate the fourth of July. A contingent of troops and officers from Fort Union, forty-five miles to the south, had also ridden in for the occasion. One of them was Maxwell's close acquaintance Colonel Henry Inman. Maxwell, Carson and the colonel quickly got together for a reunion drink.

"I think you've outdone yourself, L. B.," Colonel Inman said. "I've never seen such a party!"

Kit Carson surveyed the crowd of happy faces. "Even some of our old Indian friends are here!"

Maxwell beamed with pride. "I couldn't get any fireworks, but just wait till this afternoon and you'll see what I have instead!" He spotted the Allison brothers and McCullough sisters chatting with the Colberts. "If you'll excuse me, gentlemen, I see someone I have to talk business with."

Maxwell walked over to the group. "Well, I'm certainly pleased to have such beautiful ladies help me celebrate the holiday!"

"We wouldn't have missed it for the world!" Hannah told him.

Ben asked, "How is your wife dealing with this weather, Lucien?"

183

Maxwell waved an impatient hand. "Oh, she's fine! You'll find her around here somewhere. Nothing keeps Luz down for very long. Now, if you'll excuse me, I'd like a word with Clay." He took Clay's arm and led him a short distance away.

"I was hoping you'd be here today," Maxwell said. He took a paper from his coat pocket. "I want you to see that I'm tearing up our loan agreement, since it has been paid back in beef shipments." He tore the document into four pieces and handed them to Clay.

"Thank you, Mr. Maxwell. I'd planned to bring it up with you while I was here."

Maxwell's large black mustache couldn't hide a teasing smile. "I don't suppose there's any chance you'll go broke—I still have my eye on that fine horse of yours!"

Clay grinned back. "Not a chance in hell!"

"Well, I knew from the start I'd never get my hands on that magnificent animal—you're too good a businessman!" Maxwell took Clay's hand in a warm shake. "You've raised a little hell in this town, Clay Allison, but it's done more good than any I ever stirred up!"

Clay glanced down with embarrassment. "Whatever happened, I never asked for it." He looked seriously into the man's steely eyes. "But I do want to thank you, Mr. Maxwell, for believing in me!"

As the day came to an end, with each stomach full of delicious food and good whiskey, the shadows grew heavy over Cimarron. Maxwell rubbed his hands together and gave orders for a six-pound Howitzer to be rolled out from the storage shed.

"I've been keeping that cannon under wraps just for this occasion!" he told his friends. "We found it left over from the Mexican War."

Kit Carson and Colonel Inman watched as a hush fell over the crowd. An Army officer assisted Maxwell in preparing the monster for firing.

The Colonel's eyes narrowed. "I hope L. B. knows what he's doing. That thing's still rusty—hasn't been fired in years."

Suddenly the Howitzer roared and women screamed. The officer near the cannon's muzzle had been thrown back in a blinding flash, his left arm blasted away. He lay moaning in a widening pool of blood.

Lucien Maxwell, at the rear, held up his left hand, blood streaming down the wrist.

Colonel Inman rushed over to him. "My God, L.B.," he exclaimed, "your thumb's nearly torn off!"

Kit Carson went to kneel beside the wounded officer and frowned at the bloody mess. "This man needs attention!" Carson said, the perpetual gray mustache drooping over his somber face. "Is there a doctor here?"

Ben Colbert had been hit by the flying metal and lay dazed on the ground. Hannah dropped to her knees beside him.

Clay and John Allison rushed over with the McCullough sisters, the girls holding their ample skirts high above the dirt.

Ben raised his head. "Good Lord, Hannah, what happened?"

"The cannon exploded," she answered, holding back a sob. "Are you all right, Ben?"

He pressed fingers on his right arm and winced in pain. "Nothing broken, as far as I can tell."

Maxwell came over to look down. "Doctor Colbert, a man's arm has been torn off—are you able to help?"

"Let me see . . . " Ben struggled to get up, but dropped onto one elbow. "Drat it, I can't use my right arm!"

"Don't try it, Ben," Hannah said through tears. "You're hurt too bad!"

Clay noticed blood on Ben's coat sleeve. "The Doc's been hit, too, Mr. Maxwell."

Maxwell ignored his own bloody hand and went back to the officer who lay writhing in agony, his shoulder torn into raw bleeding flesh.

"Get this man into the house!" Maxwell ordered. "There's a bed in the room behind the kitchen!"

Ben squinted against the pain and looked up at Hannah. "Have someone go back to the house and get my bag—and all the bandages you can find. Hurry!" He gasped and raised his other hand. "Help me up, Clay. I've got to see what I can do for that soldier!"

A few men carried the wounded officer into the house and Ben Colbert followed, along with Colonel Inman and Kit Carson.

"I'm sorry," Ben said to Maxwell "but with this bad arm, there's little I can do!"

Maxwell still clutched his wounded hand, oblivious to the pain. He looked at the suffering officer. "Dammit, we need a surgeon!"

"Then I'll get you one!" Colonel Inman said. He turned to the open doorway and shouted to one of his captains, "Have a man ride back to Fort Union and bring the post surgeon here as fast as he can!"

A sergeant jumped onto his horse and kicked it into a frantic gallop. He raced out of town, south to the fort.

It took the man over four hours of hard riding to cover the forty-five miles. As soon as he reined his panting horse to a halt in front of the post hospital and dismounted, the poor animal fell dead with exhaustion.

With the disastrous end of Lucien Maxwell's holiday party, all guests departed. Only Clay and the Colberts remained to help with the wounded officer.

Ben, unable to use his right arm, administered a sedative to the injured man and then gave orders to Hannah and Clay who did their best, cleaning and wrapping the wound with bandages. The bleeding, however, continued.

In a corner of the room, Luz Maxwell tried to sooth her husband while ignoring his stream of oaths.

Just before midnight, the military physician from Fort Union reached Cimarron and walked into the room. It now carried the ugly smell of blood.

Ben Colbert greeted him. "Thank God you could make it,

Doctor!"

The physician looked at Ben's bloodied shirt and limp arm.

"I'm all right," Ben said. "It's this man over here who needs urgent attention!"

The surgeon went to the wounded officer and worked quickly, first sewing up the hole where the man's arm had been torn away. After the bleeding had been stopped and a tight bandage applied, the surgeon examined Lucien Maxwell's shattered thumb.

"Lucky it was only your thumb," the physician said. You could have lost the hand, as well!"

Maxwell downed two more glasses of liquor while the surgeon did his best to reassemble the thumb, then wrapped it with clean linen.

"Let's hope I've been able to save it," the surgeon said, "but I don't think you'll ever use that thumb again!"

Maxwell growled under his breath. "What would I use the thumb on my left hand for, anyway?!"

The wounded officer, wrapped in a blanket, lay sedated in a wagon as it trundled with the physician back to Fort Union.

Hannah took Ben home and helped him down into his easy chair. "Are you going to be all right, Ben?" she worried.

He shook his head. "No broken bones. But you'll have to help me fashion a sling. I won't be able to use this arm for a while."

After two restless nights of pain, Ben arose in the early morning, trying not to waken Hannah. In her concerned half-sleep, however, she got out of bed to find him with the arm still in the sling and trying to get into his coat.

"Ben! Where are you going?"

"I really should check on Lucien Maxwell."

"But Ben, you're in no condition!"

"Hannah, It's just an arm injury. I'm not an invalid!"

She knew it was useless to argue and put the coat around his shoulders.

Arriving at the large house, Ben found Lucien Maxwell still in a dark mood from the tragic incident. The stubborn man softened, however, on seeing the doctor.

"Ben, you didn't have to get off your sick bed to come here!" he said.

"No problem. I still can't use my right arm, but if your wife will help, I'd like to change that bandage."

Luz Maxwell assisted and they unwrapped the bandaged. Ben cursed under his breath at what he saw—the ugly wound was festering out of control. "I don't like the looks of it," he had to admit. "My personal opinion is to have your thumb removed—but I can't do it with my dratted arm like it is!"

Colonel Inman made a suggestion. "L. B., I could take you to the hospital at Fort Union, if you'd like."

Maxwell's face, now red with fever, knew something had to be done. "With all respect to you, Doctor Colbert, maybe I should be treated at a hospital!"

Colonel Inman and Kit Carson rode with Maxwell in his coach during the tedious journey to Fort Union, Lucien raving feverishly all the way.

Upon their arrival, the post surgeon scowled at Maxwell's infected thumb. "You're risking your life, Mr. Maxwell, if you don't let me amputate! I'll give you a sedative, first."

"That isn't necessary!" Maxwell told him and seated himself in an office chair. He held out the wounded hand on a table. "Go ahead and cut the damned thumb off!"

With heavy gray clouds dimming the sun, Colonel Inman and Kit Carson each held a kerosene lamp while the surgeon began.

Perspiration broke out on Maxwell's face as the knife did its job, but Lucien uttered no sound of pain. He watched with gritted teeth as the thumb was severed and silver-wire ligatures twisted in place.

Colonel Inman took a bottle of whiskey from the doctor's shelf and poured some into a tumbler.

"Here, L. B.," he said, offering the glass. "Perhaps this will help."

Lucien Maxwell took the glass, but the liquor never passed his lips. The stubborn bull-of-a-man slumped over in a faint.

# Chapter Twenty-Seven

*B*en and Hannah joined other townspeople gathered along the dusty street, all staring with fascination at a caravan of ten large wagons, crammed with expensive belongings, being escorted out of town by Fort Union soldiers. Lucien Bonaparte Maxwell was leaving Cimarron for good.

His old friend Kit Carson had finally died of the aneurism that plagued him for years; Maxwell had taken all the gold possible from the nearby mountains; his vast land grant was now in the hands of Santa Fe and European investors and his favorite daughter had run off in an unapproved marriage. With nothing more to accomplish, Lucien Maxwell was moving to his final home—the deactivated Fort Sumner, a hundred miles to the south, which he had purchased from the government.

The huge Maxwell home now stood like a magnificent empty shell. Not far away, Lucien's three-story grist mill loomed over the settlement, an eternal monument to the man who had given birth to the town of Cimarron.

"It's like the end of an era," Hannah remarked sadly.

"And the beginning of another," Ben added, noticing a couple of new faces in the crowd. "That's Mr. and Mrs. William Morley over there, the new owners of *The Cimarron News and Press*."

"Oh, dear," Hannah said with a frown. "I've heard rumors that the Santa Fe Ring arranged for Bill Morley to take over the newspaper!"

"Yes—he hopes to be named one of the Ring's directors. Well, as fellow citizens, we really should go introduce ourselves."

They made their way through the crowd and Ben put out his hand. "Welcome to Cimarron, Mr. Morley. I'm Doctor Benson Colbert and this is my wife Hannah."

Morley smiled, giving him a warm shake. "Pleased to meet you, Doctor and Mrs. Colbert. This is my wife Ada."

A young and very pregnant Mrs. Morley demurely took Hannah's hand.

"We understand you've taken over the newspaper," Hannah said. "I'm sure everyone's eager to see the first issue."

"Thank you, Mrs. Colbert," Ada Morley replied. "Bill and I have worked hard getting everything ready."

Morley turned to look at the departing wagons. "I suppose things will be different around here, now that Lucien Maxwell is gone. Looks like we have our work cut out for us!"

Ben's eyes narrowed. "Yes, I'm sure we'll be seeing a lot of changes."

"You're correct about 'changes,' Doctor," Morley said. "I've already written an editorial. People will have to realize, now, that they need to pay for being on someone else's property."

His wife squeezed his arm eagerly. "I didn't know you'd finished the article so soon, Bill. I'll start setting the type right away!"

The dam broke sooner than expected. Ben Colbert read the first newspaper editorials and paced the floor with worry.

"The miners taking gold from Mount Baldy are told to give a full statement of their claims or be evicted," he told Hannah. "There's been rioting in Elizabethtown, with government offices destroyed —they've even called on Fort Union soldiers to quell the violence!"

Hannah shuddered. "I'm so glad we left E-Town when we did. Can you imagine what it must be like, living there, now?!"

"It's not just the miners who are affected," Ben told her. "The ranchers and farmers will be next!" He shook his head. "I wonder how Clay Allison will react to this?!"

Clay, rounding up strays, wiped late afternoon sweat from his face as a neighboring rancher rode up. The man waved a newspaper at him. "Have you seen the latest issue?"

Clay took the paper and read it. His eyes narrowed with anger. "They have no right! The deed is still being contested—they can't say which acres are theirs and which belong to us!"

"Well, that damned Cimarron newspaper ain't helpin' any!" the rancher growled. "They're a part of that Santa Fe Ring and somebody oughta step on 'em!"

Retaliation stirred in Clay's gut. "Somebody oughta put 'em out of business."

"You're right." The rancher grinned. Why don't we ride into town tonight and take care of it?!"

Two more ranchers joined them. At sundown, the four rode into Cimarron's quiet streets, stopping first at Lambert's saloon. After fortifying themselves with two rounds of whiskey, the group rode to the darkened newspaper office. All but Clay jumped down from their horses.

"Break down the door!" he ordered.

The men threw themselves against the wooden entrance, crashing into the office. Clay urged Ebon forward, ducking his head as the horse carried him into the building.

The men wasted no time, shouting with glee as they overturned tables, cupboards and the printing press.

Clay dismounted to grab some sheets that had been printed on one side only. He dipped a pen into red ink and scrawled CLAY ALLISON'S EDITION on the blank side of each one, then stuffed the pages into his coat pocket.

He climbed back into the saddle and threw his lariat around a cabinet containing trays of lead type. A gig on Ebon's flank took him out of the office, dragging the metal container behind. Clay rode over to the Cimarron River bridge and, with angry satisfaction, pushed the cabinet into the dark rushing water.

The other men, having finished their dirty work, came out of the ruined office with excited faces as Clay rode up.

"I have a delivery to make!" he yelled.

The men got onto their horses, all whooping as they followed him back to the Saint James Hotel.

Clay jumped down from Ebon and burst into the lobby. He plopped the newspaper pages onto the desk in front of a startled Mrs. Lambert and said, "Tell Henry to sell these to everybody in the saloon!"

Mrs. Lambert looked at the papers scrawled with CLAY ALLISON'S EDITION. "At what price?" she asked, confused.

"A dollar each, and we'll give it to somebody who needs the money!"

Clay ran back to join the other men and they raced their horses through the street with exultant yells. Adding to the mayhem, they waved their six-shooters in the air, filling the night sky with wild gunfire.

Ben and Hannah Colbert were among the frightened citizens peering from their windows as the vandals rode out of town.

Ben shook his head with a wry laugh. "Now I know how Clay Allison would react to those editorials!"

John Allison knew his older brother had ridden over to a neighbor's house the night before, but didn't know they had gone into town. He found out the next morning from Deputy Case Gordon who showed up at the ranch.

Case shook his head with exasperation. "That was quite a show you put on last night, Clay!"

John gave his brother a hard look. "What's he been up to, now, Case?"

"Everybody saw Clay Allison and three other men wreck the newspaper office last night, then shoot up the town on their way out."

John's silence demanded an explanation.

"Well, somebody has to take action around here!" Clay said in anger. "Otherwise, all us little people are gonna get run out of the Territory!"

"Destruction of private property isn't the answer," Case told him. "That's against the law, and I ought to take you in."

John stood up for his brother. "Case, we all agree with how Clay feels about the Santa Fe Ring. He may be a little headstrong in his convictions, but he means well. How about us paying for the damage—would that justify everything?"

Case gave it consideration. "If it's agreeable with the Morleys. But Clay'll have to come back to town with me so I can make sure!"

"If you don't see me by sundown," Clay said ruefully to John, "then you'll know I'm back in that durned jail!" He got onto Ebon and followed Case into town.

Clay and Case got off their horses in front of the newspaper office where a group of curious citizens stood mulling over the devastation. They stepped aside, letting the two men enter.

Clay looked with dismay at the ruins; he hadn't realized the damage he'd done. In the midst of all the debris a woman stood crying into a handkerchief, her long dress bulging out in the last term of pregnancy. Case waited at the front door as Clay walked over to her.

"Kind of a mess, I reckon," Clay said with a shamed face to the woman.

She turned her reddened eyes to him. "Just look at what that

194

Clay Allison has done . . . after Bill and I had worked so hard to make a go of this newspaper!"

"Bill Morley?"

"He's my husband. I helped him set the type and run the press." She gave a little sob. "But, now, we can't do that anymore!"

Clay took out a wad of bills. "How much you suppose it'll take to get runnin' again?"

She shook her head. "Maybe I can get the press working, but it's no good without the metal type."

He put the money into her hand. "Get yourself another press or whatever you need."

She looked up in surprise. "Who are you?"

"My name's Clay Allison—and I don't fight women!" He turned and left the office.

Case Gordon gave the dumfounded Mrs. Morley a tiny smile, tipped his hat and followed Clay out to the street.

Dora McCullough had joined the onlookers and met Clay and Case at the door. She gave her parasol a twirl of disapproval. "Clay Allison, I thought you wanted the little people treated right! Few of us agree with what the Morleys have been printing, but this action is quite out of line!"

Clay opened his mouth, but couldn't think of anything to say.

Case came to his rescue. "Hold on, Dora. Clay has just apologized to Mrs. Morley and paid her for all the damage he's done. Mrs. Morley is happy, now, and the matter's been taken care of."

Dora blushed lightly. "I'm sorry if I spoke out of turn. I should have known you'd be kind enough to do that, Clay. But I still think the way you express your opinions is a little outrageous!"

"Seems I owe you an apology, too," Clay finally said. "I'm sorry if my actions have offended you."

Her face softened. "You have a big heart, Clay Allison. You just have a strange way of showing it! I'm on my way to visit the Colberts, now. I know they'll be pleased when I tell them what you've done for atonement!"

Clay and Case tipped their hats politely as she walked down the street.

Hannah Colbert greeted her guest with delight. "Dora McCullough, you came at a good time—I've got a fresh cake cooling. Come in and we'll try it with some coffee!"

The two women entered the living room as a farmer with his arm in a sling came from the doctor's office, Ben Colbert close behind.

"Just keep that arm at rest for the next two weeks and come back to see me," Ben told the man.

The injured farmer nodded politely at the women on his way out the door.

"Ben, do you have time for coffee and cake with Dora and me?" Hannah asked and went to the kitchen.

"I always have time for that!" Ben took Dora's hand in greeting. "Your family must be in good health. I haven't seen any of them for some time."

"Sorry we're not adding to your income," Dora replied with a small laugh. "We're getting along just fine."

Hannah came in with a tray of coffee cups and sliced cake. "If accident-prone farmers keep coming into the area, Ben won't have to worry!"

They seated themselves at a small table to enjoy the refreshment.

"I just saw Clay Allison on the way over," Dora said as they ate.

Hannah's eyes rolled heavenward. "That boy! Everyone's talking about last night!"

"I don't think he realized he was doing any real harm," Dora said. "When I saw him this morning, he had just apologized to Mrs. Morley and paid her for all the damage he'd done."

Hannah smiled with relief. "Now, that was nice of Clay. You can tell that his mother gave him a good upbringing!"

Ben gave Dora a mischievous wink. "Are you two getting along any better?"

Dora looked at him with embarrassed concern. "I like Clay very

196

much, and I know he likes me. But every time we get close, he just seems to put up a shield." She shook her head in discouragement. "I don't understand it, Ben—am I being too forward?"

Hannah put down her coffee cup. "Maybe it's because he doesn't want to see you get hurt."

"How could I get hurt?"

Ben gave Hannah a sharp look. "We agreed not to talk about that, dear!"

Hannah felt like a child caught doing wrong. "I'm sorry, Ben, but it isn't fair to Dora, not knowing."

Dora shook her head in bewilderment. "What on earth are you two talking about?!"

Ben leaned back to explain. "Now, what I'm going to say is just between us, Dora. You see, Clay received a blow to his head years ago. The injury created a slight epilepsy. Whenever he touches liquor—or becomes angry or excited—something in his brain tells him to act without caution."

"You mean, he's dangerous?"

"Oh, no, he'd never do you physical harm. In fact, he has the highest regard for women and would fight anybody who thought otherwise."

"So, what are you trying to tell me, Ben?"

"Clay's main problem is alcohol. When he's under the influence, he can't seem to control those negative things his brain tells him to do. What Clay Allison needs is someone to keep him in control, someone he can respect." He smiled wisely. "A woman, perhaps!"

# Chapter Twenty-Eight

*W*es held a heifer's legs while Clay pushed red-hot metal into its side. A wisp of smoke rose in a sizzle and the small animal bleated, then Wes let it jump up to join its brothers in the pasture.

Clay and Wes shaded their eyes at a horseman appearing in the distance. From the way he sat in the saddle, Clay knew the rider was Case Gordon.

"What's that on the mule he's leading?" Wes muttered.

Clay put down the branding iron and they waited until Case rode up. Clay's heart skipped a beat—draped over the mule behind Case hung the body of Reverend Tolby.

"What the devil, Case?!"

"Found him on my way to E-Town. The reverend was probably on his way back to Cimarron when somebody ambushed him."

Clay walked over to study the lifeless figure. "He's been shot in the back! Who did it, robbers?"

Case shrugged. "Wasn't that. He still has money in his pockets and the saddlebags weren't even touched."

Wes had been staring in awe. "Then it was just plain murder! Who'd want to kill a preacher?"

Clay gritted his teeth. "I think Case and I know. It was somebody fronting for the Santa Fe Ring—Reverend Tolby's been preaching against them up and down the Territory!"

"Don't start getting riled up, Clay," Case warned. "We don't know that for sure."

"Well, what are you gonna to do about it?"

"Investigate. First, I have to find a man named Cruz Vega. He was a substitute mail carrier between Cimarron and E-Town yesterday, most likely the only one in the area when Tolby was killed."

"I wanna help you get that man!"

Case shook his head. "Hold it, Clay. When everybody hears the reverend's been murdered, I'll have my hands full keeping peace in the area . . . and I don't want you stirring them up any more." He started his horse forward. "Thanks for your offer, but I'd rather you let the law handle this!"

Clay doubled his fists in anger and watched Case continue on his way to Cimarron, Reverend Tolby's body jostling ominously over the mule's back.

John Allison, hearing of the tragic event, knew Clay would want revenge. "If you even set foot into that town," he told his brother, "you're apt to get blamed for something! Now you promise me you'll stay here on the ranch and let Case Gordon take care of it."

Clay went to his work grudgingly. He burned for vengeance on the man who had killed Reverend Tolby. But out of respect for his brother, he vowed not to become involved.

It came as no surprise, however, when Case Gordon appeared at the ranch the next morning asking about Clay's whereabouts the night before.

"Some men found Cruz Vega before I did," Case told the Allison and Calley brothers. "They forced him to tell what he knew and then strung him up. I'm just trying to find out who did it."

"Well don't look at me!" Clay declared. "I've been here ever since I saw you yesterday!"

"He's right," John said. "The Calleys and me can back him up."

Clay still fumed. "Did you learn what Vega told those men before they killed him?"

"He accused Manuel Cardenas of being paid by the Santa Fe Ring to kill the reverend."

"Just like I said! Have you found Cardenas?"

"Got him in jail, now. He's awaiting trial."

"Trial?!" Clay banged a fist against his leg. "You know the Ring will find a way to get him off!"

John gave his brother a warning look. "It might not go that way, Clay. Now, we're all going to stay here at the ranch until this thing's cleared up!"

John was glad he didn't let Clay out of his sight during the next few days, otherwise, Clay would have been suspected of another murder, for Wes came back from town with startling news.

"I heard while they was movin' Manuel Cardenas from the hearing room back to the jail, a hidden gunman put a bullet through his head!"

John relaxed. "Well, looks like all the trouble's out of the way, now. Clay, I guess it's all right for you to start delivering the beef again."

# Chapter Twenty-Nine

*I*t steamed Clay to think he was a suspect every time somebody got shot, but he drove the next wagon of beef into Cimarron. By late afternoon the meat had been unloaded and he went to the Saint James Hotel to take a room.

Dora McCullough, on her way home from shopping, spotted him and called out, "Hello, there, Clay!"

He waited at the hotel door while she walked over.

"Clay, we haven't seen you in days! Are you staying overnight?"

He relaxed for the first time in weeks, for she always made him forget his troubles. "Thought I would. I'm just going to get a room."

"Then you've got to take supper with us—Hannah and Ben Colbert will be there and I won't let you say no!"

He had no reason to refuse, and didn't want to, anyway. "That's mighty nice of you, I could use a good meal for a change!"

It seemed like being home again, sitting around the large table with good friends enjoying a delicious supper.

"Things are picking up real good in the east, now," John McCullough said. "The girls and I heard from a friend in Tennessee. He wants me to come back and work for him."

"But Daddy doesn't want to leave Cimarron," Dora said, passing the fried chicken. "I'm glad, because we all like it here. Although we do have our share of shooting and killing!"

"Well maybe all this violence has ended," Bettie added. She handed the chicken plate to Clay.

He gave a joking glance at Ben Colbert, "I guess it's creating a little more business for you, though, isn't it, Doc?"

Ben scowled. "It's the undertaker who's getting rich!"

"Oh, let's talk about something more pleasant!" Hannah remarked.

"I agree," Bettie said. "Clay, Dora and I haven't been out to your place since you finished the house. I imagine you've improved it a lot by now."

"Haven't done any more with the house. We've been working too hard to make a profit."

John McCullough looked up from his plate with a knowing smile. "I would guess it needs a woman's touch . . . or should I say, the touch of *two* women?"

Dora saw Clay's embarrassment and spoke up quickly. "Daddy, why don't you tell Clay about your plans on expanding the post office—and *please* pass the mashed potatoes!"

The full moon hung like a big Japanese lantern in the night sky as Clay and the Colberts prepared to leave. Dora handed Clay his hat and maneuvered him to the porch while the Colberts were saying goodnight.

A softer feeling had been growing in Dora's heart, now that she knew of Clay's malady. She wanted to help, but didn't know where to start.

"Maybe Daddy's right," she told him gently. "Bettie and I could come out and do something with your ranch house."

"I'd like that."

She put a hand on his arm and the gentle touch ignited a burning urge to take her in his arms. But the Colberts came out.

"Come on, Clay," Hannah said, "we'll walk you to the hotel."

Clay reluctantly said goodnight to the McCulloughs and joined Ben and Hannah on their way to the Saint James.

"The McCullough girls are such sweet young ladies," Hannah said as they walked in the warm night air. She glanced at Clay. "Bettie and John seem to have eyes for each other—you think they'll get married, Clay?"

He looked down, embarrassed. "Oh, I don't know. John never talks about it."

Ben sensed what Hannah was getting at. "We should keep our noses out of it, Hannah. I'm sure if John's serious, he'll pop the question when the time's right."

"Then there's Dora and Case Gordon," Hannah persisted. "Maybe he's waiting for the right time, too . . . unless someone else beats him to it!"

Ben cleared his throat pointedly. "If Case wanted to get married, he would've done it long ago. Maybe he thinks it's not the right thing for a man in his line of work."

They arrived at the hotel and stopped to say goodnight.

Hannah gave Clay a little hug. "Sleep well, Clay. I understand Henry Lambert has comfortable rooms here."

"Yes, they're right nice." Clay shook Ben's hand in goodbye. "I'll drop in on you next time I'm in town."

The Colberts gave a little wave and continued walking toward their own house.

"It hurts me to see the look in Dora and Clay's eyes each time they get together," Hannah said thoughtfully. "There seems to be a kind of agony—like they're trying to break invisible chains."

Ben put a loving arm around her. "Give them time, Hannah. I have a feeling those chains are getting weaker. Maybe they'll snap sooner than you think!"

Clay entered the Saint James to go to his room, but a man stopped him in the lobby. The suave-looking Mexican, wore fine-looking trousers and maroon satin vest. A gun in its tooled leather holster rested ominously on his hip. "You're Clay Allison, aren't you?" he asked.

"That's right, I am."

"Then I want to talk to you for a moment. My name is Pancho Griego."

The name put Clay on guard. Pancho Griego was Cruz Vega's uncle, a well-known enforcer for the new owners of the Maxwell Land Grant. Clay knew Griego's reputation for killing several innocent people in the Territory—even a rancher's wife, which added to Clay's loathing of the man.

"I don't have anything to say to you," Clay told him.

"Just for a moment. Come, let's go to the barroom. The drinks are on me!"

Clay felt a tinge of curiosity as to what the man had to say, and besides, a drink sounded good after the long day. "All right, but just one drink."

Only four men occupied the saloon, drinking and smoking cigars at a table, as Clay and Griego went to the bar.

"Good evening, gentlemen," Henri Lambert said from behind the counter and gave Pancho Griego a suspicious look. He obviously knew the man. "I warn you, it is slow tonight and I am about to close."

"We just want a couple of whiskeys," Griego said.

Lambert sighed and put a bottle with two glasses on the bar. "Then help yourselves—I will be in the kitchen, putting away my pots and pans." He tightened an apron around his waist and left the room.

Griego picked up the bottle and filled their glasses. "You knew that my nephew Cruz Vega was lynched by a mob here not long ago," he said casually.

Clay took a good swallow of the warming liquor. "I heard, but I didn't have anything to do with it."

"And I suppose you don't know who killed Manuel Cardenas?"

"I wasn't in town when it happened." Clay felt intimidated and downed the remainder of his glass.

Griego drank his liquor in one swallow and immediately refilled the glasses. "Everybody knows you had a grudge against both of them."

"I'm not the only one. 'Most everybody in the Territory had a grudge against them—*and* the Santa Fe Ring they worked for!"

Griego reacted as if slapped in the face. "You should be careful who you're accusing!"

Clay finished the second drink. "You know who the guilty ones are. Now, if you'll excuse me, Mr. Griego, I'm going to bed."

Clay started for the door, but Griego put a hand on his arm. "Not so fast, Mr. Allison, I'm not through, yet!"

In the kitchen, Henri Lambert finished lining his pots and pans in a neat row, then carefully turned out the kerosene lamp. Suddenly three muffled gunshots caught his ear.

With curiosity, he took off his apron and went to the barroom to investigate, but found it completely empty. He shrugged. The gunfire must have come from outside, but he was not about to get involved.

Since the last customer had left, he extinguished all the lamps and went upstairs where he undressed wearily, glad to crawl into bed beside his warm loving wife.


Early the next morning, Henri Lambert yawned and forced himself downstairs to sweep out the barroom since he was short of help.

However, the little Frenchman never started his chore. As he moved back a table and four chairs from the corner, his sleepy eyes widened in horror and the broom dropped to the floor. In a pool of coagulated blood lay the stiff body of Pancho Griego.

# Chapter Thirty

"You're crazy, Case! Why would I shoot a man and then come upstairs to bed with him still layin' dead in the bar?!"

Case Gordon looked down at Clay Allison sitting on the bed in his underwear. "I admit, Clay, it isn't like you."

Clay rubbed his eyes, still groggy from last night's whiskey and also being awakened so early in the morning. "Why don't you talk to those other four men who were in the barroom?"

"Henry Lambert didn't know who they were, so I can't find them."

Clay looked up in exasperation. "So why pick on me?"

"Because you were the last one seen with Griego."

Clay spewed a breath of resignation and plopped back onto the pillow. "All right, dammit! Reckon I can't talk my way outta this one!"

"Then you did it?"

"Yes, I shot the bastard. But I had to—he pushed me into it, even pulled his gun on me!"

"One shot wouldn't have done it? Griego had a bullet hole in his right temple, one in the right breast and another in the abdomen!"

Clay looked up with a burning hatred. "Guess I was thinkin' of one bullet for each person he's killed!"

Case raised an incredulous eyebrow.

"Well, everybody knows he even gunned down innocent women!"

"Those four men at the table, did they see you do it?"

Clay took a deep breath to stifle his anger. "No. They left just before it happened. Griego and I were alone."

"You should have reported it to me, or at least to Henry Lambert."

Clay put a hand to his head. "I'd had one too many drinks, I guess . . . and I was boiling mad. I just came on upstairs and went to bed." He looked up through bleary eyes. "What are you gonna do, now, put me back in that stinkin' jail?"

Case heaved a sigh. "I could do that and run you through a trial, but with no witnesses, you'd be in trouble." He shrugged. "I'll put in the report that you shot in self-defense and let it go at that."

Clay sat up in surprise. "Then you'll let me off?"

"I didn't say that. You'll still have to come to the sheriff's office with me and sign the report that you acted in self-defense." Case's stern look faded. "But there's not a soul in the Territory who'd say Griego didn't deserve it. You actually did us all a favor!"

Clay dressed and went with Case downstairs where a worried Henri Lambert met them in the lobby.

"I hope you will understand," the rueful Frenchman said to Clay, "but I had to tell the deputy you were with that Griego man last night!"

Clay put a hand on the little man's shoulder. "That's all right, Henry. It's all over, now."

Lambert's sad eyes brightened. "Then Deputy Gordon isn't taking you to jail?"

Case gave him a tight smile. "Clay acted in self-defense, so he's free."

"Good, good! That Griego was *mauvaise poisson*—a bad fish. We are all happy to have him out of the way. Now, to show my gratitude, let me prepare you a breakfast. It is early, you must be hungry!"

They accepted and Lambert showed them into the dining room.

On entering, Case glanced with amusement at the ceiling. "If your customers keep shooting up the place, Henry, you'll have to start putting in a new ceiling!"

Clay looked up at the many bullet holes and wondered which ones were his.

"I'm thinking of that," Lambert said. "But it will need reinforcing with very hard wood—the upstairs guests are tired of dodging bullets!"

Pancho Griego's body had been removed and two Mexican laborers, on their hands and knees with a pail of soapy water, worked at scrubbing away the blood. Lambert discretely seated Case and Clay on the opposite side of the room. The Frenchman disappeared for only a moment and came back with their breakfast.

"We sure never have eggs like this at the ranch," Clay said as Lambert placed a warm plate in front of him. "What do you call it, Henry?"

"Eggs Benedict. It is only a simple dish, egg and ham on a muffin with Hollandaise Sauce." The Frenchman poured coffee and set the steaming pot on a trivet. "Enjoy your breakfast, gentlemen. I am at the bar if you need anything more."

Clay realized his hunger and didn't hesitate to dig in. "Case, this is another time you've let me off the hook," he said while they ate. "How come you're being so nice to me?"

"Maybe it's because we're alike in some ways."

Clay paused in surprise. "How do you figure that? You're so calm and sure of yourself—and me, I go running around, raisin' hell!"

"We both believe in justice and rights for everybody." A faint smile tipped the deputy's mustache. "It's just that you're a little too extravagant in showing it!"

"So you became a deputy sheriff, to prove your point?"

Case Gordon's coffee-colored eyes softened. "I did it because of my mother and father."

"They talked you into it?"

"No. They were killed by outlaws."

Clay ate with slow curiosity as Case continued.

"I grew up on a little farm near Taos. My folks saw to it that I had good schooling in town, and when I was seventeen, ready to go out on my own, some men rode into our farm. I saw them from the field where I was working. They were crazy with whiskey, shooting into the air. When Mama and Daddy came out of the house, the men gunned them down . . . right there on our front porch."

Clay asked in a low voice, "Did they ever catch those men?"

Case shook his head. "They got away. But right then I knew what my destiny was. I became a deputy in Taos. It took me two years, but I tracked those men down. We had a shoot-out and I killed them." Case shrugged and began eating again. "But getting revenge didn't cleanse my soul like I thought it would. I'm still trying to make this Territory safe from men like that."

"I think I know how you feel, Case. My mother died of a broken heart because the Yankees destroyed our home. Maybe I'm trying to get revenge against people like that, too . . . the same as you are."

Clay signed the report in Case's office, then drove the wagon quickly back to the ranch. The news about Pancho Griego would get around fast and Clay didn't want his brother to hear it second hand.

Wes and Jim Calley had already gone to their chores and John was getting ready to go out when Clay arrived.

"Before you get started, John, I've got to tell you something."

John took in a long breath. He wasn't sure he wanted to hear it.

Clay blurted it out. "There was a shooting at the Saint James last night. Pancho Griego got killed."

John studied his older brother for a moment, knowing there must be more. "And you were there, of course?"

Clay nodded.

"Well . . . did you do it?"

"Yes."

John could only give him a cold stare.

Clay huffed impatiently, "All right, dammit, just let me explain!" He sat down at the little table and ran fingers through his hair. "We were drinking at the bar. Griego was getting real nasty about his nephew's shooting. I wanted to leave, but he kept pushing. He was making me mad and I knew I had to get away before anything happened. I tried to go twice. The second time Griego stopped me, he came right out and said I'd killed his nephew. He pulled a gun on me, but I drew mine and got him before he could hit the trigger. The next thing I remembered was Case Gordon waking me up in my room this morning, telling me that Pancho Griego had been shot in the saloon."

"And why didn't Case arrest you?"

"There were no witnesses, so Case put in the report that it was self-defense."

John slumped down into the other chair like a half-empty feed sack, his dark blue eyes fixed on nothing in particular.

Clay stared at his brother, realizing for the first time how much older he looked. "You feelin' all right, John?"

John leaned back and shook his head. "On top of working my butt off making a go of this place, I have to worry every time you go into town, wondering what's going to happen next!" He let out a long slow breath. "I'm just tired, I guess."

Clay felt a sudden remorse. Being the older, he should be looking out for John. But, now, it was the other way around—John had come with him all the way to New Mexico just to make sure Clay didn't get into trouble. And trouble was the only thing Clay had brought his little brother.

"You need some fun for a change," Clay said. "I heard there's gonna be a fandango next Saturday at Las Animas in Colorado. You like to dance. Why don't we go up there and forget about all this!"

"We can't leave the ranch."

"I've already been to market. Wes and Jim can run the place for a few days. Besides, with me away from Cimarron, maybe people will stop talking." Clay put a hand on his brother's shoulder. "Come on, John. What do you say?!"

# Chapter Thirty-One

*C*lay felt better already. They had ridden nearly the whole day to reach Las Animas, just across the border in Colorado, but John didn't seem to share Clay's relief.

"I heard tell the Vandiver House is a fine hotel," Clay said, hoping to cheer up his brother. "It might cost a few pennies, but heck fire, we've earned it!"

John shifted in his saddle. "If they've got a soft bed, I'll go for it."

They put the horses in the hotel stables and checked into their room.

Clay opened his saddle bags and took out a pair of gray pants and a fancy shirt. He held them up for his brother to see. "I got these at the store in Cimarron. Haven't even worn them yet! You think the ladies will take to 'em, John?"

John gave them a dour look. "Yes—maybe some of the wild ones!"

Clay swallowed the criticism and watched John pull out his own dressy but conservative clothes—dark trousers, a charcoal coat and string tie.

"Well, you're gonna look like a real dandy, John. Sure won't have any trouble gettin' a pretty little *chiquita* to dance!"

The two had recently bought new Colt .45 Peacemakers and Clay strapped the gun belt around his waist.

John watched him in thought. "You really think we oughta wear guns to a dance?"

Clay patted his forty-five. "We don't know this town—better keep 'em with us just in case!"

John buckled his own gun belt beneath the coat and the two left for the Olympic Dance Hall.

The wooden building shook with the sound of good piano-and-fiddle music to entertain the cowboys, ranchers and farmers who had come for miles to enjoy the fandango and dance with their lady friends. An abundance of young Mexican girls stood by, ready to fill in when necessary.

Clay and John made their way through the crowd, getting a feel for the room, and stopped beside a thin mustachioed man who tipped a bottle to his mouth. He gave Clay a smile and offered the bottle. "Need a little fire to get you goin'?" he asked.

"Sure thing!" Clay took the bottle for a gulp. "Mind of my brother has a little, too?"

The man shrugged.

Clay handed the container to John who took a small drink and gave it back to his brother. Clay took another hearty drink before returning it to the friendly stranger.

The man looked down at their guns. "You two might wanna put them pistols away," he warned. "Sheriff Faber don't allow guns at fandangos!"

"They stay with us," Clay said. "Besides, we're not here for trouble—just to have a good time!" He turned to his brother. "Go ahead and enjoy yourself, John. There's lots of pretty little gals over there just waitin' to dance!"

Two young Mexican girls walked over to them. "You like to dance?" one asked John.

John smiled and took her arm, moving out into the crowd.

The other girl looked with expectation at Clay.

"What the heck!" he said and took her hands.

The whiskey gave Clay courage enough to try some steps, but his clumsy foot kept stepping on the girl's toes.

"You hurt my feet!" she exclaimed and pulled away.

He grabbed her hand. "Come on, *Chica*, I'll do better!"

They began stumbling around the floor and soon Clay felt a hand on his shoulder. He turned to face a big mustache and shiny tin badge.

"I'm Sheriff Charles Faber," the man said. "You'll have to take that gun off or else leave the dance hall!"

Clay was now feeling light-headed and carefree. "The only time my gun goes off is when it's smokin'!" he replied.

Not far away, John saw his brother talking to the sheriff. Sensing trouble, John left the surprised *señorita* and walked over.

"Any trouble here?" John asked.

Sheriff Faber looked at the gun belt showing through John's open coat. "Nobody's allowed to wear a gun at these fandangos. You two'll have to take 'em off or leave!"

Clay was adamant. "We're not lookin' for trouble, Sheriff, but we're keepin' our guns. Now, why don't you just relax and enjoy the party!"

Sheriff Faber gritted his teeth and stomped away. Clay gave him a laugh and said to his brother, "Don't worry, John, he's not gonna stop us from havin' some fun!" He took the girls' hand again for another dance.

It didn't take long for the rebuffed sheriff to reappear—only this time, he carried a double-barrelled shotgun.

The music stopped and a hush fell over the room as dancers cleared a path between Sheriff Faber and the Allisons.

John realized the sheriff meant business. He moved his hands down to undo the gun belt.

Faber, thinking he was going for his gun, pulled a trigger and the room shuddered from the blast. Buckshot slammed into John, throwing him against a wall.

Clay erupted in blind fury. He drew his Peacemaker and fired three rapid shots of hot lead at the sheriff. One caught Faber in the chest and he fell, but his shotgun roared again, sending pellets tearing into John's leg.

The room broke into bedlam with women screaming and scrambling for the door.

Clay ran through the pall of acrid gunsmoke to his brother who lay on the floor with hands clutched to his side. Blood poured through his fingers.

Clay dropped to one knee. "John! My God, what'd he do to you?!"

John couldn't answer; his breath came in short gasps and his eyes glazed over.

Clay stumbled back to the dead sheriff. He grabbed the man's collar and dragged him over to John. Tears flowed from Clay's eyes.

"John, here's the man that shot you!" he cried. "Look at the damned son of a bitch! I killed him!" He turned to the remaining crowd that stood watching in shocked silence. "Is there a doctor in this damned town?" he sobbed. "Somebody get a doctor—my little brother's dyin'!!"

Some kind soul got hold of a doctor and two other men helped Clay take John back to the Vandiver House where they placed him onto a bed in the hotel room.

"Is he going to live, Doc?" Clay asked in a weak voice. He had stopped crying, but a hard knot stuck in his throat.

"Looks bad," the balding little doctor said. "I'll take out as much of this buckshot as I can. A lot of it, though, is deep. No telling what it'll do!"

While the doctor worked on John, two deputy sheriffs arrived to arrest Clay for murder. Too grief-stricken to resist, Clay went quietly with them to the jail where they locked him in a cell to await trial.

For three days, Clay paced the cramped jail cell in anguish, not for himself, but with guilt and concern for his brother's life.

At last, the judge arrived in Las Animas to consider Clay's fate.

"You're a lucky man, Clay Allison!" the judge told him. "There were enough witnesses at that dance to say you shot in self-defense, even though it was a sheriff you killed!"

Clay walked out of jail a free man and went directly to the Vandiver House to check on John. He found the doctor wrapping fresh bandages around John's chest and stomach.

The doctor stood up with a heavy sigh, which didn't sound reassuring. "So far, your brother is lucky," he told Clay. "But he can't walk and needs to stay in bed for at least two more weeks.

John rolled his head on the pillow. "I don't want to stay in this rotten town another day!" he muttered.

"But you can't walk!" Clay argued.

"Just get me on my horse and take me home—I'll be all right!"

The doctor glared down at John. "I had to do a lot of cutting on your insides, Mr. Allison. Riding a horse could tear you open again!"

John's eyes flared in a mixture of pain and defiance. "Clay, I said take me home—*now*!"

The exasperated doctor added some extra padding to the bandages, then with Clay's help, they eased John out of the hotel and carefully lifted him into the saddle.

After paying the physician, Clay had to take the reins from his weakened brother's hands and lead the horse behind as the two rode slowly out of town.

It took them two grueling days, plodding back to New Mexico, with stops for John to rest. His face had become ashen as they finally struggled into the ranch and the Calleys ran out to meet them.

"John's in bad shape," Clay said. "Help me get him into the house!"

The men carried the semi-conscious John inside where they placed him gently onto the bed. Clay opened his brother's coat.

"Good Lord!" Wes Calley breathed in shock.

John's shirt had become an ugly red mass of blood seeping through the bandages.

# Chapter Thirty-Two

*B*en made sure he had all the necessary supplies in his little black bag, then closed it with a snap.

"I don't know how good a job that doctor did in Las Animas," he said to Hannah, "but I'd feel better if I had a look at John Allison's wounds."

The whole town had been talking about Clay Allison killing the Colorado sheriff, that John Allison had been seriously wounded with Clay being arrested, then released to bring his brother back to their Cimarron ranch.

"Do you want me to go with you?" Hannah asked with an anxious face.

"No, dear, that won't be necessary. I'll be back before dark."

Ben started for the door and heard an urgent knock. He opened it to see a distraught Bettie McCullough.

"Oh, Ben," she wailed, "I just heard that John's back at the ranch . . . if he's wounded as bad as they say, I'd like you to go check on him!"

"That's just where I'm headed, Bettie."

Her face relaxed. "I'm so worried about him, Ben . . . would it be all right if I went with you?"

Clay had been mentally wringing his hands ever since the incident. With John back home, Clay and the Calleys tried to patch up the ugly wounds, but John's bleeding persisted.

"Dammit, John, you need a doctor," Clay finally said. "I'm gonna go get Ben Colbert!"

He strode out to throw a saddle on Ebon just as Ben and Bettie McCullough arrived in the little buggy.

Bettie jumped down and grabbed Clay's arm. "Everybody knows what happened, Clay—how is John?"

"Not good. I was just goin' to fetch Doc Colbert."

Ben took his little case out of the buggy. "Let's go have a look."

They entered the bedroom and Bettie gasped at the sight of John lying delirious on a bloody sheet. She rushed to kneel at the bedside and took his hand. "Don't worry, John, Ben Colbert's here, now!"

He moved his head on the pillow, not hearing her words.

Ben frowned at what he saw and began removing the sticky blood-soaked bandages. He glanced over his shoulder. "Bettie, fetch me some hot water and clean towels, please!"

"Of course, Ben!"

Bettie rushed to the kitchen and stoked the iron stove, then poured water into a pan. She wiped tears from her cheeks while waiting for the water to heat. It seemed to take forever until she finally returned with the steaming pan of water.

Clay had grabbed some towels and Ben dipped one into the hot water. He began gently cleaning the wound while Bettie knelt down to help. Clay stood watching with a blanched face.

"He's going to need some stitches," Ben said with a calm voice, holding a towel over the wound. "There's silk thread and a needle in my case, Bettie."

She rummaged through his black bag and produced the material.

"Now, if you'll hold the towel to keep the blood away," he told her, "I'll sew up this hole."

Bettie followed his instructions while Ben threaded the needle and dipped it into a bottle of carbolic acid solution. Never wincing, she watched as Ben pushed the needle through John's flesh.

After the sutures had been made and bleeding stopped, Ben sterilized the wound with more carbolic acid, then applied clean bandages. He stood up with a worried sigh, looking down at his patient. "He's going to need a lot of rest—and those bandages will have to be replaced every day."

Bettie, still on the floor at John's side, looked up. "I'll stay and do that. You have to get back to Hannah, Ben. If John gets worse, we'll send for you."

Ben gave her a tender smile. "That's very good of you, Bettie. You've seen how I do it, so I needn't worry."

"Ben, would you please tell Dora and my father where I am, and that everything's all right?" She looked up at Clay. "It *is* all right, isn't it?"

Clay felt a great relief. "Of course, Bettie. You can sleep on my bed here next to John. I'll bed down on the floor in Wes and Jim's room."

The following week, Ben Colbert pulled his buggy to a stop in the bright mid-morning sun and Dora McCullough hopped down. Bettie, having seen them arrive, rushed out to hug her sister.

Dora laughed. "You're certainly giving the town a lot to talk about, Bettie, living out here with four men!"

"Well, I don't care, let them chatter!"

They went to John's room and he looked up with embarrassment. "If I'd known visitors were coming, I'd have dressed up!"

"You're looking good, John," Dora said. "Daddy and I've been worried about you!"

Ben looked pleased with his patient's recovery. "John couldn't have made it without Bettie's help. She makes a good nurse!"

With professional ease, Bettie began helping Ben undo John's bandages while Clay and Dora watched.

Dora smiled impishly. "Come on, Clay, let's leave them alone to play doctor."

Clay followed her out to the tiny front porch and they leaned against the house, taking in the fresh sweet smells drifting from a stretch of green pasture land. After a quiet moment, Dora spoke.

"From what Ben says, John's ranching days are over, with all that buckshot still inside him . . . does John know that?"

Clay's tormented eyes remained on the horizon. "Yes, he knows."

"What's going to happen to all of you, now?"

He lowered his stricken face. "This is all my fault! I don't know what's going to happen. I just don't know!"

"They're already saying in town that you're too quick with a gun."

She had used kind words. People were really saying that Clay Allison had turned into a cold-blooded shootist and would kill anybody who got his dander up. But she knew it was only because of his troubled mind. She studied his agonized face and her heart overflowed with pity. He needed help and she longed to take him in her arms, to shield him from all the bad things being constantly thrown in his path.

"I got a good idea what they're saying," he told her. "But I don't want to talk about it, now. Come on, let's go get some coffee."

Ben Colbert and Bettie McCullough finished their job in the bedroom and John could sit up, looking like a new man.

"Well, John, that ought to hold you till I come out again," Ben said.

Bettie laughed. "You won't have to, Ben. I can take care of him from now on."

Ben, seeing the love in her eyes, thought it best to leave them alone. "I think I smell fresh coffee. If you'll excuse me, I'll go get a cup."

After Ben had gone out, Bettie sat on the bed and took John's hand.

"John, Ben says you won't be able to work on the ranch anymore, like you used to."

He shook his head. "That's been bothering me. I can't just sit around and watch Clay, Wes and Jim run this place."

"I've been thinking about it for the last few days. Daddy could get you a job with his friend in Tennessee. All you'd have to do is sit in an office and give orders!"

"Well, I think I've about had it with this country, anyway." His love had grown under her devoted care and now he gazed into her warm brown eyes. "But if I went back to Tennessee, I'd still need somebody to look after me for a while—and the Doc says you're a good nurse."

She caught her breath. "John Allison, is this a proposal?"

"I reckon you could call it that!"

"Then the answer is yes!" She bent down, planting a loving kiss on his lips.

Dora had just poured cups of fresh coffee for Ben and Clay and they all looked up as Bettie waltzed into the kitchen area. "Guess what!" she exclaimed, her face glowing with delight. "John just proposed—we're going to be married!"

After a moment of stunned silence, everyone broke into jubilant congratulations.

However, Clay felt even more lost than before. He went to John's bedroom. "Just heard you're gettin' married," he said.

John looked sheepish. "I would've told you, but I didn't know, myself, till just now. I'm no good here, anymore. Bettie and I plan on going back to Tennessee. I'll get a job there where I won't have to ride a horse or round up strays."

"Sounds good. I think the Calleys and me can run the place without you. But we'll have to figure some kind of agreement to pay you for your share."

Regret clouded John's eyes. "That doesn't bother me. The only thing I'm worried about is you, Clay. You need somebody to hold you down. I know Dora loves you. Why don't you two get married?"

Clay reddened. "You know why. People are already calling me a killer. I don't want to hurt her when I go wild and gun down another man!"

"The worst part of your trouble is liquor. Dora would keep you from drinking."

"I'll think about it. When's your wedding?"

"Bettie and I thought we oughta wait till I had a job opening in Tennessee. Then, we'd keep it simple. Have a justice of the peace come out to the ranch, since I can't walk good yet."

The job offer came sooner than expected. Bettie and Dora worked quickly, making plans for the wedding, which was simple, the way John wanted it. Only a preacher, the Colberts and Case Gordon came from town for the short ceremony. Wes and Jim Calley surprised everyone, dressed in clean clothes, with their usual unruly hair slicked down nice and shiny.

After the vows had been said, they all sat down at two makeshift tables for the wedding feast, which Dora worked all day to prepare.

"Before we start," Case announced, "we need a toast to the bride and groom!" He brought out two bottles of champagne. "I got these from Henry Lambert—and Henry sends his congratulations, by the way!"

Case popped open a bottle and filled each glass to everyone's delight.

Dora's heart ached as she saw Clay move away from the group to sip his champagne in stony silence. She wanted to go to him, but thought better of it. This was a time when he needed to be alone.

# Chapter Thirty-Three

*H*annah Colbert held two mugs of coffee as she peeked into Ben's little office. He had taken off his glasses and now sat in the big chair, staring out the window.

"Maybe some coffee will help," she said gently. "It'll get your mind off whatever's bothering you."

Ben turned with a kind look. He realized again how lucky he was to have Hannah at his side when he needed comfort.

"I'm sorry, dear. I didn't know my bad mood was rubbing off on you."

She came in and set the mugs onto a table, then began rubbing his tired shoulders. "That's what a wife's for. Your worries are my worries. Do you want to talk about it?"

She thought he might be brooding over Steve slipping through his fingers and, now, probably gone forever. However, Ben's answer surprised her.

"It's just that I hate to see things disintegrating. I guess it all started when John Allison left two months ago."

224

Hannah recalled the happy moment. A small group bade farewell to John Allison and his bride Bettie when they took the stage to Cheyenne. The train then whisked them away, leaving Clay and the Calley brothers to run their ranch. Hannah, too, had felt a sense of loss. She wondered where things would go from there.

"That's good," Ben said, feeling relaxed under Hannah's tender hands. "I'll have my coffee, now."

She took the chair opposite him and picked up her coffee mug. "Don't you think Clay will make a go of it, Ben?"

He took a sip of coffee and shook his head. "I know he could, if it weren't for the dratted Santa Fe Ring. The new owners of Maxwell's land grant are demanding steeper rent from all the ranchers and farmers—and Clay's is the highest. They're trying to push him out of the Territory."

Hannah gave a small laugh. "If I know Clay Allison, it'll take a lot of pushing!"

"That's just it, Hannah. If he won't budge, they'll resort to deadly violence, like they have with all the others who've stood in their way!"

Hannah cringed at the thought of Clay Allison being shot down in cold blood. "Maybe you can talk him into moving someplace else, Ben."

She didn't want to say it, but leaving Cimarron had been gnawing at her own mind. It seemed that violence had followed them from Elizabethtown and she wondered if any place in the Territory was free of it. Maybe Las Vegas, a large growing city to the south—it had more law and lay closer to Fort Union with all the government troops.

Sooner than expected, Hannah and Ben had a surprise visit from Clay Allison.

"Clay!" Hannah said with delight. "Do come in—I thought you'd be so busy with that ranch, we wouldn't see you for a spell!"

Clay took off his hat and walked into the sitting room. "I had to

225

come into town on business . . . and to tell you some news."

Hannah wondered at his sober face. "Well, I hope it's good news—but wait, let me fetch Ben."

She went to the study door and opened it. "Ben, Clay Allison's here, he wants to tell us something important!"

Ben came out with a puzzled look and shook Clay's hand.

"I'd stay here and fight the Ring," Clay told them, "but it's too big for me alone. They've cut off my market, now, so the only thing I can do is to move out."

Hannah felt a sudden relief, but her heart ached to know she'd probably never see Clay again.

Ben asked with concern, "Where do you plan to go, Clay?"

"Me and the Calleys are movin' our herd to Texas, a place in the Panhandle called Mobeetie. It's sort of the crossroads of activity."

Hannah put her arms around him. "Oh, Clay, you've been almost like a son . . . we'll miss you something terrible!" She wiped at a tear. "You know, there's another person here in Cimarron who'll be devastated to know you're leaving. Have you told Dora McCullough yet?"

Clay looked down with embarrassment. "I'm goin' there, now. But I wanted to say goodbye to you all first."

"We've got to stay in touch, Clay. Promise you'll write and let us know how you're doing."

Ben gripped Clay's hand. "I told you once, you were just as good as any man. I still mean that, Clay. I know you'll make good at whatever you do!"

Clay dreaded going to the McCullough house; he knew it would be the last time he'd see Dora. With reluctance, he trotted Ebon to their home and knocked on the door.

Dora appeared in the doorway, her face breaking into happy surprise. Before she could speak, Clay put a finger to her lips and led her by the hand to a secluded spot on the porch.

"Just wanted you to know," he said, "I'm leaving Cimarron. Me and the Calleys will be movin' our cattle to Mobeetie, Texas, by the end of the week." He averted her pained face. "I wish things could've worked out different."

Tears filled her eyes. "They didn't have to turn out like this, Clay . . . not altogether!"

"What do you mean?"

"Oh, I don't mean your trouble with the Ring—nobody could stop them! It's about us, Clay . . . Ben Colbert told me about your problem, but it was for my own good. He knew I loved you. I know you don't want to hurt me . . . but, Clay, I'll die inside if you leave without me!"

He shook his head in frustration. "I love you, too, Dora, but it wouldn't work. Look at what I did to John—I almost got him killed! I'd never forgive myself if I did anything to hurt you."

She swallowed her pride. "If I were your wife, that wouldn't happen!"

"But, Dora, everybody's calling me a cold-hearted shootist—and there's more than one man who'd like to see me dead. You don't want a husband with that kind of reputation."

"Let them talk, I know it isn't true!" She put her arms around him and cried against his chest. "Clay, I love you and want to help you . . . please give me that chance!"

Her soft body in his arms and the words she spoke gave him a strange rush of freedom. The wall he had built around himself began to crumble and he realized that Dora was his last hope. Only with her love would he be able to survive. He gently raised her face to kiss her trembling lips.

"In that case, Miss Dora McCullough, I'd like to formally ask for your hand in marriage!"

A smile broke through her tears. "On one condition." She ran her fingers through his shaggy whiskers. "If you'll get rid of this beard. I want to see just how handsome you really are!"

# Chapter Thirty-Four

*B*en let the reins hang slack as the mule, by habit, took his little dark buggy across the Cimarron River bridge and onto the street where Hannah waited at the house.

He felt all empty inside, probably just burning out with old age. Losing so many good friends didn't help. First, Lucien B. Maxwell who seemed to hold the town together; then John Allison and Bettie McCullough, followed by Clay and Dora along with the Calley brothers. He and Hannah would probably be the next to disappear from Cimarron.

Suddenly, he yanked the reins to a quick stop and the mule raised its head in surprise.

With a pounding heart, Ben narrowed his eyes at three men dismounting in front of the Saint James Hotel. He hadn't seen his boy in over ten years, but he could tell by the way one of them walked—it had to be Steve.

The men entered the hotel and Ben guided his buggy over to the hitching rail. He didn't bother to tether the mule and walked quickly inside to the lobby desk.

"Three men just came in," he said to Mrs. Lambert, "did they go to the saloon?"

"Yes, Doctor," the dark-haired woman replied and nodded toward the door.

Ben opened the door only enough to look inside. Three Negro soldiers from Fort Union were drinking beer at one table, while near the door the three newcomers occupied another table with their glasses of whiskey.

One of them appeared tall and well-dressed, one thin with a laughing carefree look and the youngest had stringy red hair to match the freckles on his cheeks. A short red beard couldn't hide the fact that he was Steve Colbert.

Ben walked back to the desk. "Mrs. Lambert, would you do me a great favor?"

She gave him a puzzled smile. "*Certainement,* Doctor. What is it?"

"Those three men—could you go inside and ask one of them to come out and see me? It's urgent that I talk privately with him!"

"I'll be glad to . . . but which one is it?"

"The youngest one, with red hair and beard."

Mrs. Lambert left the desk and went inside. Ben paced the floor until she returned with the young man.

"Thank you," Ben said to Mrs. Lambert.

"I'll leave you alone to talk." She respectfully disappeared into a hallway.

Ben and Steve appraised each other for a moment. Finally Ben spoke.

"You look all grown up, now. And with a beard, too."

"The lady said you wanted to talk to me," Steve told him without emotion. "Is that all you wanted to say?"

"I tried to be a good father, Steve, and I know I failed somewhere along the way. After the war I promised myself things would be different, but Chunk got to you first. He's gone, now, and you still have a chance . . . Steve, please let me help you be the son I can be proud of!"

"You never helped me before," Steve answered with derision, "and I don't need your help, now!"

"Don't you know the law is looking for you?"

"Sure, I know it."

"But if the sheriff sees you here, he'll take you in!"

"I won't be here long. We're just stoppin' for some whiskey. Besides, me and my friends can take care of anybody that tries to lay a finger on us!"

Ben scowled. "Friends? Just who are those men?"

"Davy Crockett and Gus Heffron."

Ben thought a moment. "You pick strange bedfellows! That's the famous Davy Crockett's grandson. Everyone knows about him shooting up towns all the way from here to the Mississippi!"

"Well, they're waitin' for me." Steve turned to go.

"Wait, Steve. Won't you stop running around with that kind of men? Deputy Case Gordon is a good friend of mine—if you'll give yourself up, I can talk the law into going easy on you."

Steve frowned with menace. "There's two men who'd see me hang if I gave myself up—Case Gordon and Clay Allison. When I get the chance, I'm gonna send both of them to the hole in the ground where they belong. Then maybe I'll consider your offer!"

Steve gave his father an impudent look and went back to the saloon.

Ben stood helpless; there was so much more he wanted to say. With nothing else he could do, he uttered a dejected sigh and left the hotel to ride home.

Steve walked back into the saloon and joined his two friends at the table. They had just finished their drinks, so Steve tossed his down quickly.

Davy Crockett looked at him with suspicion. "Who was it you talked to out there?"

"Just an old man I used to know back east," Steve replied.

"Then we better get outta town before he tells the sheriff you're here!"

They screeched their chairs back, getting up from the table, and Davy went to the bar.   He paid Henri Lambert for a bottle of whiskey, then the three men started to leave.   As they reached the door, it opened abruptly and a Negro soldier stepped inside, bumping into Davy.

Crockett's face reddened in anger.   "Watch where you're goin', Nigger!"

The man gritted his teeth.   "Sorry, mister, I didn't see you."

"Then get outta the way and let us white folks pass!"

The soldier moved back, but only a step.   Davy growled and pulled his revolver.   The soldier instinctively went for his own gun just as Davy fired, spinning the Negro around.   The man slipped to the floor and Davy turned on the other Negro soldiers who rose quickly from the table with their guns drawn.

Davy fired three more shots and two of them grabbed their chests before collapsing over the table.   A bullet had struck the third one's hand, making him drop his gun.

Henri Lambert stared petrified from behind the bar.

"Come on!" Davy yelped and the three rushed out of the hotel.

Sheriff John Turner, having heard the gunshots, came running across the street. He saw the men leap onto their horses. "Stop!" he yelled, drawing his gun.

They gave him a glance and kicked their horses into a fast gallop.

Turner took aim and fired.   He thought the distance was too great, but Davy Crockett grabbed his arm and fell off the horse while his two friends disappeared across the bridge.

Henri Lambert ran out of the hotel. "That man," he called to Sheriff Turner, "he killed three soldiers in my saloon!"

"Then we'll have to lock 'im up!"

Lambert followed the sheriff over to Davy Crockett who lay clutching his wounded arm.

Turner yanked the man to his feet and clicked handcuffs around the wrists. "You'll be my witness, Lambert!" he said.

Davy Crockett sneered through his pain at John Turner. "You won't keep me in jail for long, Sheriff. My friends'll get me out—even if they have to kill you to do it!"

# Chapter Thirty-Five

*H*annah turned from the stove to see Ben come in with his little black bag. He always had an anxious look, returning from a call, and she often wondered if he was praying that the patient would recover. But now he seemed even more disturbed.

"You're tired, Ben," she said with worry. "Sit down and rest. I'll have your supper ready in a minute."

He dropped into a chair and took off his glasses to wipe them with a handkerchief. "It's just that the whole town's on edge after those killings at the Saint James . . . and I have to go to the jail and treat that outlaw Davy Crockett who did it!"

Hannah knew there was more to his concern than that. Everybody had been talking about the town doctor's son being involved. She couldn't stifle her hatred for a boy who would bring such misery to his father.

"Did the mail rider come through today?" Ben wondered aloud.

Hannah's face brightened as she took a roast out of the iron stove. "I nearly forgot! Dora Allison wrote. She and Clay are expecting!  I stopped at the post office and John McCullough gave me her letter.  It's there on the table."

"Well, it's nice to have some good news for a change!"  Ben put on his glasses and picked up the paper to read Dora's fine handwriting.  "I see Clay's already sold a few steers in Kansas," he mumbled.  "Seems like things are going well in Mobeetie."

Hannah wiped her hands on an apron and gave him a troubled look.  "I don't know, Ben.  If you'll go over that letter again and read between the lines . . . I wonder just how the situation really is in Mobeetie?"

# Chapter Thirty-Six

*A* small herd of cattle stood munching sparse green grass on the outskirts of Mobeetie, Texas, while the Calley brothers sat with boredom on their horses.

"This Texas country sure ain't like New Mexico!" Wes said. He shifted in the hot saddle and took off his hat to wipe sweat from the inside rim.

Jim licked his dry lips and squinted at the flat horizon. "They's not a mountain for miles. I sure miss them Sangre de Cristos!"

Only the addition of Clay Allison's new wife to the partnership eased their discomfort in this new environment. With Dora maintaining a clean house and serving them proper meals, they were like a family, which would soon gain another member when the Allison baby arrived.

"Well, this here Panhandle didn't rightly turn out to be a gold mine after all," Jim continued to grumble. "But ol' Clay don't let on like he's too worried."

"That there Dora keeps him so snowed under with lovin' care, he

235

don't have time to worry," Jim added. "Don't think I can remember the last time I seen him take a drink. When we went to town last week, he walked right past them saloons without even turnin' his head!"

"Yeah, but you ever notice the sheriff is just a step away, with a hand on his gun? Clay Allison's reputation has got as far as Mobeetie—maybe even clear to the east, by now!"

While the Calleys worked the herd, Clay sat at the kitchen table, going over the dismal finances.

"You're frowning again," Dora said and walked up behind him to put a loving hand on his shoulder.

His old friends back in Cimarron would have a hard time recognizing Clay now, with only a thin mustache and short goatee. It was Dora's tonsorial creation, which she thought gave him a dignified appearance.

"It's just that we're not showin' a profit on this place!" he said.

Her smile faded. "Is there anything we can do?"

"I've already talked to the Calleys about sellin' the ranch, but you know how scarce money is, now!" He put a hand tenderly on his jaw. "And if this durned tooth would stop achin', maybe I could think of a way out!"

"I don't want to nag, but I wish you'd see a dentist in town before it gets any worse."

He leaned back with a smile. She always knew best. "All right, sweetheart, I'm not gettin' anywhere here. I'll go saddle up Ebon. Tell the boys I won't be back till late."

Mobeetie thrived with many businesses but the town now functioned under an air of apprehension, knowing that the infamous Clay Allison had a ranch just a few miles away. Aware of the guarded atmosphere whenever he came to town, Clay felt determined not to create trouble.

Two dentists had offices on the main street and Clay pulled Ebon to a halt at the first one. He draped the reins over the saddle horn and went inside, placing a hand against his pestering jaw.

"I got a powerful toothache," he told the small man in a white coat. "Can you do somethin' for it?"

The little man had just enough hair to be pomaded down on his glistening head and he rubbed eager hands together. "Best thing to do with a tooth hurting that bad is to pull it! Why don't you sit down in the chair and let me take care of it."

Clay didn't feel comfortable with such a snap diagnosis, but he took a seat in the strange-looking chair.

The dentist held a small pair of pliers and bent over Clay's face. "Now, open wide, please."

"It's on the bottom, left, second one from the back," Clay told him and opened his mouth.

"You don't have to tell me," the man said. "I know 'em when I see 'em!"

The whole thing seemed odd to Clay as the dentist reached in, feeling around with the pliers.

"Aha!" the man said with glee. "I believe this is it!" He clamped the instrument around a tooth and started to work it loose.

"Ahhhhh!" Clay tried to yell and jerked the hand out of his mouth. "You damned fool, that's the wrong tooth!" He jumped out of the chair, pushing the man aside. "Get away from me, you imposter—whoever said you were a dentist?!"

The doctor stood holding his pliers with a mixture of shock and disappointment as Clay stormed out of the place.

He saw the other dentist sign a short distance away and stomped fast on his limping foot down the board walk to burst into the office.

The tall doctor, wearing wire-framed glasses, turned in amusement. "Well, sir, this must be an emergency!"

"That charlatan down the street tried to pull a good tooth!" Clay growled. "If you can't pull the right one, this town's gonna be minus two dentists!"

The man chuckled. "I'm afraid you chose an unschooled

practitioner. He's had nothing but complaints. If you'll calm down, maybe I can help you."

The dentist's professional manner had a soothing effect and Clay put himself into the chair. "It's this second lower one from the back, on the left," he said once again and opened his mouth wide.

The doctor made a quick investigation. "Yes, I see it must be infected. It'll have to be pulled, but I must have your permission, first."

Clay made a go-ahead motion.

The dentist picked up pincers. "I warn you, it may hurt a little."

With a few gentle tugs the tooth came out, taking the throbbing pain with it, and the hole was packed with cotton.

Clay got to his feet. "You did a good job, Doc. How much do I owe you?"

"Two dollars for a simple extraction."

Clay pushed some bills into the man's hand. "Here's five, and it was well worth it!"

With revenge shooting from his eyes, Clay clomped back to the first office and stormed inside. He pushed the frightened little man backward into the chair.

"I didn't pay you for your trouble!" Clay growled and grabbed the pliers. He forced the man's mouth open with one hand and jammed the instrument inside to grab a tooth, any tooth.

A richly dressed man and his wife had just arrived at the office door. Hearing screams, they peered inside at a man trying to yank a tooth out of another one who kicked and yelled in protest.

"My word," said the lady, "You certainly don't want *that* dentist working on you!"

"It's the first time I ever saw a dentist wearing a gun!" her husband answered.

He rushed inside and dragged Clay off before any harm had been done. Clay wrenched himself free and walked outside to lean against the building, catching an angry breath.

The wealthy-looking man came out and joined his wife. "I was about to have that dentist check my teeth," he said with a hesitant smile, "but now I don't know . . . "

Clay forced himself to simmer down. "That scoundrel's no dentist—if you want to keep your teeth, go see the other one down the street."

"I appreciate the recommendation. My name's Bob Laird, and this is my wife Ethel, Mister . . . "

"Allison. Clay Allison." He nodded politely to Mrs. Laird. "I hope you'll excuse my uncivilized behavior, ma'am, but I was just gettin' even for that man tryin' to pull the wrong tooth."

Ethel Laird chuckled. "Well, we're fortunate in meeting you, Mr. Allison. We're new in town and Bob needed someone to look at an aching tooth. Would you mind showing us to the other dentist?"

"Glad to." Clay began walking them down to the next office.

Bob Laird looked around with interest at the little metropolis. "This seems to be a nice town. Ethel and I sold our eastern holdings and we're looking for some property in the west to develop. Perhaps you could give us some more of your sage advice, Mr. Allison."

Clay couldn't believe the golden opportunity. "Just so happens I have a small cattle ranch outside of town you might want to look at. But I have to warn you, the cattle market's pretty much depressed right now."

"Yes, I know. But it'll pick up again. Ethel and I have enough to live comfortably until it does." He looked into the second dentist's office. "After I have my tooth checked, we'd be happy to ride out and look at your place."

The sun had lost its glare as Clay rode back on Ebon, accompanied by the Lairds in their buggy. Wes and Jim came in from the pasture and Dora stepped out onto the front porch.

"Mr. and Mrs. Bob Laird," Clay said, "I'd like you to meet my wife Dora and my partners, Wes and Jim Calley."

Everyone took the introductions with a friendly smile and Clay added, "Wes, why don't you and Jim show Mr. and Mrs. Laird around the place before it gets too dark."

Wes and Jim guided the Lairds in their buggy out to the pasture while Clay took a confused Dora inside.

"Clay, what's going on?" she asked.

"Honey, we're in luck. We're just breaking even on this durned place, and in another month we'll start going in the hole! Now, the Lairds are looking to buy a place, even though they know this one's not making a profit. But they've got money and don't care!"

Dora looked around at the house she had worked so hard to turn into a cozy place to live. "Clay, you mean you're selling our home?!"

"We'll get another one and start over, but not so big. By the time the market picks up again, we'll be on our way to building a better ranch."

"But where will we go?"

"I don't know yet—someplace where just stayin' alive won't cost an arm and a leg till the market picks up again!"

"Clay, our baby's due soon!"

His mind worked fast. "We'll go back to Cimarron first. You can have the baby there and we'll figure something out."

She gave in with elation. "Oh, I'd love to be with Daddy when the baby comes—and Ben Colbert can help with the delivery!"

Wes and Jim brought the Lairds back to the house and Ethel Laird fell in love with the place. Now that it had turned dark, she helped Dora prepare a nice supper for everyone. Afterwards, the men got together and went over the negotiations, with the selling price split between Clay, Wes and Jim.

Dora felt like she'd been swept off her feet by one of those frightening tornadoes that so often raced through the area.

"Not everything is settled yet," she announced. "Wes, what about you and Jim? With Clay and me going to Cimarron, do we have to say goodbye to you two, after all this time?"

Bob Laird cut in. "I'm going to need hired hands. Until I can find some, I'd be happy to pay the Calleys a good salary!"

"I hate to say goodbye to a couple of good partners," Clay said. "Wes, could you two hang on here till I get another place? I'd sure like us to keep working together."

"I don't like the idea of splittin' up, either," Wes told him.

Jim added, "It shouldn't be too long, anyway. Just let us know when you got somethin', Clay, and we'll come a-runnin'!"

Time came to leave and Dora, with a sad heart, packed her belongings for the men to put into a wagon tied behind the buckboard. Even though she was eager to see her father again, Dora's eyes filled with tears as she hugged Wes and Jim Calley.

"I told Ethel Laird if she kept your bellies full, you two wouldn't give her any trouble!"

After Dora climbed into the buggy beside Clay, he jiggled the reins and Ebon started them forward.

Dora didn't want to look back to see Wes, Jim and her home fading away behind them. If she did, she knew she'd burst into tears.

# Chapter Thirty-Seven

*C*lay and Dora crossed the Cimarron River bridge in their buckboard and wagon full of belongings, only to find an eerie blanket of silence.

Dora, half asleep with her large abdomen bouncing at every turn of the wheel, brushed hair from her eyes to look around. "Something's wrong, Clay. I've never seen the town like this—there's not a soul on the streets!"

Clay, too, had an ominous feeling. "We'll stop at the Colberts first and see what's up."

An air of tension had filled the Colbert house as Hannah sat in the front room working on her crochet; she hoped it would keep Ben from seeing the concern in her face. At the sound of a wagon pulling up outside, she stiffened and went to peek through the window curtains. "Ben, someone's just driven up!"

He came to her side and looked through the window with a smile. "No need to be afraid, my dear—it's the Allisons!"

He unlatched the door and Hannah followed him out to the

wagon.

"Clay," Ben said, "good to see you! We got your letter just last week." He helped Dora down from the wagon. "How are you, Dora?"

Weariness vanished from Dora's aching body at seeing good friends once more. "I'm just fine, Ben . . . for someone in my condition!"

Hannah took her arm. "Come inside, Dora, you must be exhausted!"

They all went into the house and Ben secured the door behind them. A chair was moved for Dora to sit on.

"Looks like you're about due, young lady!" Ben remarked.

"I probably waited too long to bring Dora back," Clay said. "We were hoping you'd help deliver the baby."

"I'd be honored to do so! But you came at a bad time, I might say."

Clay noticed that Ben had latched the door behind them. "Just what's goin' on here, Doc?"

Hannah answered with a grieved face, "Cimarron's been taken over by a gang of outlaws—everyone's afraid to leave their homes!"

"What about Sheriff John Turner and Case Gordon?"

Ben shook his head in defeat. "Case is in Santa Fe on a trial right now, and those men shot poor old John Turner—nearly killed him, getting their friend Davy Crockett out of jail. There's three of them. With John Turner laid up, there's no law here. They've been coming into town, shooting up the place and taking anything they want." Ben wiped his glasses. "The worst part is . . . one of them is my boy Steve!"

Dora had been listening with growing fear. "What about Daddy, is he all right?"

Hannah gave her an assuring pat on the arm. "He's just fine, Dora. So far, nobody's been hurt or killed."

"I've got to see him!" Dora moaned. "Clay, please take me to the house!"

"Sure, Dora." He helped her out of the chair.

Hannah took her by the hand. "Ben and I will come over tomorrow, first thing, and stay with you till the baby comes." She walked Dora outside to the wagon.

Clay started to follow, but Ben stopped him at the door.

"Clay," Ben said in a low voice, "Case Gordon is due back in town tomorrow. When Steve finds out that you and Case are both here in Cimarron, he'll have just what he wants."

"What do you mean?"

"Steve has sworn to kill you and Case to get even for what you did to my brother Chunk."

Clay gritted his teeth. "Doc, I killed your brother in self-defense and I don't want to have to kill your boy. But if it comes to that, I hope you won't hold it against me!"

Ben gave him a futile look. "I understand. What has to be, has to be!"


Ben and Hannah Colbert appeared at the McCullough house early next morning with a few belongings to carry them through Dora's childbirth. They had just gotten settled as Case Gordon rode up.

John McCullough went out to greet him. "Case! We're mighty glad to see you in town again!"

Case got down from his horse. "I hear Cimarron's in kind of a mess!"

"Mess isn't big enough a word! Come in, you're just in time for breakfast."

Relieved to have Case Gordon back in town, everyone gathered around a large table to eat and discuss the situation.

"Case, you can't take on those men all by yourself," McCullough said. "If you'll make me a deputy, I'll be glad to help!"

"Count me in, too," Clay told him.

Dora moaned. "Clay, please don't get involved—not at this time!"

"It's three against three," he told her. "And I wager we're better shots, so don't you worry."

"Maybe we could set up an ambush," John McCullough suggested. "Catch them unaware as soon as they get to town."

"We don't know which way they'll come from," Case Gordon said, "and I don't think we ought to split up."

"They've always come in over the bridge. I think they've got a camp somewhere in Ponil Canyon."

The three men checked their weapons, McCullough with a shotgun and Case and Clay with rifles and their six-shooters. Each made sure he had extra ammunition.

Before leaving, Clay gave Dora a kiss, but her eyes were full of dread.

"Clay, do you have to leave me, now? I'm so afraid!"

He hoped he wasn't doing the wrong thing, with their baby due any moment. "This won't take long." He kissed her again. "I'll be back before you know it!"

The town appeared lifeless in its silence as the three men went quietly to the river bridge. A nearby farm offered good concealment; John McCullough hid at the barn while Case and Clay took places behind a haystack.

They had to bide their time. While waiting in the quietness, Case grinned at Clay. "You look mighty good with that new goatee!"

Clay chuckled. "It was Dora's idea. She thinks it's dignified." He became serious. "Case, I never got a chance to tell you . . . I hope you don't hold a grudge against Dora and me getting married."

"Of course not, why should I?"

"I always thought you had your mind set on Dora. You would've made a better husband."

Case's brown eyes glistened in the morning sunlight. "I admit, I did have a soft spot for Dora. But, you're wrong. With the job I have to do, I'd only bring her grief. I know she's happy, now. Let's just say I came out a loser!"

Finally, in late morning, three riders approached and trotted their horses over the bridge.

John McCullough stepped out in front of them. He raised his shotgun with a shout. "I'm a deputy—throw down your guns and raise your hands, or I'll shoot!"

Davy Crockett only laughed. "Then go ahead and shoot, old man!" He whisked out his gun and fired.

The bullet tore through McCullough's arm and he answered with a blast from his shotgun.

Crockett, hit in the chest, fell back in his saddle, grabbing at the horn.

The other two wheeled their horses around as Case and Clay jumped out from behind the haystack, firing their rifles. Gus Heffron dropped from his horse and Davy Crockett slumped forward, both men dead. The third one, Steve Colbert, made his escape across the bridge.

Clay and Case went quickly to John McCullough who stood holding a bleeding arm.

"How bad is it?" Clay asked.

"Enough to keep me from using a gun for a while!"

"Take him back to the house," Clay said to Case. "I'll go after Steve before he gets too good a start."

"No, Dora's waiting for you. You take John to the house and I'll get Steve."

John McCullough growled at them. "Will you two stop cackling like a couple of wet hens?! Go ahead, both of you. Hell, I can make it back by myself. Doc Colbert can tend to me and we'll both be there with Dora!"

John McCullough, able to ride back to the house, found Dora in the first stages of labor. Ben and Hannah stood vigil at her side.

Ben, wondering if Steve had been killed, asked McCullough, "Did you get them?"

"All but your boy," John told him.

Ben saw his bloody shirt sleeve. "You've been hit. Let me look at that."

"What happened to Clay?" Dora asked through her pain. "Where is he . . . and Case?"

"They went looking for Steve Colbert," her father said while Ben dressed his wound. "But don't worry, if he can't be found, they'll be back before dark."

Long afternoon shadows stretched ominously through the tall swaying pines as Clay and Case checked Ponil Canyon. They soon found where the three outlaws had made camp.

"Maybe Steve's gone north, into Colorado," Clay said.

Case shook his head. "I don't think so. He knows it'd be too easy for us to find him on the trail. I have a hunch he'll hide out till we get tired of looking."

"Where could he hide around here?"

"E-Town's deserted, now. It's as good a place as any!"

Elizabethtown had become a ghost town with nothing but a scattering of empty, buildings drying in the hot morning sun; shells that once echoed with the lusty voices of miners, tradesmen and prostitutes.

Clay and Case rode cautiously to the edge of town and reined to a stop. Before them, the large town hall of sculptured stone loomed on a higher slope like a skeleton guarding the dead. Clay remembered a woman's beautiful voice echoing from its perfectly-arched windows that glowed with the light of a hundred kerosene lamps. Now, buzzards roosted on the gaping black openings like harbingers of death.

"That's a perfect hiding place," Case said. However, there was no sign of life. "If he's in there, he's got his horse out of sight."

Clay studied the two-story building's once-proud facade. "I'd guess he's seen us ride up, but he can't guard both ends at the same time. You sneak around back, Case, then I'll draw his fire. While I keep him occupied, maybe you can get him from the rear!"

They tied their horses at a vacant weathered saloon near the town hall. Clay stayed hidden while Case eased his way past a building, keeping out of view. A gust of wind broke the ghostly silence, whispering through streets now overgrown with dry grass. Somewhere a door creaked mournfully on rusted hinges.

Case reached a spot directly behind the hall and saw Clay step out of his hiding place, just long enough to be seen. *Putting his life on the line*, Case thought.

A shot rang out and birds flew shrieking from the windows. Clay jumped to another area for cover as a second bullet kicked the dust behind him.

With Steve obviously standing at one of the big front windows, trying to get a bead on Clay, Case rushed to the back door and stepped inside. He found Steve's horse waiting beside a dark stairway that led to the upper floor.

A third shot broke the dead air, but this time it was Clay's gun—bits of stone sprayed from the upstairs window.

Case drew his forty-five and crept up the stairway. Almost at the top, a loose board thumped beneath his foot and he caught his breath. Hearing no sounds of footsteps above, he continued slowly upward until his eyes were just above floor level.

The upstairs banister had been torn away and he gripped the opening to pull himself up, easing his gun barrel over the edge. No one stood at the large open windows and he knew in an instant that his rear was unprotected. An explosion shattered the air and he gasped as a bullet tore through his back and out his chest. The gun dropped from his hand, clunking down the stairwell. He held on to the floor's edge to keep from falling and looked up through bleary eyes.

Steve Colbert glared down, a smoking pistol aimed at Case's head. "This'll take care of one of you!" he snarled and pulled the trigger. It only clicked—he'd used his last bullet. With a curse, he stomped a heavy boot on Case's fingers.

Case uttered a groan and tumbled down the stairway to fall on his back at the rear door. Each breath burned like fire and he choked on blood flowing into his mouth. Through glazed eyes he saw Steve

Colbert step over him, jump onto the horse and ride out the doorway. Then a quick darkness fell.

Case didn't know how long he'd been out, but opened his eyes again to see Clay staring down with an ashen face.

Case spit out blood to talk. "Did you get 'im?"

"I let 'im go when I found you . . . where'd he shoot you?"

"In the back . . . guess I came out a loser again."

"Never mind that, I'm gettin' you back to town!"

"It's no good, Clay—I can't ride."

"You'll ride with me!"

Clay put an arm under Case's shoulders and gently raised him to his feet. Case coughed up more blood as Clay helped him down the slope to their horses.

In order to get Case into the saddle, Clay had to move Ebon to a lower part of ground. Case put a weak hand on the saddle horn to keep from falling and Clay jumped quickly behind. He wrapped an arm around his friend.

"Just hold on, Case. Doc Colbert will fix you up!"

He nudged Ebon forward and they started slowly back to Cimarron. Case slumped forward and Clay held him closer, trying to remember the last time he'd said a prayer.

Darkness had settled as they finally trotted up to the McCullough house, but Clay knew for the last few miles he'd been holding a dead man.

The once-elegant stone town hall at Elizabethtown, NM. Photo taken in November, 1967, by Richard A. Gray. Much less of the edifice remains today, since it is fast deteriorating.

*Courtesy Museum of New Mexico, Neg. 5328*

# Chapter Thirty-Eight

"*C*ome see your daughter," Hannah told Clay softly.

Ben Colbert and John McCullough had taken Case Gordon's body to the front room and placed it onto a couch. Clay's mind seemed numb with remorse as he followed Hannah to the bedroom where Dora lay holding a small bundle.

"Thank God, you're all right!" she told him in a weak voice. "What about Case?"

"I had to bring him back with me, on Ebon . . . he's dead."

She bit a finger, but it didn't stop a sob of grief.

Clay sat down beside the bed. He wiped a tear from her cheek. "What about you?"

She choked back her sadness. "Ben did a fine job. He helped bring us a little girl." Her forehead wrinkled. "But Ben says her right foot is twisted. He might be able to fix it when she's older." She opened a blanket at her side.

Clay looked down. The sight of his daughter's small, red face washed the dark clouds from his mind. He relaxed and gently took

251

hold of the baby's tiny fingers. "What are we going to call her?"

Dora gave a chagrined smile. "I thought of calling her Patti. While I was carrying her, sometimes I could hear the patter of her little heart. Is that all right with you?"

"Anything you want, honey." He bent to kiss her forehead.

Hannah stayed with Dora at the house while most of the town assembled in the graveyard for Case Gordon's funeral.

On the way back to the house, Clay, Ben Colbert and John McCullough walked together in a somber mood.

"Too bad the way things turned out," Ben said, "but I'm just glad Steve didn't get you, too. With him still at large, though, you're going to have to watch out for yourself, Clay."

"Don't worry, Doc. He likes to shoot men in the back, but I won't give him that chance!"

"What are your plans, now, Clay?" McCullough asked. "You and Dora plan to stay in Cimarron?"

Clay shrugged. "I feel the same way my brother, John, did. I've had it with this part of the country—I wanna get away as soon as I can!"

"You got another place in mind?"

"Back in Texas, if I have the money."

"I might have an answer for you," McCullough told him. "A while back, Case Gordon acquired some land down south, just across the line, in Pecos, Texas. He told me he was holding it in case he ever got married." He chuckled. "I kind of think he had Dora in mind, but of course, you beat him to it. I guess he gave up the notion of ever using that land because he put it in both my name and his, so it'd be mine if anything ever happened to him." He gave Clay a warm smile. "I think Case would be real proud to let you and Dora have it. Sort of like a wedding present."

The gnawing agony swelled in Clay's heart. Case Gordon had saved his neck more than once, and now he seemed to be reaching from the grave to do one more favor.

"I don't know," Clay said. "Let's talk it over with Dora."

With tears of love and gratitude, Dora agreed to accept Case Gordon's land. "You do what you think is best," she told Clay. "Patti and I will follow, wherever you go."

Her father said with concern, "Let's not be too hasty, Dora." He turned to Clay. "There's a house and windmill on that property, but the place hasn't been lived in for years—you know it'll need a heap of fixin' up. Maybe Dora and the baby oughta wait here while you go down there and be sure it's all right for them to follow. Just let us know and I'll bring them down to Pecos for you."

John McCullough signed the papers over to Clay so he could get started as soon as possible and Clay found it difficult saying goodbye to old friends once again.

Ben Colbert tried to brighten the situation. "Don't think you two are getting away completely! Hannah and I are thinking about moving down to Las Vegas—we'll be a little closer, anyway!"

"Wonderful!" Dora said. "Then you can help again when Clay and I have another baby!"

Clay blushed. "Dora, remember what they say about not countin' your chickens!"

Before leaving Cimarron, Clay spoke with Ben privately.

"Doc, I want you to do something for me." He drew some money from his pocket and put it into Ben's hand. "I want Case Gordon to have a decent marker on his grave. Could you see to it for me?"

Ben's eyes grew soft. "Of course, Clay. But I'd have done it, anyway. We all loved Case Gordon!"

As Clay rode south out of Cimarron, he thought of the time he'd left the Tennessee valley so many years ago. Both places had given him love and happiness in the beginning, but fate had a mean way of turning it all sour in the end. Maybe after Dora and the baby joined him in Pecos, Texas, he could rebuild that peaceful world again. This time, however, he was determined to hold on to that happiness, no matter what fate had to say about it.

# Chapter Thirty-Nine

*C*lay reined Ebon to a stop on his newly-acquired land and regarded it with grim eyes. John McCullough wasn't talking through his hat—the place needed a heap of fixing up, all right.

The large house had four rooms and seemed in good shape to have been unoccupied for so long. However, the roof needed work and mounds of dust would have to be cleaned out.

He walked over to the windmill and saw that it, too, had to be put back into running order. A small barn looked to be serviceable, but he noted with discouragement that he'd have to construct a corral from scratch.

Just beyond the barn he saw a horse and buggy kicking up dust as it moved toward him on the road. A man and woman sat on the hard seat, shading their eyes with expectancy and the man pulled his vehicle to a stop in front of Clay.

"Good mornin'," the stranger said. "Do I have the pleasure of addressin' Mr. Clay Allison?"

"That you do," Clay answered with curiosity.

"The land office in town said you'd taken over this parcel." The man got down and put out his hand. "We're your neighbors, Earl and Mary Crump.

Clay took Crump's hand in a shake and guessed the two must be about his own age. However, their leathery faces showed the scars of battle from years of fighting a stubborn land.

Mary Crump peered out of a sunbonnet, which she held down against a sudden breeze. "We've been watchin' for you, Mr. Allison. Saw you ride by our place and just had to come over and say 'Howdy!'"

Her husband added, "You prob'ly saw our little farm when you rode in, two miles back." He waved his arm to the north.

Clay couldn't help smiling at their friendliness. "Well, I'm glad to see I've got neighbors," he said. "What kind of farming do you do?"

"Oh, it ain't much, with just the two of us," Earl said. "We sell some corn, tomatoes and melons to the town store. Gets us by comfortable-like. What you plannin' to do with this here land of yours, Clay?"

"I'm gonna buy some cattle later on and start up a ranch."

Earl looked around. "Looks like you got your work cut out, but reckon it could be worse."

Mary took off the sunbonnet and stringy dark hair fell around her shoulders, giving a smoothness to the tiny wrinkles on her cheeks. "Would you be havin' a family comin' with you, Mr. Allison?" she asked.

Clay caught a hopeful longing in her voice. "My wife Dora and daughter Patti are coming down as soon as I can get this place fit to live in."

Mary's face glowed as if another log had been put on the fire. "My, that's good news! The only people I ever get to see is when we go into town."

"Well, I want you to know," Earl said, "we're here to help. That's what neighbors are for!"

"Till you get your place liveable," Mary put in, "you're welcome to stay at our place."

"That's a mighty kind offer," Clay told them, "but I'd like to get an early start on this fix-up. I can sleep here in my blanket."

Earl looked at the lowering sun. "I know how you feel. But I ain't so busy I can't give you a hand. I'll come by tomorrow mornin' and help you get started. I got all kinds of tools you're gonna need."

"Oh," Mary exclaimed, "I nearly forgot!" She reached behind her in the wagon and brought forth a basket. "Here's some fried chicken —you might want to have it for your supper." She handed it down to Clay.

"Well, thank you, ma'am, that's real thoughtful. I can sure use it!"

"I'll come along with Earl tomorrow and bring some vittles. With all the work you've got ahead, you'll need somethin' to stick to your ribs!"

Earl Crump climbed back into the buggy and they drove off with a wave, disappearing back up the road in a swirl of Texas dust.

The Crumps hadn't spoken lightly, Clay discovered the next morning. He'd just washed his face at the house pump when they rattled up in the buggy, which was filled with all kinds of implements. Earl produced a ladder and a wooden box containing hammer, saw, nails and other necessities while Mary climbed out armed with a broom, water pail, soap and various cleaning aids.

While Mary went to work ridding the house of dust, Clay and Earl started patching the roof. After devouring a simple but satisfying noon meal, which Mary had prepared in the cleaned-out fireplace, the men next went to work on the corral and windmill.

Earl Crump turned out to be a God-send. However Clay wished the Good Lord could have slowed down the man's tongue just a bit. Crump never let up, even while sawing wood. By the end of the day, Clay had heard the man's complete history of coming to New Mexico and struggling with a hostile land.

It seemed a miracle. Within only a week, the house and barn were in good shape and the windmill was pumping fresh clear water. Clay rode into town and sent a letter to Dora to have her father bring her and Patti down as soon as possible. He then purchased the essential bed, table and chairs and had them sent out to the house. Now, he could hardly wait for his family's arrival.

# Chapter Forty

"*O*h, Clay," Dora cried, "we mustn't ever be apart again for such a long time—I thought I'd die without you!"

It had been a long trip for Dora, her father and little Patti, but they stopped in the large city of Las Vegas and other smaller places along the way, which broke the monotony. Now, Dora was back with her husband again and she warmed in Clay's loving embrace while John McCullough took the bags inside.

"The house is beautiful, Clay," Dora breathed, holding Patti in her arms.

"Come on, let me show you the rest of it." Clay put an arm around Dora's waist and led her into their new home.

Dora walked with delight from room to room. "I didn't know you had it in you, Clay—you've done wonders!"

He looked down, embarrassed. "Well, I can't take all the credit. Our neighbor lady Mary Crump did most of it."

"I was so happy when you told me we had neighbors. I thought I'd be stuck alone out here. I'm dying to meet them!"

"Don't be surprised if they show up any minute—I know they must've seen you and your father drive in."

Sure enough, the Crumps arrived in their wagon a short time later, Mary toting a basket of baked goods. Clay showed them in and made introductions.

"Land sakes!" Mary Crump said. "I'm so glad to see somebody else livin' out here." She beamed at the baby in Dora's arms. "And this must be your little girl—just what's your name, little one?"

"Her name's Patti," Dora said.

Mary gave Patti a delicate kiss on the forehead. "Well, you're ever' bit as pretty as your mother, Patti!"

"Do you have children?" Dora asked.

Mary's happy face showed a hint of sadness. "After we lost our first two, I found I couldn't have any more. A blessing, I suppose. Raising children in this harsh land takes a lot out of a woman!" She realized how her words might have been taken. "Oh, but you're young, Dora. You needn't worry, especially with me and Earl around!"

Dora's heart ached when her father prepared to drive back to Cimarron. She gave him a loving hug before he climbed into the buggy.

John McCullough reached down to shake Clay's hand. "You've got a real nice place, Clay. I won't have to worry about Dora, now. When do you think you'll get your herd of cattle?"

"I'm goin' up to the Panhandle soon as I can and buy a few head. I already wrote Wes and Jim Calley to join me, and they're rarin' to go!"

Clay put an arm around Dora and they watched as her father disappeared down the road on his way to Cimarron.

# Chapter Forty-One

$\mathcal{H}$annah put on her new spectacles and muttered with irritation. Ben had chided her since their move to Las Vegas to see an eye doctor in the city, and she finally agreed. Now, although the glasses were a nuisance, she could at least read in comfort, especially the letter that Ben had just brought home. It was from Dora Allison.

Hannah tore open the envelope and read the letter with increasing delight. "Dora's expecting again!" she cried. "She wants us to be there so you can help with the delivery!"

Ben's eyes lit up behind his own spectacles. "Well, well—just when is this happy event going to take place?"

"It won't be for several months. Clay's up in Texas, now, getting his first herd of cattle. He's coming back with the Calley brothers next month . . . but here, you can read about it." She handed him the first page.

Ben settled carefully into a big chair, silently cursing the increasing pains that always rode on the wings of age. He began to read the letter and thought how much faster things happen as one gets older. It seemed only yesterday, that John McCullough had taken Dora and the baby to join Clay at their Pecos, Texas, home.

Hannah finished the second page with excitement. "And they're coming here to Las Vegas when Clay gets back! Clay wants you to do something about Patti's foot."

Ben took the next page and continued reading, but with a pang of futility. The world seemed to be racing ahead with no regard for the poor humans struggling to hold on and he knew it was about time he retired from medical practice for good. He wondered if he'd be able to do anything with little Patti Allison's foot.

# Chapter Forty-Two

*P*atti Allison played in the dirt under a bright south Texas sun while her mother pinned sheets on the clothesline. Mary Crump had come over to help with the washing and stood beside a large tub, stirring clothes in the hot wash water.

"Thank goodness for neighbors!" Dora said. "It certainly would've been lonesome here without Clay, if it weren't for you and Earl."

"Well, it works two ways," Mary said. "You bein' here has brightened up our lives, as well!" She wrung out some wet underwear and handed it to Dora.

Dora pinned it beside the sheet and wiped her forehead. "I'm so anxious to see Clay again. I just pray every night that he'll come back safe." Suddenly, the ground began to shake and her eyes widened.

With a distant roar of plodding hoofs, the silhouetted herd of cattle appeared on the horizon and the two women looked in wonder.

"Patti, your Daddy's back!" Dora cried and quickly tied back her stringy hair; she couldn't let Clay see her like this after being away so long!

In a moment, Clay rode up, heavy with trail dust. He jumped down from Ebon and picked up little Patti in his arms, then gave his wife a kiss. He wiped a smudge from her cheek. "Sorry I messed up your face!" he apologized.

"I want it on me, it's part of you!" Dora's eyes filled with joyful tears as she kissed him again. "Oh, Clay, I'm so glad you're back—did you see Daddy when you stopped in Cimarron?"

"Yes, and he sends you his love." He turned to Mary Crump. Howdy, Mary. Glad to see you've taken such good care of my wife for me!"

Mary Crump had been watching with admiring eyes. "Dora was just sayin' she prayed every night you'd come home safe—and now you did!" She walked over and gave Clay a quick welcome embrace.

Dora looked at the cattle being calmed down to graze. "Is that Wes and Jim?" Then she saw their familiar faces and waved. They paused in their work to yahoo and whirl their hats overhead.

"Hope you've got extra food on hand," Clay said. "Me and the Calleys sure got some empty stomachs right now!"

"Why you all must be starved!" Mary exclaimed. "Come on, Dora, let's get started—by the time them other two come in, we'll have a big welcome home dinner!"

Earl Crump had seen all the activity and knew Clay was back home. He jumped into his buggy and appeared at the Allison ranch in time to sit down with everyone at the large table.

Mary Crump's face shone with excitement. "I don't think there's ever been an occasion like this in these parts. Clay, this is your house, why don't you say Grace before we start?"

Earl cut in. "Clay, I recall you sayin' even though your daddy was a preacher, you never was one to be very religious. With your kind permission, I'd be pleased to say the Grace."

Clay nodded with chagrin. Dora stifled a giggle and everyone bowed their heads.

Earl Crump raised a stentorian voice in prayer. "Lord, we thank you for all the good things you've allowed us to have, especially for us neighbors to be such good friends. We ask that you keep your good hand over Clay and Dora's heads, helping them and Patti to make a go of this here place. Amen."

"I haven't been this happy in a long time!" Dora said as they began passing the plates. "It's like having my family back again!"

Wes looked pleased, also. "Well, Jim and me never thought we'd have our own house! We gotta thank you, Clay, for buildin' it for us."

With Earl Crump's help, Clay had constructed a small two-room home for the Calley brothers next to the main house before he left to buy cattle.

"I thought it was the safe thing to do," he told them. "If we all had to live under one roof, it wouldn't be two days before we'd be chasin' each other with pitchforks!"

The men had put in a long day, so the Crumps said an early goodnight and returned to their farm. The Calleys went to their little house and Clay crawled into bed before Dora got on her nightgown.

She checked to see that Patti was asleep in her small cot, then extinguished the lamp and snuggled next to Clay under the warm comforter.

"It's like a new beginning, isn't it, Clay?" she murmured.

He yawned and kissed her cheek.

She realized her own exhaustion and breathed a tired sigh. "While you were in Cimarron, did you see anybody else we knew, besides Daddy?"

After a long silence, she thought maybe he'd already dozed off. But Clay's mind had gone back to that gray afternoon in Cimarron. There were lots of clouds and it was probably raining or snowing in the Sangre de Cristos. He had to remember where the grave was, but found it with little trouble. He thought it would be prettier; however, it was quiet and kept up. The new gravestone was nothing fancy, but it had his name, the year he was born and the year he died: *CASEY GORDON, 1845 - 1883.* What a waste!

"No," Clay finally answered Dora's question. "I didn't see anybody else."

"Clay, now that you're back, when do you think we ought to take Patti to see Ben Colbert?"

He mulled the situation. "Well, Las Vegas isn't too far. We'll take her up there soon as we get those steers settled."

They were too tired to do any more than just hold each other; but there would be many nights ahead. She closed her eyes in satisfaction. Just their being together again was enough.

# Chapter Forty-Three

$B$y the time things were going well enough at the ranch for Clay and Dora to take Patti to Las Vegas, Dora had reached the seventh month with their next child.

"I still don't think it's a good idea takin' you on a trip when you're like this," Clay said.

"But if we wait till the baby comes, who knows when we'll be able to take Patti to see Ben Colbert?"

"He's plannin' on bein' here for the next birth. He could look at Patti then."

"But if she needs treatment, she'll have to be there." Dora laughed. "Now, don't worry, I have plenty of time left. Why, we could even go back east if necessary!"

"I hope we don't have to go that far," Clay said. "I'll go see if Wes and Jim can keep things runnin' without me for a few days.

They drove the buggy into bustling Las Vegas, New Mexico, and Dora felt even more satisfied with her little house on the Texas prairie, far from the noise and problems of a big city. She and her father had stopped in Las Vegas on their way to Pecos, Texas, and it still seemed as if she were entering a canyon. On each side of the street, buildings towered in Italian brick-and-stone architecture with large windows, cast iron columns and pressed sheet metal ornamentation around the tops.

Clay guided the wagon past rumbling wagons full of everything a growing metropolis needed to survive until they finally came to the plaza, the hub of town with streets radiating outward like spokes of a giant wheel. A low, white picket fence enclosed the center, all covered with cool green grass.

"Oh, there it is!" Dora said. She spotted the address Ben and Hannah had written in their last letter.

A modest sign on the front of a building read, DOCTOR BENSON COLBERT - GENERAL PRACTITIONER.

Ben greeted them warmly as they entered the small office.

"Ben, it's so good to see you!" Dora said, giving the kindly man a loving hug.

He looked at her rounded waist. "Are you having any problems with the new one?"

"None at all. You'll still come down before it's due, won't you?"

He chuckled. "Of course—that's all Hannah talks about! And she can't wait to see you. You are staying with us, aren't you?"

Clay shook the doctor's hand. "We've already made arrangements, Ben."

"We're staying at that beautiful new Plaza Hotel across the street," Dora said.

"But you must have supper with us at the house. Hannah is expecting you!" Ben looked down at Patti who had limped in alongside her mother. "And how is this big girl? The last time I saw you, you were just a little baby!"

"We really hope you can do something with her foot," Clay told him.

"Well, let's just take a look at this little foot." Ben lifted Patti onto a high-built chair and removed the shoe and stocking, then turned the ankle gently and felt all the bones. His forehead wrinkled. "If only we had the magic of looking through the skin to see what's wrong with these bones. The only real way of finding out is to open it up."

"I was afraid you'd have to operate," Dora said.

Ben looked up with reluctance. "I wouldn't do such a procedure unless I was sure about it."

"But you operated on my foot," Clay said.

"That was an emergency and a gunshot wound." He smiled with assurance. "I really believe it would be better if you could take Patti to specialists in Denver or, if necessary, as far as New York."

Clay's face turned to disappointment. "So there's nothing you can do for her?"

"I hate that you made the trip up here for nothing, but I wouldn't want to take a chance and fail. Especially with such good friends as you! Why don't you let me find the right surgeon. It may take a few weeks, but I'll write as soon as I hit on the best one."

Clay seemed determined. "Please do, Ben. I don't care how much it costs, I want Patti to run and play just like other children!"

The Allisons checked into the Plaza Hotel and that evening, Ben picked them up in his buggy for the short ride to his house at the edge of town.

Hannah met them with happy tears. "I was afraid we'd never see each other again!" she said. "You two haven't aged a bit—and just look at me, now, with spectacles already!"

After a delicious meal, Dora and Hannah sat with little Patti, chatting about Cimarron, while Ben and Clay stepped outside.

"I hate to bring up an unpleasant subject," Ben said as they stood on the porch. "It's about Steve."

Clay had almost forgotten about the boy. "Have you seen him?"

"No, but I heard from that new sheriff in Cimarron, Mace Bowman, that Steve was seen last week at Wagon Mound. That's just north of here, you know."

"You reckon he'll get down this way—maybe look you up?"

Ben gave a scornful laugh. "Steve doesn't ever want to see me again. It's you I'm worried about. If he's still roaming around this part of New Mexico, it's likely he'll find out where you are."

Clay gave him a grim smile. "Don't worry, Ben. I told you before, I won't give him a chance to shoot me in the back!"

The next morning, Dora finished dressing in their upstairs Plaza Hotel room and Clay drove his buggy around front for their bags to be loaded.

Across the street, the circular plaza buzzed with children playing on the neatly-trimmed grass while men and women chatted on white-painted benches.

One young man with freckles, auburn hair and a short red beard, watched with interest as Clay helped Dora into the buggy and then drive away.

The man went quickly to the hotel registration desk. "I believe I just saw two good friends checking out," he told the clerk. I haven't seen them in years. Were they by chance the Allisons . . . Clay Allison?"

"Why, yes, they were," the clerk replied. "You just missed them. They're on their way home."

"That's too bad. I'd like to see them again, but I don't know where they're living, now."

The clerk looked at his book. "They signed in as being from Pecos, Texas."

Steve Colbert's face turned to an eerie smile. "Thanks. You've done me a big favor!"

# Chapter Forty-Four

"*H*ere's your mail," Wes Calley said to Dora and climbed down from the wagon. "I'll put your supplies in the kitchen."

"Thank you, Wes!" She took the few envelopes with anticipation. It was always exciting to get mail from town, and today even more so. One of the letters was from Ben and Hannah Colbert. She opened it with eager fingers and began to read as Clay rode up for a drink at the water pump.

"Clay," she said with dancing eyes, "Ben and Hannah are coming next week! I was afraid they wouldn't get here in time for the baby!" Then she frowned. "My goodness, I've got to start getting the house in shape!"

Clay finished his drink and put the dipper back on its hook. "Now, calm down honey, that house is always neat as a pin."

His words passed over her head as she looked back at the kitchen where Wes had placed sacks of flour and sugar. "I wish I had known before Wes went into town. Now, we'll have to get a few more things before the Colberts arrive!"

Clay shook his head with stubbornness. "I'm not going to make Wes go back to town. Let's wait till Ben and Hannah get here. If we need anything, I'll go get it for you."

With her baby due very soon, it didn't prevent Dora from bustling around the house, making sure the extra bedroom was fit for company.

At last, the washing had been done with a closet full of clean ironed sheets, just in time as Ben and Hannah pulled up in their buggy.

Dora ran to greet them. "I hope you didn't have any trouble finding the place!" She embraced first Hannah, then Ben.

"Somebody in town said to just follow this road out," Ben told her. "It was easy."

After they had gone inside, Ben gave Dora a quick appraisal. "Looks like you've been taking good care of yourself, young lady. This next one should be a snap!"

Patti came in from her bedroom, the little girl walking with difficulty. Ben put out his arms and she went to him for a welcome hug.

"Well, my girl Patti just gets bigger each time I see her!" He set the child on his knee and examined her foot. "Dora, when do you plan to see that specialist I wrote you about?"

Dora moved a frustrated hand across her brow. "I hate to keep putting it off. I wanted to go to Denver right after we got your letter, but Clay won't take us till after the baby arrives. Said it'd be too hard on me."

"And he won't take Patti without you?"

"He insists on being here when I have my baby. I think he still feels guilty because he wasn't with me the last time, at Cimarron!"

Hannah insisted on helping Dora prepare supper and they put an extra leaf in the table so Wes and Jim Calley could join them.

Late in the evening, after the Calleys had retired to their little house, Dora made sure the Colberts were comfortable.

"Clay likes to get up early," she told them. "But don't let that disturb you. Sleep as late as you want!"

Clay had already slipped between the sheets when she came to the bedroom. He watched with amusement as she pulled a nightgown over her large body. "If we keep having babies, maybe we ought to lay in a supply of bigger nightgowns!" he joked.

She climbed into bed and gave him a playful swat. "Easy for you to poke fun—you men don't have to go through all this!" She snuggled beside him and closed her weary eyes.

He put a gentle hand on her rounded stomach. "Have you decided on a name yet?"

"Yes, as a matter of fact. I think you should have a Junior. We'll call him Clay Allison, Junior."

He chuckled in surprise. "What makes you so sure it'll be a boy?"

"Well, if it's a girl, we'll call her Clay Pearl Allison!"

He lay back on the pillow with a satisfied smile. "If you think you can put up with two Clays in this household!"

She turned to kiss his cheek. "I'm so happy you've settled down and we have a real home."

"I couldn't have done it without you." He touched his lips to hers. "I'm really grateful, Dora. If it weren't for you, I'd have gone to hell for sure. It's like you saved my life. I want you to know, I'll always love you . . . no matter what happens."

She put her arms around him and pulled his warm body close. She was glad he couldn't see her face in the darkness. A happy little tear had found its way to her cheek.

# Chapter Forty-Five

*B*en had expressed a desire to see the Allison ranch, so the next afternoon Clay took him in the buggy on an extended tour. They returned to the house just as Dora and Hannah finished baking several loaves of bread.

Dora stepped out onto the porch. "We're almost out of coffee and a few other things we'll need for tomorrow morning," she said to Clay. "Do you think one of the boys could go into town?"

"They're busy with the new heifers," he said. "I'll go, but I want to be sure this'll do it for a spell!"

Dora already had a list of supplies and gave it to him. "I hate for you to go when it's so late," she worried. "It'll be dark by the time you start home, so be careful!"

Clay took her in his arms for a lingering goodbye kiss, then climbed into the wagon. She watched with concern as he rode away in the long dark shadows spreading across the ranch.

Pecos, being a small town, had only one store with a good flow of business and the owner stayed open as long as they kept coming.

"Reckon you're my last customer," the store keeper said. I was just about to close up."

"My wife will be mighty pleased I caught you in time!" Clay told him.

Clay helped the owner load supplies into the wagon, then paid the man and said goodnight. Kerosene lights began to flicker behind curtained windows as Clay rode out of town and onto the dark road leading to the ranch. He had never driven the road at night, but knew the way like the back of his hand.

Soon, hoofbeats sounded behind him and he pulled the mule to a stop. However, the night prairie lay quiet with only the ghostly shapes of cacti and sagebrush on the horizon. Clay shrugged—probably another wagon pulling onto the road a mile or two back.

He urged the mule forward and the wagon started with a jerk, rolling a keg of molasses at his feet. Clay bent down quickly to keep it from falling out of the buggy—Dora would have a fit if she didn't have molasses to put on her morning biscuits. He heard hoofbeats again and started to sit up, but a heavy blow to the back of his head sent him sprawling face down.

The Colberts had already gone to bed, but Dora paced the floor. Clay should have returned from town at least an hour ago. She went out to the Calley's little house and knocked on the door. "Wes, are you and Jim in bed yet?"

Wes came to the door, embarrassed; he had quickly pulled a pair of pants over his long johns. "Is somethin' wrong, Dora?"

"Clay hasn't come back from town and it's past bed time—do you think somebody ought to go looking for him?"

Wes rubbed his chin. "I wouldn't worry, Dora, but if it makes you feel better, I'll saddle up and take a ride back."

Dora returned to the house and waited anxiously until, at last, she heard the sound of wagon wheels. She clutched the robe around her neck and rushed outside.

The wagon had just pulled up with Wes the only one in the driver's seat. His horse stood tethered behind.

Fear stabbed at Dora's heart. "Wes, why are you driving Clay's wagon? What's happened?"

Wes took off his hat, a tragic look in his eyes. "I found Clay, Dora." He nodded to the back of the wagon. "I got him there. He was half way back, layin' in the road. Looks like he fell outta the wagon and the wheels ran over his neck!"

"Clay!" Dora screamed and clutched the sideboard to look over at Clay's figure lying in the dark wagon bed.

Jim Calley came out, buttoning his shirt, and the Colberts appeared in their robes.

"What is it, Dora?" Hannah called. "What's happened?"

"Clay's been hurt!" Dora sobbed.

Jim looked into the wagon and frowned. "Let's get 'im inside, Wes."

They all followed as Wes and Jim toted Clay into the house and laid him gently onto the bed. Dora took Clay's hand and looked at the lifeless face while Ben forced one of Clay's eyelids open, then bent to put an ear to his chest.

"Is he all right, Ben," Dora sobbed. "What is it?"

Ben examined a nasty wound on Clay's head and the misshapen bruised neck. He looked up sadly.

"His neck's broken, Dora . . . Clay's dead!"

# Chapter Forty-Six

*H*annah asked Wes to drive over to the Crumps and notify Earl and Mary of the tragic event. They came back with Wes and everyone sat up with a grief-stricken Dora through the terrible night.

The next morning Ben rode with Wes Calley, taking Clay's body into town. It was necessary to report the death and also make the funeral arrangements. They left the body with an undertaker and went to the sheriff's office.

"You sure there wasn't any foul play?" the Pecos sheriff asked.

Ben couldn't answer the question with complete satisfaction, wondering how Clay's neck could be under the wagon's wheels when he fell. "Wes Calley found the body," he said. "Let him tell you what he saw."

Wes cleared his throat, reluctant to talk about such a tragic event. "Dora Allison asked me to ride up the road to see if anything had happened to her husband. It was at night and real dark. I rode 'bout half way to town when I saw Clay's wagon standin' in the road, but there wasn't anybody in it and the mule was still hitched. A few yards behind it, I saw a man layin' real still and figured it must be pore ol' Clay."

Ben and the sheriff waited patiently while Wes cleared his throat to continue.

"When I got down and looked, I found out it *was* Clay Allison—his head was twisted, kinda awful-like. I figured he must've fell out of the wagon and the wheels ran over 'im. Well, I put Clay in the wagon and took 'im back to his ranch, with my horse hitched behind."

The sheriff mulled Wes' account and turned to Ben. "And what was your conclusion, Doctor, after you examined the body?"

"Although there was a head wound, the cause of death was due to a heavy object crushing the deceased's neck."

"By a wagon wheel?"

"The wheel of a heavy wagon could do such a thing if it rolled over a man's neck."

The sheriff looked bemused. "Sounds like you you're hedgin', Doctor."

Ben frowned in irritation. "No one saw it happen, so no one can say with certainty how it happened. I am telling you only what I have concluded from my examination."

The sheriff thought a moment. "I've known Clay Allison ever since he came to Pecos. He never seemed like the kind of man who'd just fall out of a wagon." He gave Ben Colbert a hard look. "Clay Allison had a bad reputation all over this part of the west. Killed several men. They say he not only loved his six-shooter, but he had a taste for good whiskey, as well. Do you think, Doctor, that he might've tied on a few in town and been pretty well greased on his way home last night?"

Ben firmed his jaw. "His wife can attest to the fact that Clay Allison hadn't touched liquor since the day they married. I examined him only minutes after his untimely death and there was no indication that he had been near liquor."

The sheriff's eyebrow raised slightly in question.

"Look, Sheriff," Ben said, "I've known Clay Allison since before he left Tennessee. When he came out west he wasn't looking for trouble. Trouble just seemed to find him. He didn't kill all those men people would like to believe. But when he did kill, he was forced to do it."

"So you think he was on the straight and narrow?"

"Yes. But few others thought so. He married a devoted woman who was helping him erase a bad name, and he was succeeding. Until last night, unfortunately."

"Well, with his reputation, I'll wager folks'll still say that Clay Allison had to be mighty drunk, else why would he fall out of a wagon?"

Ben shrugged. "That's something I can't do anything about."

The sheriff heaved a final sigh. "All right, now, I've got to see the body before the undertaker starts working on it. Will you two gentlemen please come with me?"

They stepped out of the sheriff's office, but froze at the roar of two gunshots from a saloon across the street. The sheriff instinctively drew his gun as a bartender ran out of the saloon.

"Sheriff!" the man yelled. "Two men have just shot each other!"

The sheriff glanced at Ben. "Better come with me, Doc, in case somebody needs medical attention."

Ben and Wes followed him across the street.

The bartender explained, "They were playing poker and one accused the other one of cheating. They both pulled their guns and fired at the same time!"

The men entered the shadowy saloon to find a small group of customers looking down with curiosity at two bodies lying beside a poker table.

Ben knelt down to examine the first victim. "This one's dead," he told the sheriff. "A bullet through the head."

Someone said, "This one over here's still breathin'!"

Ben moved quickly to the other man. His heart skipped a beat on seeing the freckled face of Steve Colbert. Ben dropped to one knee and studied a nasty bullet wound in the heart area. He took Steve's wrist The pulse was weak.

Steve looked up through hazy eyes. "You never did help me, Pa, and you can't now."

Ben's throat tightened; he couldn't remember the last time Steve had called him "Pa." But only seconds remained and, after all these years, it was time for the truth.

"Steve, there's something I should have told you a long time ago. I'm not your Pa—Chunk Colbert was your real father!"

Steve blinked. "The hell you say!"

"When you were born, Chunk didn't want you, so I raised you."

Steve's mouth formed a weak smile. "I should've figgered that. The biggest difference between you and Chunk . . . he had a rock for a heart!" Steve closed his eyes and whispered, "At least I know Clay Allison got his, for killin' my real Pa!"

Ben flinched. "Are you saying you killed Clay Allison?"

There was no answer. Steve's mouth suddenly filled with blood and Ben turned the boy's head, but too late. Ben checked the pulse again and slowly got to his feet. "This one's dead, too, Sheriff!"

"I couldn't make out what he said, Doc. Did he tell you who he was?"

"He was my brother's son, Steve Colbert."

The sheriff's jaw dropped in surprise. "Your nephew?! I'm sorry about that, Doc. But I guess you know they've been looking for Steve Colbert up north in New Mexico."

Ben removed his glasses and wiped them with a handkerchief. "Well, they can all relax, now. But there's another matter. Steve Colbert swore some time ago he would kill Clay Allison—I think he accomplished that last night, Sheriff."

"Did he say that?"

"No. But only a few of us knew Clay Allison was dead, and Steve just told me he was glad about it. It wasn't coincidence, Sheriff, that Steve Colbert and Clay Allison were in the same place at the same time."

The sheriff shook his head. "But if Steve Colbert wanted to kill Clay Allison, why didn't he just shoot him? Why run a wagon wheel over him instead?"

Ben had been putting the pieces together. "Steve hated Clay for killing my brother Chunk. I believe Steve wanted to hurt Clay as much as he could . . . even to the point of ruining his name after he was dead."

The sheriff looked puzzled. "By rolling a wagon wheel over his neck?"

"When I examined Clay's body, I also found a serious head injury. I don't think it was because he fell out of the wagon. My hunch is that Steve followed Clay out of town last night, surprised him and hit him over the head before Clay could use the shotgun he always carried in the wagon. Then Steve dragged Clay out of the wagon, placed him on the ground, and ran the wheel over his neck. Steve must have thought that when Clay was found, it would be assumed he was so drunk he fell out of the wagon!"

The sheriff shook his head. "And that's just what people are gonna say, Doc. There's no way you're ever gonna prove otherwise."

Ben let out a heavy breath. "I'm afraid you're right, Sheriff. Steve Colbert will get all the revenge he wanted, now—even from his own grave!"

The sheriff heaved a sigh. "Well, let's get on to the undertaker's. He'll be right happy to know he's got two more customers!"

# Chapter Forty-Seven

*"I*t's going to be another beautiful day," Dora said quietly. "Clay would be pleased."

Earl and Mary Crump offered to stay at the ranch with Patti while the others put on their best clothes for the ride into town where Clay Allison would to be laid to rest in the Pecos cemetery. Wes and Jim took the buckboard while Ben drove the buggy with Hannah and Dora at his side.

Ben sat quiet with a stony face as he turned their horse and buggy onto the dirt road. Finally, he cleared his throat. "After the funeral, Dora, I'll let Hannah take you back to the ranch. There's another funeral in the afternoon I have to attend."

Hannah turned in surprise. "Ben, we don't know anybody else here in Pecos . . . whose funeral is it?"

"Steve Colbert. He was killed yesterday in a saloon gunfight."

Hannah could only gasp.

Dora stirred from her grief and moaned. "Oh, Ben, I'm so sorry—after all these years looking for your boy. Did you see him before he died?"

Ben could see no reason to continue the charade. It would all come out soon, anyway. "There wasn't much time," he replied, "but I had a chance to tell him his real father was my brother Chunk."

Hannah smothered her astonishment. "Ben, why didn't you ever say anything?"

"Steve was born out of wedlock and Chunk didn't want him. My wife Nora couldn't have a child and I wanted a son—it seemed only right for me to take Steve as my own. I wanted to protect him from a no-good father, so, God forgive me, I never told him the truth."

Two dust-brown sparrows chased playfully through haggard wind-blown trees in the cemetery, unmindful of the small group of mourners gathered below in the hot morning sun.

Ben and Hannah helped Dora Allison to the grave side while Wes and Jim stood a respectful distance away, hats in hand and unruly hair waving in the breeze. After the local preacher read the service, Dora poured a handful of earth onto the wooden coffin and then went with the Colberts to the buggy.

Ben said to Hannah, "You take Dora home, dear, while I stay here for Steve's funeral. Wes said he'd wait and take me back later."

"I wouldn't leave you at a time like this!" Hannah turned to Jim Calley. "Jim, you take Dora in the buggy, we'll ride back with Wes in the buckboard."

There were no services for Steve Colbert. Two grave diggers lowered his coffin into the ground in silence, alongside the unidentified man he had cheated and killed in the saloon.

Wes sat in the buckboard, waiting outside the little Pecos cemetery while Ben, Hannah and the sheriff stood watching dirt being shoveled into the grave.

"Sorry to learn he was your nephew, Doc," the sheriff said to Ben. "But he was a killer, and now that I know he's in the ground, I'd best get back to town." He tipped his hat to Hannah. "Pleased to've met you, Mrs. Colbert."

Hannah still wondered about Steve's birth. After the sheriff had left, she took Ben's arm. "You didn't say who Steve's mother was, Ben. Did you know?"

His sad gaze remained on the grave, now almost filled. "A servant girl who worked for my father. After Chunk got her into trouble, he refused to marry her. Steve was born just before father died. When Chunk and I were there to settle the estate, the girl told us she couldn't keep the baby and Chunk didn't want it either."

Hannah knew the rest. Ben took Steve for his own son and tried to raise the child properly, but Steve grew more rebellious each year. When Chunk Colbert showed up again, he must have taken his son away from Ben as a form of vengeance—turning Steve into a ruthless killer.

Hannah knew Ben blamed himself and she gently squeezed his arm. "I'm sorry it had to end this way, Ben. But it wasn't your fault, or even Steve's. It was your brother Chunk, from the very beginning."

Ben shook his head. "I thought by not smothering Steve with love and not giving him everything he wanted—like my father did me—by making Steve work for everything he got, he'd be different. But I was wrong."

Hannah patted his hand. "Steve had Chunk's bad blood. If Steve had really been your son, he would've turned out different."

"I wonder."

"You did what you thought was best."

"So did Clay Allison. And where did it get either of us?"

Hannah's eyes filled with loving tears as she watched Ben take out a handkerchief and remove his glasses. She wondered why he always cleaned them in times of stress. Maybe it helped him see things in better perspective.

Ben donned his spectacles and put an arm around Hannah's waist. "Well, my dear, we'd better get back to the Allison ranch. I have to bring another life into this damnable world!"

# Epilogue

Although Cimarron today is skirted by a modern highway, much of the small town remains the same as in the days of Clay Allison.

A few original buildings sit under the clear New Mexico sky, including the Saint James Hotel, which has been renovated and now open to the public. And, yes, bullet holes are still in the dining room ceiling. Guests can sleep in the same rooms occupied by such famous names as Clay Allison, Jesse James, Bat Masterson and many others. Certain rooms are said to be haunted by the ghosts of their former occupants.

Lucien B. Maxwell's house has long ago vanished, however the three-story stone grist mill stands as if determined to last for centuries. The huge building has been turned into a fascinating museum crammed with thousands of original artifacts and information about the old west. One can climb to the top floor where Maxwell's daughter Virginia and her loving Captain Alexander Keyes were secretly married.

Elizabethtown, twenty miles away, had two lives. After Mount Baldy's gold ran out, the thriving town was abandoned, however for only a short time. With the discovery of a new vein of gold, people once again filled E-Town's buildings. But that gold also vanished and a fire destroyed most of the town before everyone deserted it for good. Today, a tourist must look carefully to spot what remains of the two-story town hall of Elizabethtown. About the only remaining structure, the walls are slowly crumbling away to join its occupants in oblivion.

Lucien Bonaparte Maxwell, unhappy since leaving his beloved Cimarron, lived to the age of fifty-five, dying of uremic poisoning at his new Fort Sumner residence on July 25, 1875. His grave lies almost unnoticed in the Fort Sumner cemetery, only a few steps away from that of the west's more famous legend, Billy The Kid.

John Allison, never fully recovering from the shotgun wounds received from Sheriff Charles Faber in Colorado, died on January 7, 1898. John's grave is in the Allisons' home state of Tennessee.

Robert Clay Allison died on July 3, 1887, just two months short of his forty-seventh birthday, and was buried in the Pecos, Texas, cemetery. His widow Dora McCullough Allison later gave birth to Clay Pearl Allison. Dora stayed at the ranch for three years, then married J. L. Johnson and moved to Fort Worth where she died on November 16, 1939.

On August 28, 1975, eighty-eight years after his death, Clay Allison's remains were exhumed and reinterred at a specially ordained cemetery next to the *West of the Pecos Museum.* His new resting place now carries two markers, a wooden one reading:

**CLAY ALLISON**
**GENTLEMAN GUN FIGHTER**
**1840-1887**
**R. I. P.**

And one of granite reading,

**ROBERT CLAY ALLISON**
**1840-1887**
**HE NEVER KILLED A MAN**
**THAT DID NOT NEED KILLING**

**END**